THE YELLOW TOWER

BOOK FOUR OF THE FIVE TOWERS

THE YELLOW TOWER

a novel by

J.B. SIMMONS

ISBN 978-1-949785-06-7

Published in the United States by Three Cord Press

www.jbsimmons.com

No coward soul is mine
No trembler in the world's storm-troubled sphere
I see Heaven's glories shine
And Faith shines equal arming me from Fear

Though earth and moon were gone
And suns and universes ceased to be
And Thou wert left alone
Every Existence would exist in thee

There is not room for Death
Nor atom that his might could render void
Since thou art Being and Breath
And what thou art may never be destroyed.

— Emily Brontë

THE FIVE TOWERS
RED
BLACK
GREEN
THE SCOURING
BLUE
YELLOW

1

THEY ORDERED ME to shut my eyes and stay silent and touch not a drop of my power. They tied my hands and blindfolded me and led me out of the Scouring like a slave. Don't they know ropes and blindfolds are pointless? With the collar around my neck, I have to obey whether I like it or not.

I march steadily and blindly ahead. The stone under my feet gives way to dirt—lots and lots of dry, crumbly dirt. Birds sing in the distance, but no one speaks a word. I feel sunlight on my face, but I can't even crack my eyes to peek at the blindfold. All I can do is think, and that's gotten me into enough trouble already.

Emma let them do this. She handed me over to the Yellow Tower without any warning, without any resistance. We agreed to go to Yellow together, but I never signed up for a collar. All Emma said was, *I'm sorry, Cipher. This was the only way.*

She's *sorry?* After all we've been through, she owes me more than that. And why is this the only way? I have my doubts. I always have my doubts.

The sunlight suddenly dims. The dirt under my feet feels firmer. The rope stops pulling me forward. It's quiet. The air is still. I am still.

I tense at a slight sound of motion. Something touches the back of my head. The blindfold shifts, then falls off.

"Open your eyes," says a girl's voice, silky but strong.

I expect a prison…or worse. But as my eyes blink open, I see no prison bars. I'm in a quaint little room. The earthen walls and thatch ceiling glow soft and yellow. Light pours through a window and beams down onto a loaf of bread on a small wooden table. Steam drifts lazily from the golden crust. A fire burns in an earthen hearth in the corner. It's almost pleasant.

"He is surprised," the girl says. "And hungry."

She stands before me bright as an angel. She's the one who collared me. She's my master. Her face is made of steep lines, framed by straight black hair under a silver crown. She wears a yellow dress and slippers, delicate and refined and entirely out of place on the plain dirt floor.

"No wonder," a boy says. "They do not feed them in Green."

He stands in the doorway, silhouetted by the light outside. His features are hidden, but not his crown. He's the tall boy who led the Yellow team into the Scouring. He made the trade that landed me in a collar. And, even if he looks as young as the rest of us in this place, he's Emma's father. I want to shout at him—*where is she?*—but the cold metal link at my neck allows no word. If only I could use my power…

"Do not provoke him," the girl says. "He is angry."

"We can use anger," the boy replies. "Tell him what to do so we can return. I tire of this dirt."

"Very well. Come with me." The girl unties the rope around my wrists, then takes my hand, gently. The boy steps aside as she leads me out.

The flat ground around the little hut is cracked and yellow-grey, with a few scattered weeds. There is a gentle breeze. The suns shine down without any tree or cloud to block the light. I shade my eyes and scan the surroundings. In the distance, fields of grasses and grains grow in patchwork patterns. There are other small huts like the one behind me. Beyond the fields rises a tall palace—the Yellow Tower—dazzling as crystal. We must have walked past it, out of the Scouring and to this field.

A massive flock of birds swoops overhead. I turn and watch them soar away until they form a single dark pattern in the bright blue sky. Between the earth and the sky, a wall extends across the horizon, as if enclosing the land. I remember this wall. It's the wall that Emma and I sailed to together from the Blue Tower. The same wall where the Green Tower's forest ended. The wall that Yellow's archers patrol, allowing no one to enter. Except now I'm within the wall, remembering the pain of an arrow through my leg. Emma had healed it quickly. Emma healed so many things for me. But now she handed me over to be enslaved. *This was the only way*, she said. Why? For her father? She wouldn't betray me, would she? No, not Emma…

"What is *this* you feel?" The girl leans close, her wide-set eyes peering into mine like she's reading an open book. "Very interesting. You have so little fear."

"It takes only a little fear to be a coward," the boy says.

The girl turns sharply to him. "This one is different. I am sure of it. Rarely does one with such courage come to Yellow."

"All who come have fear," the boy says. "He will remember it. Or he will be reset."

The girl faces the boy with her back to me. Her shoulders show rippling tension under her yellow dress. "We must force nothing," the girl says. "You know what Elijah and the Widow command."

"But they are not here anymore, are they?"

"They will return," the girl snaps. "Nothing is covered that will not be revealed. But *we* cannot reveal anything. Only the light can do that."

"The light! You sound just like them…" The boy grins at her, sly and playful. "Maybe they really have gone for good."

The girl shakes her head, making her black hair swing like a curtain across her back. "They could be here even now, listening to us. You grow too bold."

"Too bold, or scoured?" he asks.

The girl glances back at me. The collar tells her what I feel—curiosity and confusion and anger.

"You reveal too much," she tells the boy. "We will speak more of this. Shall I give the orders?"

The boy holds out his arms innocently. "By all means."

"Pick up some dirt," the girl commands me. "Study it."

I bend down and scoop up a handful of the soil at our feet. The dirt looks grayish brown in my palm. Little clumps crumble as I roll them between my fingers, dry and dusty as they fall to the ground.

"Smell it."

The earthy fragrance is thick and stale, like the dirt has been baking under the three suns for eternity. It has none of the moisture or decay of the floor of the Green Tower's forest, and none of the red hue of Red's mountains.

"You begin as a Serf, the first level of the Yellow Tower," the girl says formally. "You will stay on your plot of land and work the earth. You may not leave. The animals will bring all that you need. Learn to grow your crop and you do well. Trade with your neighbors and you do better. Bake a loaf of nine grains and you will advance."

"If, and only if, I approve," the boy says, adjusting the crown over his golden locks. "No one advances without the king's permission. That would be me."

The king. His smug grin tells me this won't be easy. But he's Emma's father. She knew about Yellow. She should have prepared me for this. I have to bake a loaf of bread? I should be ready for anything after the other towers—I plunged into a lake in Blue, faced a dragon in Red, and dangled in a net in Green. But baking bread? Why?

"So curious!" the girl says, interrupting my thoughts. "You must focus on what is before you. Anger will not help, especially not against William."

The boy suddenly grabs the girl's arm. His knuckles are

white as he squeezes. "Are you challenging me?"

"No." The girl shrugs away from his grip. "But you are not the only one who grows bold."

"Enough, *Joan!*" He says her name like an accusation. "Finish the instructions and we go."

She looks to me. Joan. Black hair, dark eyes…so gentle, and yet so strong. Who was she on Earth?

"You know your task," she says. "Once we leave your land, you are free to do whatever you like on your plot. But only obedience leads to advancement. Only obedience pleases the king."

The boy, the king, William, releases her and holds out his arm formally. Joan slips her arm—marked by red fingerprints from his clenched hold—through his. The two of them walk together, with formal elegance, away from me and toward the Yellow Tower's glistening spires in the distance.

I try to follow, to shout. I can't. The commands hold.

Once we leave your land, she said, *you are free…*

I wait until they enter the edge of a field of tall grasses, then try again. This time my legs instantly surge into motion. I chase after them, and I summon the wind. The blue threads of power flood in and through me, racing like rapids. It is a thrilling rush. My power is back. I can get out. Weaving all the threads I can, I blast the wind at the king and the queen.

The power slams into something hard. The force of the collision knocks the threads away. The power stopped, but I'm still moving, still free.

I summon the air again. I carefully prod with the wind until it reaches an invisible barrier, a few steps ahead of me. It rises in a straight line along the dirt. My power can't penetrate it, but whatever it is, the boy and girl walked through easily. I run after them.

The invisible wall meets me hard as stone. I collapse to the dirt with a loud grunt. A cloud of dust billows up around me.

"Wait!" I shout. "Joan!"

The girl pauses and glances back over the tall grains. "You may not leave," she calls out. "Work your own plot. Courage begins there, and Yellow needs it."

2

I SIT ON the dirt, hurting, and watch as William and Joan walk away toward the palace. The plot before me, on the other side of the invisible wall, has parallel lines of grains. They are tall and golden and ripe for harvest, and soon they hide the glinting crowns of the boy-king and girl-queen.

The golden field has no weeds. No gaps. Whoever sowed it must have an ordered mind to plant thousands of grains like this. Other patchwork fields spread all around, with little huts like mine at regular intervals. In the distance, close to the Yellow Tower, there are a few two-story buildings like manor homes. Maybe Emma waits in one of those, lounging in silk, with a host of collared serfs, ready to greet her father and serve nine-grain bread and a tall glass of iced tea…

Focus, Cipher. This isn't your first tower. Find a way out.

I stand and dust myself off. The collar feels tight around my neck, but my master, Joan, has left no command. Only an instruction: *Bake a loaf of nine grains and you will advance.*

It's very strange, but it can't be so hard.

First I need to test my limits. I summon the wind and weave the threads into a gentle breeze against the wall. The air meets the barrier and glides along it, but not a molecule passes through. I press my hands to the surface. It feels smooth as glass and doesn't budge when I shove. I won't try running through it again any time soon. Using the threads to explore, I follow the invisible wall as it goes left a couple hundred feet, then it turns in a ninety-degree angle, then turns again, and again, forming a perfect square around my plot of land. Going up, the barrier rises vertically until it is far above the ground, then it turns inward like a flat ceiling. I don't have a way to measure, but my guess is that it's a perfect cube around me. A perfect prison.

I figure the plots around me are enclosed in their own invisible walls. Each plot matches the shape of mine, and they look like dozens of separate little serfdoms. Some plots have tall, ripe grains. Others have vibrant green shoots. A few are fallow dirt like mine. One nearby has blooming sunflowers scattered randomly across the plot. The plots are set in a grid, meaning eight would border mine. Eight other serfs, plus me. That's nine people, nine fields…and nine grains.

Bake a loaf…

It won't be easy if I can't set foot off my own plot. No one is in sight, but my neighbors must be in the surrounding huts. Blue made us work in teams and rise in classes. Red gave out tasks and paired boys with girls. Green sent us out into the wild in tribes. It could be

Yellow's way to make us cooperate. They want me to bake a loaf of bread…unless that's only what the boy-king wants. Joan mentioned another command, by two people she called Elijah and the Widow. But the boy said they could be gone for good. Who are they? The leaders? Emma probably knows more. Maybe she had a reason for what she did. I desperately want to believe it.

Whatever it takes, I will not give up. I stare down at my scarred hands and foot. I earned the three crisscross scars in three other towers—Blue, Red, and Green—as I discovered my past. I was Paul Fitzroy, an American doctor, a father, a husband, and a mess. Somehow I died on Earth and came to the Five Towers. Here there is only one way out—the White Tower. I saw my mother go up into it, through the light in the Scouring. But I couldn't follow her. I remember what Green's leader, Daniel, told me. There are five of us with scars. The marked ones. When we find out why we're here, Daniel said, then we can enter the White Tower. That's what I have to do, but that doesn't mean I'm going to play by Yellow's rules.

I concentrate again on the wind. This time I weave it methodically, testing the wall in every way I can. First I funnel it into a massive gust. The wall doesn't bend. Then with scalpel precision the air slices at the barrier, but it might as well be a plastic knife against a diamond. Finally I prod every square foot of the invisible encasement, searching for some gap, some pinhole. There's not a single opening or weak spot.

By the time I finish, I'm exhausted and only more

certain of my confinement. But I do not panic. Not that I want to be stuck on this acre of dirt, but this is no worse than the starts I had in the other towers. It might even be better: an invisible wall and grains to grow. It beats hanging in a net, and no one has tried to drown me or send me after dragons.

I return to the hut and walk around it, counting five strides to pass each side. It is made of pale brown stucco, with only two openings—an open window on one side, and a plain wooden door on the other. Inside, the floor is the same dirt as outside, if packed a little harder. A pallet of straw lies along one wall, opposite from the earthen hearth where coals still burn. There's a stack of chopped wood and a large clay jar on either side of the hearth. The jar is full of small, yellow kernels. I scoop out a handful and sniff. It's corn.

A small wooden table and chair are in the center of the hut. The chair holds a stack of neatly folded clothes. I unfold them—light brown cotton pants and a yellow linen shirt with long sleeves. They will be more comfortable than the buckskin shorts and vest from Green. I change and find that the clothes fit well, as if made precisely for me.

The golden bread no longer steams on the table. The cast iron pan that holds it is cool to the touch. I sit and pull off a bite with my fingers. It's cornbread. It tastes good. I spot a glass container of milk on the floor beside the straw pallet. I drink it to wash down the bread.

When it grows dark, I lay on the pallet of straw. Sleep comes, but it's fitful. I dream of a vast cave lit by only a few small candles, and I know that it is my job to find someone there. Maybe Emma, or someone from my own past. Maybe Samantha. I search and call for them but hear only echoes. Small flying creatures emerge out of the darkness, flapping like bats. They dive at me. I try to fight them back, but they are relentless. They snuff out the candles' flames one by one. I have no way to relight the candles. Smoke blinds me. The bats surround me and smother me.

I wake up screaming in the dark. The hut is cold and quiet. The temperature fell sharply as I slept. The hearth holds only the faintest embers. I shuffle to the door and step outside.

The bare dirt around me looks like the surface of the moon, soft gray in the starlight. I stare up at the countless pricks of light. I see no bats. I wonder…

Emma, are you there?

I send the thought up, remembering how we spoke through the stars in the Green Tower. She knew her father was going to put the collar around my neck. She led me right into it. But she's still Emma. *This was the only way*, she said. Can I still trust her?

Emma…

I call out for her many times, focusing on the stars, but eventually shiver with cold and give up. I return into the hut and summon the air to move three logs from the stack of wood onto the coals. Breaths of wind bring the fire to life, flames licking up the logs. Warmth drifts out. I curl up on the bare dirt floor and sleep again.

A distant hammering sound wakes me. Morning light gathers in the room, spilling through cracks in the wooden door and the single window on the opposite wall. Cold lingers along the ground. I put three more logs on the coals and drag the table closer to the hearth. The last of the cornbread breaks the night's fast. There's no milk left to wash it down.

They do not feed them in Green, said the boy-king, William.

Maybe not, but the forest had food some of the time. And the Green Tower had the Jubilee feast. All I have now is a jar of corn kernels. Joan said the animals would bring what I needed. I imagine mice scurrying into the hut and depositing cheese on the table, but the thought only makes me laugh. I search the hut and find nothing new, so I go outside.

The three suns have crested the horizon. For the first time I see others out on the surrounding fields. The hammering sound comes from a hut set amidst a field of high, golden grains. I go to the border between the fields, studying the crop. Their tassels are thick and ripe at the end of each grain. Wheat, maybe. I reach forward slowly but my hand hits the invisible wall. For good measure, I try the wind and get the same result as the day before: nothing.

"Hello?" I shout. "Is anyone there?"

The hammering stops.

There is no motion from the field of golden wheat, but to my left a boy approaches and stands at the corner of his plot of dirt. He watches me as I walk toward him. His black hair hangs straight. His eyes are narrow and hard, just as they were in Blue, Red, and Black.

"Cipher," he grunts.

My fists clench. "Max."

3

"AND I THOUGHT it couldn't get worse…" Max glares at me. We stand within reach of each other at the corners of our fields, wearing the same soft Yellow garb.

I'm wielding the wind, ready for anything, but the blue threads can't pass through the invisible wall between us. Neither can Max. The barrier meets here at a square angle, marking the separation of our fields. Dirt is under my feet. Small green shoots under Max's. The rising suns cast shadows so long that his figure and mine seem to meet in the distance.

The last time I saw him was when Emma and I went to the Black Tower's land to save my mother. Black had captured Max from Red, after I'd taken his place as Alpha. He had been with Kiyo in Black, in a small village. She had called him Lord. He'd remembered nothing of what had happened in Red. The look in his eyes tells me he remembers now.

"How did you get here?" I ask.

"*You…*" The word leaves his lips like venom.

"What about me?"

"I was the Alpha. You let Black catch me."

"We had a deal," I say. "We divided Red's Scouring team fair and square. You picked your six. You got caught."

"You're the reason I'm stuck here." The muscles of his jaw, unbearded as he was in Black, tense and strain like he's chewing a lemon. "You have no idea how many days I've wasted away in this place."

"It seems better than that Black village. How'd you get here?"

He shakes his head. "I see you haven't changed."

"But I have," I tell him, as if he cared. "It hasn't been easy for me either. I got caught by Green. I got killed, and wiped, *twice*." My hand goes to the collar at my neck. "Emma tricked me."

Max's clenched jaw turns into a grin. "Serves you right."

Taking a deep breath, I remember the blade at my neck in the dark room on Black's land. This boy wanted to kill me. He would try again if he could get through the wall, but I could take him. I defeated Baron, who was stronger in Green than Max ever was in Red. *But I have changed...* Max must have something in his past worth discovering, like Baron and his giving, like me and my research.

I make my voice as calm as I can. "How did you get here, Max?"

"Betrayed, like you," he says. "Kiyo did it."

"Kiyo?"

"Your friends are not as reliable as you thought. Or

maybe they're just as selfish as you are."

"There must be a reason," I say, but it comes out weak, unsure. Emma couldn't *betray* me. She said it was the only way…

Max leans forward with his hands pressed against the invisible wall. "There's one nice thing about you being my neighbor."

Something in his face, his closeness, makes me step back.

He bends down and uproots a tender green shoot from the soil beneath him, then slaps his hand to the wall, pressing the green shoot to it. "This is rye. You need nine grains, and this is one of them. I will see to it, personally, that you never get it. Better get used to being a serf."

He drops the green shoot on the ground, then turns and walks off. The uprooted plant is only a foot away, but the wall stops my hand. I call after him. He doesn't slow or glance back. I sink to the ground, feeling confused and defeated.

"Hey!" someone shouts. "You!"

A boy approaches from the left, plodding along slowly. Like Max and me, he wears a yellow tunic—though his shows dirt and sweat stains. I stand and watch him carefully, wondering if I'll recognize him, too, but I don't. His eyes look tired and his hair is a short stubble.

He stops five paces short of the line between our lots. He leans on the staff of a hoe, pressed against the dirt. There are only a few grains around him, growing at different heights and in different places with no obvious pattern. He smiles slightly, which makes his ears protrude from the sides of his head and gives him a playful, goofy look.

"I'm Drew," he says. "I'd shake your hand, but you know…"

"Right, the wall. I'm Cipher."

"Max don't like ya much." The boy yawns. "Ya alright?"

"Not exactly." I point along the line of the invisible wall. "I don't like being trapped."

"Eh, ya get used to it. Whoa, where'd ya get that scar?"

I lower my hand. "It's a long story."

"Ya got one on ya foot, too. And ya other hand. They all look the same." He studies me curiously. "Most folks wake up clean and healthy here. Ain't much room for pain, or scars…"

"How long have you been here?" I ask.

He starts counting on his fingers. "One, two, three—" Then he laughs like it's some big joke. "Who knows? Maybe fifty years?"

"*Fifty?*"

"Eh, could be a lot more. Easy to lose track."

"Did they tell you to bake a loaf of bread?"

"Sure did," he says. "Nine grains. Now, one or two grains, no sweat. But nine, ain't that the devil?"

"How many grains do you have?"

"Once I had five." He shrugs, as if he doesn't care. "It's hard to grow ya own grain, much less get it from y'all neighbors." He smiles toward to the wall between his land

and Max's. "Looks like ya already learned that. Anyway, life out here ain't so bad. Better than the palace, that's for sure. I hear they gotta fight there. Here nobody's gonna mess with ya. So I reckon it's best not baking any of that fancy bread. Ya got a grain jar, right?"

Better than the palace? They have to fight? My gaze shifts to the Yellow Tower in the distance. How could anyone *not* want to go there?

"Hey, ya listenin'?" he says. "What's in ya grain jar?"

"A jar, yes… In my hut there's a clay pot full of corn kernels. Is that what you mean?"

"Yessir. Mine's full of oats. Everybody's got they own grain, but them jars is the best. They never run out. Ya eat it down, then it's full again in the morning. So we got food, we got shelter, and the good Lord's sunshine. I reckon we're in heaven, or about as close as we gonna get."

The boy smiles wide, like he's as content as he can be. It's baffling. As far as I know, no one in the five towers has ever thought the place was heaven.

"Have you been in any other towers?" I ask.

"What towers?"

His easy tone makes me smile. If I didn't know about the other towers and the Scouring and everything else about this place, maybe this fertile plot of land wouldn't be so bad…other than the invisible walls.

"Do you remember anything before this place?" I ask.

"Oh yeah! Ya really wanna hear about it?"

"Sure, what's your story?"

His face comes alive with energy, like a schoolboy

picked first for show-and-tell. "Just about every dream I've had since comin' here starts like this."

4

DREW'S FACE WAS pressed into the mud, hands over his helmet for cover, when the first bomb hit his platoon. The ground shook violently. Dark jungle dirt fell like snow. Then Drew heard the next incoming hiss. He ignored every bit of training and got up and ran. The second blast sent him flying into a palm tree with thick bark like teeth. By then he didn't feel any pain. The fumes went into his nostrils like spirits bent on sucking out his life.

But a man named Captain Hughes somehow found Drew and hoisted him on his shoulders. The last thing Drew remembered was those spirits infiltrating his nose with the smoke and the jungle green swallowing him while all around it sounded like the world was ending.

He woke up on a cot with a bandage as thick as a pillow around his foot. The smoke was gone, and only one spirit had seen fit to stay in his nostril. Drew named the spirit Napalm. They got along alright most of the time, but Napalm sometimes said mean things to Drew.

"You ran from your men!" Napalm would accuse.

"I was scared!" Drew would reply.

"That's why I found you…"

Drew imagined Napalm grinning and rubbing his hands when he said this, but he never saw the spirit's face. They mostly just talked to each other, keeping company during the day.

After the pillow came off Drew's foot, taking two toes with it, Drew got on a plane and came back to the United States of America. It was a blessing from the good Lord. Even if he had to bring Napalm back with him, Drew knew America was the land of the free and just about the best thing that ever happened to the world. Even Napalm admitted the country's freedom was something to be admired.

Drew settled in the nation's capital, where some men told him his brain didn't work quite right anymore so he could leave the Army and learn to pay his rent and his taxes with the money he earned at an old building called the Treasury Department. It had the longest, straightest halls Drew had ever seen. And it was his job to keep the floors of those halls spit-shine clean. On Monday morning he would start on the first floor at the northwest corner of the building. Around Tuesday he would get to the second floor, leaving no trace of dust.

"Boy," he'd tell Napalm, "them floors can shine if we keep scrubbin' 'em clean."

Drew knew, of course, that Napalm wasn't doing any scrubbing himself, but he kept Drew company so it seemed like a team effort all the same. He'd keep on shining on Wednesday and Thursday, and by Friday at 5 pm, sometimes at 4 pm, if Drew really got working, he'd finish the top floor and take his bucket down to the first floor, ready for Monday again. It was just about the finest work Drew could imagine. Napalm agreed.

Nice as those working days were, Drew's favorite thing to do was to sit in this big cozy chair in a nice little apartment on Sundays. He'd pull a lever on the chair, and out came a footrest, simple as that. Sometimes the right foot, missing the two toes, reminded him of the blasts in the jungle and the smoke and the spirits going up into his nose, but Napalm told him not to worry about that anymore. He'd take good care of Drew. Whenever it seemed like Drew would get too close to that old smoky memory, he'd have a sip of Coca-Cola and flip on a screen that showed football all day. Nobody bothered him a lick in that chair. Not even Napalm. It was just great, Drew thought. Sometimes he'd even say it out loud.

"God Bless America!"

To which Napalm would reply, "And the pursuit of happiness!"

Drew didn't keep much track of time, but he figured years passed like that. He got to where, when he stood, he couldn't see his two missing toes anymore unless he bent way over. His stomach got so full of Coca-Cola that it blocked his view. He also lost a little bit of his hair, but it never bothered him much. He could still keep those long hallways spit-spot clean.

Things changed a bit when, one spring Saturday evening, while Drew was watching baseball—it not being football season, after all—two men knocked on his door and Napalm said they were fine men and so Drew let them in and they watched baseball together for a while.

Drew figured they were nice enough, even if they did have funny accents. One nice thing they did was offer Drew a whole bunch of money so he could buy a bigger television and order as many pizzas as he wanted and maybe even go to a real ballgame. The only thing they wanted was for Drew to do a little errand. Napalm said it was a good deal, so Drew smiled and shook their hands.

The errand was this: Drew needed to copy something that the men had accidentally left behind in the Treasury Department. They told him it was very important, and had to be done right away, even though the game wasn't over. Drew didn't like leaving before the end of the game, but a deal was a deal.

"They need your help!" Napalm told him. "Don't be a coward, like when you ran from your men."

Drew had to admit Napalm was right. He'd been afraid in the jungle, with the enemy hiding everywhere, and that's how he'd lost his toes and somehow let Napalm inside. Anyway, Drew sure was the right man to help these guys, because he had the biggest ring of keys you could imagine—more keys than he could count. He knew where all the keys worked. Sometimes he had to go inside offices and empty trashcans and clean the floors. But this time the men knew right where the paper to copy was, so Drew just needed to go get it. They told him it was so important that he shouldn't even tell anyone about it.

"If somebody stops you," they said, "just tell them you get paid a little extra for working on Saturday."

It was almost true—Napalm assured him—but Drew never had to say that anyway. The building sure was quiet on a Saturday, especially late at night. Almost spooky, Drew thought. He might have been too scared if Napalm wasn't with him. But he did just what they asked. He went to the top floor and found a folder in a desk drawer like the men said. Then he made copies of all the papers in the folder and put the folder right back where he'd found it.

When Drew got back to his little apartment, the men thanked him and took the copies and gave him a stack of cash.

"They're not very smart," Napalm told Drew after they left. "The paper they gave you is worth a lot more!"

Drew got a chuckle out of that, and he got a new television with the cash. It sure made the ballgames look nice.

He kept on doing little errands like this, and soon enough he had a new chair and a new apartment, too. He even started going to the movies, where he could buy all the Coca-Cola and popcorn he wanted. His favorite movie was Star Wars. But there was one big problem. He didn't live to see *The Return of the Jedi*.

There was a Tuesday in August, one of those hot and sticky days when walking to work made Drew feel like he was wading through maple syrup, when he was mopping the floor spit-shine clean, same as always. A few men came up to him with badges and guns. They didn't look nice.

"Are you Andrew Forrester?" they asked.

When Drew told him that he was—he was an honest man, after all—they told Drew he was under arrest and before he could even ask why they put handcuffs on his wrists.

"They should pad those things!" Napalm shouted inside Drew's mind. "This isn't fair!"

But Napalm's complaining didn't do any good. The men led Drew out of the building. They made him leave his mop bucket right there in the middle of the floor. He still doesn't know who finished his work that morning.

The men put him in a police car outside. He kept thinking they'd turn on the blue light and siren, like police always do, but the car just drove down the street like any other car, not in any sort of rush. As they drove off Drew tried to figure out what he'd done wrong. He was a good citizen, as far as he knew. He paid his taxes, followed the speed limit, and even went to church on Sundays before the football games started. Napalm said it was probably about time Drew got punished for fleeing during a battle, for being a coward. Drew remembered something his mom had always told him before he ended up in that jungle, running, afraid. *Ya sins gonna catch up with ya*, she'd say.

So Drew, sitting handcuffed in the back of the car, asked the police if that was the reason. "Is this because I ran away in the jungle?"

They only stared at Drew, confused. They wouldn't talk.

The police car stopped at a red light, then all of a

sudden a big black truck rushed to a stop right beside them. Drew remembered the sound of the truck's tires—braking and squealing—and the smell of burnt rubber, not quite so bad as the fumes in the jungle, but he wanted some fresh air all the same. Sure enough, a man helped him out by smashing something through his window. The air came in, even stickier and warmer than the morning, and a man stood there looking angry. This was odd, because he was one of the nice men who had the deal with Drew, paying him to do little errands. Now the man pointed a gun at Drew. There was a loud bang, like a hammer hitting something. Then Drew woke up right here, on this nice plot of land that he reckons is heaven.

5

"THANKS FOR LISTENIN'," Drew says with a carefree smile. "How about you? Ya die too?"

"I think so," I say.

"How?"

"I don't know."

"Don't wanna talk about it, eh? Can't blame ya. Most folks round here are the same, and they don't listen much either. You were mighty kind to let me talk." Drew yawns and stretches his arms high. "Beautiful day, ain't it?"

I gaze around and can't help but smile. The three suns are high overhead. There's a warm breeze and not a cloud in the sky. Drew is…different. His memory of the past is vividly clear, and tragic, but it hardly seems to affect him. *A spirit? Napalm?* In my past, as a doctor, I would diagnose some form of mental disorder, due to potentially major brain damage. I didn't have the heart to tell him that he was probably caught spying on behalf of a foreign government. His memory of Star Wars would place him in the 1970s, which means it was likely the Soviet KGB. The poor guy had been caught in the middle of something he'd never understood.

"Your story was very interesting," I say. "Did you know all that when you first came here?"

"Oh, goodness no," Drew laughs. "I came here wiped clean as those spit-spot floors. The memories come in my dreams, starting in the jungle and then eventually I'm scrubbing and scrubbing those endless hallways. I reckon I've cleaned them more times in my dreams here than I ever did on Earth."

"What about that last part?"

"You mean with the angry man and the gun? Gee, I ain't seen that but a few times, and only after a real hard day working, planting seeds or harvesting. I've learned better. No need to work that hard. You'd be amazed at how fast plants grow here. Ain't nothing like this dirt. Or maybe it's the three suns. I reckon it's a farmer's paradise."

"Why do you think you came here after you died?"

"Heck if I know! My momma always said, *if anyone don't believe in the Lord he'll be burning in hell.* She told me heaven was where I wanted to go, and I agreed. Well, this place sure don't seem like hell. Ain't hot enough, right?"

I smile. "I guess not."

"Well, neighbor, nice talkin' with ya. Here, try planting a few of these."

He suddenly tosses a handful of grains toward me. They pass right through the invisible wall without a trace of resistance. I reach forward and my hand hits the wall. It hasn't budged.

"Funny, ain't it?" Drew says. "I reckon the grains are all

that can pass through. Them and the critters."

"Critters?" I scoop up the oats scattered over the dirt.

"Boy, you sure is new! There's all kinds of critters. Cats, dogs, goats, horses. They roam the land. Didn't you wonder how you was gonna fill up ya milk jar? Don't worry, you can't miss 'em. Well, all this talkin' got me sleepy. Time for a nap. I'll be seein' ya. Wait, what's ya name again?"

"Cipher," I say. "Nice meeting you, Drew."

He waves and walks away toward his hut. I watch him all the way until he's inside the building, thinking about his story and Max and the grains and whether I will ever learn how I died.

When I turn back to my hut, I see a mottled grey and white cat strolling along outside it. The cat keeps its distance as I approach, eyeing me curiously. I go inside the hut and lay the oats on the table. Remembering what Drew said, I decide to test the jar of corn kernels. I turn it upside down over the black pan until all the kernels have poured out in a heaping pile. But that's it. The jar stays empty.

The cat watches me, as if amused, from the open window. It hops down gracefully and rubs its side along my leg, arching its back high. It purrs softly when I pet it behind the ears. Sitting back, eyeing me, it suddenly leaps up into my lap. That's when I notice the thin collar hidden beneath the thick fur of its neck. The collar is leather, not metal like mine. I feel around it and find two capsules and a tiny roll of paper. I lay them gently on the table, marveling at them.

The capsules are no bigger than my thumbnail. I open the first and press my finger to the white powdery substance. It smells and tastes plain, and I wonder if it's baking powder. The next capsule has a white, granular substance. I taste it hoping for sugar and get salt.

The paper unrolls delicately and fits easily in my palm. The tiniest, most exquisite handwriting fills every blank space. As I begin to read, I expect some description of the capsules, some instruction, but not this.

Cipher, move to the shadows. Do not read this in the light. Move now. Stop reading.

I glance nervously around the hut. It is quiet. Sunlight streams through the window, but it does not touch the table or me. I am in shadow. Still I move to the straw pallet, sitting in the darkest place in the room. I try to steady my shaking hands and read on.

Sorry it had to be this way. Daniel warned me. I couldn't tell you. Your shock had to be genuine, to keep my father's guard down. Darkness shadows him. He monitors all the light, even the stars. Do not try them again. Follow the normal path. Our leaders, Elijah and the Widow, are missing, but they told me before there is always a purpose in the stories that lead to nine grains. Find that purpose. Bake the bread. Then we will fight together. We defeated Baron. Now we must defeat my father. Destroy this paper now and tell no one. This is all I can risk now. It is everything I risk. - E

Emma.

She wrote this. Only she would know these things.

I lean back against the wall and set the note gently in my lap. It means she didn't betray me. She had a reason for not telling me. She wanted my shock to be genuine. It was.

And now, apparently, her father's guard is down. But how does he monitor the light? And how are Yellow's leaders missing? Whatever the answers, Emma and I will work together again. I still wish she'd warned me, but I shouldn't have doubted her. I should have trusted her all along.

I read the note again, then a third time. I commit the words to memory. I roll the paper and move slowly across the hut, avoiding direct sunlight. The tiny scroll feels stuck to my fingers as I hold it over the embers in the hearth.

It is the only piece of Emma I have. It is a great source of hope. I don't want to destroy it, but her warnings leave me no choice. I drop it and watch it blaze and burn to ashes.

The mottled cat curls at my feet beside the hearth. I kneel and pet it, watching the embers for a long time. Eventually I move back to the pallet of straw. I lay on my back, eyes open, thinking.

Emma couldn't tell me, because she wanted her father, the boy-king William, to think I was a normal captive. And Daniel warned her, but what exactly did he warn her about? How does darkness shadow her father? Is it because Yellow's leaders are missing? Could it be the Colorless One?

The door creaks.

I spring to my feet, back against the wall.

The door pushes open and my heart races. I summon the wind, ready for anything.

A dog pokes its head inside the hut, tongue lolling. Its tail wags as it enters. The door swings shut.

The dog moves casually past the cat, like an old friend, and comes to me. It has chestnut brown fur and its back stands higher than my knees.

"Is anyone with you?" I ask softly.

The dog pants. I move silently past it, listening for anyone outside. There's no sound. I form a shield of air around me and step cautiously through the door. There's no one in sight. I release the air and wipe a sheen of sweat off my forehead. Then I laugh. There was no threat. It's just me and a cat and a dog in a little hut. The Yellow Tower is an odd place.

I return to the dog, who has plopped down on my pallet. It wears a collar as the cat did. Petting it softly, I feel around until I find a pouch tied tight to the underside of the collar. I undo the slender laces.

The pouch holds liquid inside and has a cork on one end. Taking my empty jar, I carefully open the cork and pour out the pouch's white contents. I sniff and taste it: milk.

"Good boy," I say.

This time I know better than to down the milk all at once. Emma's note said I have to follow the normal path, to bake the bread. I might as well practice. There was cornbread before. It can't be so hard. Smash the corn and cook it, I figure.

So I pour half the corn back into the jar and use a dull rock to smash the rest into a fine dust. I mix a little of the milk, salt, and the white powder in with it, then slide the pan into the hearth and let it cook. As I step away, I glance down at the jar of corn and freeze.

The jar is completely full again.

Drew was right. An everlasting supply.

Once the hearth has the hut smelling pretty good, I pull the pan out by the handle. It cools a while, then I scoop out a handful of the sloppy mixture. It's not cornbread, but it's better than nothing. I finish most of it and give the rest to the dog, who licks the plate clean.

"Kernel," I say. "Mind if I call you Kernel?"

The dog comes to me and paws at my leg. I rub his back. He pants approvingly. Kernel it is.

Outside there's a gentle pattering sound. A steady rain begins to fall. The soft sound of running water leads me to an upper corner of the hut. A groove is set into the stucco wall, and water glides down through it from the roof. At the foot of the straw pallet there's a wooden plank I hadn't noticed before. I pull it aside and see a small well, a few feet deep, with the fresh water pooling inside it.

I lie back again on the pallet. Kernel settles close beside me, breathing deeply, sharing the warmth of his thick chestnut fur. The rain slows and eventually stops.

So I have food and water, a cat that brings me ingredients and secret notes, and a dog that brings me milk and lies by my side. I see what Drew means. If I didn't know all the things I know, this could be heaven. But I do know. Emma has not betrayed me. She wants me to help her. To fight the darkness that somehow shadows her father. This is another prison of the Five Towers, and I have to find a way out.

6

I STAND IN the middle of the operating room. I wear my white coat and have a surgery team around me, a scalpel in my hand. There's a brain on the operating table. It's only a brain, no body. This doesn't affect my focus. Nothing could. My team is breathless. My first incision is perfect. I carve into the grey mass with my gifted hands, perfected by countless surgeries where one millimeter separates life and death. I prepare the spot in the frontal lobe. Someone hands me a microchip. I give it only a passing glance, enough to confirm its size and fit. Then I place it delicately in the spot, where the circuitry of silicon and carbon can connect. I proceed to the next site, the parietal lobe. I make the next cut, focused and tense. The operation stretches on and on. Hours pass. I implant more and more chips. I'm holding the scalpel ready for another cut when, suddenly, the brain moves. *Yes, yes*, I think, *it's working*. It moves again and someone screams.

I bolt upright, shocked out of the dream. I rub my eyes, remembering where I am. My hut in the Yellow Tower. It's a relief. I'd rather be awake here than stuck as Dr. Fitzroy in a never-ending surgery on a living brain. It seems too weird to be true. It reminds me of Drew's story. He scrubbed hallways in an office building. I operated on a brain. And our dreams locked us in our work without any explanation of why. But was this dream showing me something that really happened?

It fits with some of what I've learned about my past. I was a neurosurgeon who became the leader of the most advanced medical research institute in the world. But implanting chips into a brain? Before this dream I saw bats swooping into a cave and putting out candles. That wasn't real. That was a nightmare. So what was this?

As I rise and step outside, basking in the warmth of the three suns, I think more of Drew's story. He told me he saw how he died after the days of his most grueling planting and harvesting. Maybe hard work unlocks memories in dreams? That would be no stranger than how it worked in the other towers—dunking my head in the Sieve in Blue, staring at a flame in Red, or drinking sap in Green.

I decide to test it out. If yesterday's sheen of sweat brought me into a half-dream, half-nightmare of surgery on an isolated brain, then today I will toil until I'm drenched in sweat. No shortcuts with my power, either. Just work. Even if it doesn't help my dreams, I need a field of corn so I can trade and bake my nine-grain bread and get to Emma.

I begin to plant the kernels. The memory of using a scalpel, with such precision, mocks my hands as they scoop out little holes of dirt, insert a kernel of corn, and cover it again. Yellowish brown dust wedges under my fingernails. I plant three rows, spacing out each kernel to leave room to grow. A fourth row is devoted to the oat seeds that Drew gave me. It's only two grains, not nine, but it's a start.

I use the empty milk jar to wash off my hands and then water the rows of seeds. It takes a dozen trips or more to drench the four lines. By then the three suns have heated the land. It feels fifty degrees hotter than it was at night. The temperature swings wildly in this place. I pause to stare at the half-finished rows. They look lifeless. Drew said things grow fast, but there's no use waiting to watch.

Kernel prances up to me. I pet him and feel an object fastened to his collar. I pull it off and smile. It's a small shovel, just the right size to hold in my hand.

"Thanks, boy," I say.

He cocks his head like he wants to tell me something.

"What is it boy?"

He trots off and looks back to make sure I'm following. He stops beside a small object on the other side of my hut.

It's a small brown bird, a wren maybe. It flaps its wings, but one of them is hurt. I kneel, set the shovel on the ground, and cup the bird gently in my hands. Its delicate body trembles.

Inside the hut, after confirming the cat is nowhere around, I lay the bird down on the ground near the hearth, where it's warm. The wren's beady eyes dart from me to the hearth. It pecks at the dust of corn on the hard-packed dirt floor.

Eventually I go back outside, to continue my work. My

hands become dirt-stained again, and a blister opens on my palm. But still I press on, digging and planting, digging and planting.

The rows are mostly finished and watered, and the suns are setting, when I hear a loud cawing from the hut. I rush back to it and find a crow perched in the windowsill, black against the gloaming sky. It glances at me, then at the little wren on the floor, then suddenly swoops toward it.

"No!" I shout, trying to scare the crow away.

But it doesn't flee. It lands on the hearth, oily feathers darker than night. I've never seen such a bird so close. It unnerves me.

"What do you want?" I ask, questioning my own sanity as the words come out.

"Caw! Caw!" It hops down to the floor, circling me, eyeing the wren.

I quickly scoop up the little brown bird to protect it.

"Caw!" the crow cries as it leaps back to the windowsill.

"Shoo!" I rush toward it, summoning the wind. "Get out of here! Shoo!"

"Caw!" it cries again, like a warning, then soars out of sight, its wings smoothly catching my blast of wind.

I sit in the chair by the table and study the bird in my hands. Kernel comes to my side and licks at my hand. His round eyes look up at me like he wants something.

"You know what that was about?" I ask.

He licks my hand again, studying the bird.

I feel around at its wing. A miniscule bone could be broken—too delicate for my fingers to fix. I bet Emma could heal it. She learned about healing here. She said the Healer is Yellow's facet of the prism.

I figure it's worth a try. I reach for my power. The blue threads come easily, but there's no yellow. I weave the air around the bird, but it only ruffles tiny feathers. I prod around with the wind, hoping to infuse it with light, with anything that could pull in a trace of Yellow's power, but nothing works. There's no sign of the Healer.

I give up and set the bird closer to my pallet of straw, where I can keep an eye on it, then spread more corn for it to eat during the night. The bird seems calm.

I lay back and close my eyes. My body is tired from the day's work. My thoughts are confused by the crow and the wren. The other animals have been so gentle, helpful even. But the crow seemed ready to attack. Why? Why these plots? Why these animals? Why this Yellow Tower? The string of "whys" carries me into sleep.

The golden blur looks like a rain drop under the microscope. Turn the dial, zoom there, and the blur takes on fine, glistening edges. The gold plops up in the center and ripples out, like a pond after a stone has been dropped in it, except that this shape is frozen. The molten gold cooled after the material sank into it, crystallizing into this in-motion-pond of atomic number 79. Outside the golden ring are the lethal chemical toxins. They would kill a person with the wrong dosage, but this dosage is perfectly calibrated and targeted. We've saved mice and monkeys, attacking the cancers that attacked them, and now we're ready to save humans by firing these nanotech torpedo missiles straight at the cancerous cells.

I step back from the microscope. I ask the research team around me if they're sure it's ready. They answer eagerly and affirmatively. It has been tested. It is ready. The first patients have given their approval. Normal chemo has failed them. The tumors still grow on their brains, and this is their last hope. I sign off, without seeking any other authorization. The disease that took my son will be stopped.

The next day we employ the microscopic golden missiles, loaded with toxins, into the frail bodies. No one vomits or loses hair. They hardly notice the days of assault we bring against their cancers. The first patient's white blood cell count drops noticeably in three days. The others drop within a week.

A month later, two of the patients are pronounced clean, five are doing much better, and only one is dead. Without the golden rings, they'd all be dead. It's a victory.

That night my wife Susan opens a bottle of champagne. We sit together on the balcony of our Washington apartment as the sun sets. Everything is golden—the fading light, the bubbles streaming up my glass, the ring on my wedding finger.

"You've worked so hard for this," Susan says. "How does it feel?"

"Good." But it won't bring Benjamin back.

"So many lives will be saved."

"This is only the beginning of what we could do."

Susan smiles. "It's a miracle."

She doesn't know what I really mean. Only five of my researchers, the most brilliant and trustworthy ones, know what else we have been trying. The nanotechnology has yielded amazing new possibilities. We have been experimenting, secretly, to transfuse it into brains of those who have just died. It requires the most exquisite work. Far more than any brain surgery I've done, but we are close. We have kept a brain alive without a body for an entire week. We have spliced synapses from one person's cortex to another's spinal cord. And if we can do these things together, we could keep a human alive forever.

"The miracles have only begun," I say.

"Miracles come only from God," she replies.

"Call it whatever you like. The technology is powerful. It is a good thing that it remains in good hands."

"The line between good and evil goes through every heart." She laughs lightly. "But let's not debate that again. This is a celebration. What you've done is courageous."

We sit quietly for a while. I think of Benjamin, my son who died, too young, too soon, and I know Susan thinks of him, too. Eventually I ask, "Can courage come from fear...for what we lost?"

"Maybe," she says. "Even fear serves a purpose."

7

THE NEXT MORNING I feel sore all over. There are more blisters on my hands. Kernel sleeps beside me. The injured little bird pecks at corn dust. The dream glows warmly in my mind. *Even fear serves a purpose.* I was facing my fear, trying to save others from the sickness that took my son. But my ambitions were not pure. There was something off, a dark undercurrent. If I've learned one thing about the Five Towers, it's that I'll have to face that darkness, whatever it was. It's the only way out—to learn the past, and scour it.

I rise from the straw bed and shiver from the cold. The faint coals in the hearth do not hold back the chill in the air. I summon the wind to add more wood, then pick up the wren to place it closer to the hearth.

The moment I have the bird in hand, it feels different. There's a subtle current passing from it to me. I focus on this energy, and it is like the blue threads of air, but golden. I've felt it before, much stronger, from Emma.

I follow the threads, hopeful, and they lead *into* the bird.

Its tiny heart thumps rapidly. Its tiny muscles pulse with this energy. I find the break in the wing. It is like a gap in the golden threads.

I pull the threads together, slowly, carefully, until they touch again. Then, for good measure, I coil them around each other, like splicing two ends of a wire.

A sudden motion makes me jump. The bird leaps out of my hands and hovers before me for an instant, wings flapping. It chirps, then soars out the window.

I stare after it, stunned.

I healed it.

This was completely different from what I did on Earth. There was no splint, no brace. The threads were not there last night. But this morning, after the dream, they were nearly as clear as the blue threads of air. And I wove them together *inside* a bird smaller than my hand. Amazing.

When I step outside, I feel like a new person. The air is fresh and crisp. Birds sing and swoop overhead, and I wonder if one of them is my wren. No crows are in sight. The three suns shine brightly and make the drops of dew on my newly planted rows glisten like brilliant little pearls.

Kernel barks ahead of me, and past him I glimpse a new person at the edge of the field of golden wheat beside mine. I head that way, with Kernel joining at my side.

"You know this person?" I ask the dog.

Kernel's tongue lolls. He bounces as he walks.

As I approach, the person looks up from underneath a wide sunhat. She is pretty, with a narrow face, brown skin, and large, dark eyes. There's a hoe in her hand, just like the one Drew had. Kernel walks straight to her, passing through the line between our fields, where the invisible wall should be.

The girl kneels down and pets Kernel like they're old friends. She ignores me.

"Hey, I'm Cipher."

She glances past me, as if assessing my plot of land. "You're new."

"Yes. I came from the Green Tower."

"I heard Green's a wild place. I like the peace and quiet here."

"Looks like you have a way with farming." I say, eyeing the golden stalks and ripe clusters at the top, swaying gently in the breeze. "Any tips?"

"Have anything to offer me?"

"Um, corn kernels? I just planted some."

"Come back when you got something ripe." She spits on the ground beside her.

"What's your name?"

"People call me Sally."

"Was that your name on Earth?"

She stands up straight and looks steadily into my eyes. She looks young, like everyone in the towers, except for the eyes. She looks like she's seen her share of trouble. "You first," she says.

"Paul Fitzroy. Everyone here calls me Cipher."

"Sounds American."

I nod. "Twenty-first century. You?"

"My name was Sally Hemings." She studies me, as if

expecting some reaction. "I was also American, a few hundred years before you." She looks toward Drew's plot of land. "That makes three of us here. I wonder…"

"What?"

"There must be some reason for it. They say the leader Elijah—who nobody's ever seen—picks everyone's plot."

"There could be a connection between us. It's like that in the other towers, too. Lots of people knew each other on Earth, one way or another. Are you connected to Drew?"

She frowns. "Ask him."

"Were you family or something, across generations?"

"No," Sally snaps angrily. "We look nothing alike. Why would you think that?"

"I don't know…My mother was here, in Red."

"Ah." She seems surprised. "*Was* here?"

"She went up to the White Tower."

"Bah, a myth." Sally spits on the ground again. Kernel sniffs at it, then whimpers softly before lying at Sally's feet.

"No, I saw it," I say. "We were in the Scouring. She went up through the light in the center and never came back. It's the only way out of this place."

Sally scowls as she gazes toward the Yellow Tower in the distance. "Lies they tell us. No way I'm baking any nine-grain loaf and going there. Not any tower, not any scouring. Oh, I heard about that once. They fight. They die. But here I got my land, the sunshine, everything I need. So I'm going to enjoy it in peace and not let anyone tell me otherwise."

She hoists her hoe over her shoulder and turns to walk away, holding out a hand to graze the ripe wheat above her waist. Kernel stays at her side and disappears among the tall golden grains.

I press my hand to the invisible wall. "Wait, please."

She pauses and glances back. "I *do* like corn. So when you got something fresh to trade, maybe we'll talk."

She leaves and I return to my hut without Kernel or any new grain. The suns bear down on me. The morning cold has quickly given way to heat so thick it makes the horizon blur in a haze. The Yellow Tower looks like a wavering mirage in the distance.

Back in the hut, a new cat is waiting, curled up in front of the hearth. This one is black with a streak of white fur down its nose and slitted green eyes. I move toward it, hoping for more supplies, or better yet, another note.

The cat rises lazily.

A grey shape darts away from it, but the cat pounces. The grey creature twitches then falls still. The cat moves away proudly, leaving a small dead rabbit on the dirt floor. The cat's green eyes look up to me, blink, then turn away. The cat leaps smoothly up to the open window and out, leaving the rabbit.

Faced with another meal of mushy cornbread and milk, I decide to accept the cat's gift. It's messy work, but I watched enough meat cooked in the forest of the Green Tower to know how to turn the creature into a little feast. There's even some salt to season it. The meat tastes pretty good, with leftover cornbread on the side. With my belly full, weariness settles over me. It's still too hot for work outside. I lay on the pallet of straw for a nap.

My dream is fitful. I operate again on a brain on a table, with a team gathered close, in white coats like mine. Just when I think I'm finishing the work, setting the scalpel down, another brain appears and it starts all over.

I lose count of how many times I repeat the motions. My eyes strain. My hands shake. I can't go on. I peel my eyes away from the wrinkled flesh and the operating table. The team stares at me, waiting.

"We're ready," I say. "Let's transfer it to the body."

8

THE GENTLE SOUND of rain wakes me. Water runs down the chute to the small reservoir by the pallet. No new critters inhabit the hut this time. I shake away the dream and peer out the window. Through the soft sheets of rain there's a person working in the distance, near the edge of my field. It's the plot of land opposite Drew's, and to the corner of Sally's. It's another potential source of grain.

I head out. My feet squish lightly in the moist soil. The rain quickly soaks my linen shirt and pants.

The girl stands calmly, watching me approach. She has a broad round hat that drips water from the brim like a curtain of rain around her. Plants rise to her knees, with thick stalks and leaves. Behind her a few of the stalks rise higher than my head and hold bright yellow sunflowers.

"Hello," I say, waving.

She gives me a friendly wave back. "Hi. I'm Li Min."

The rain and the invisible wall do not block her energy or warmth. She has a wide, genuine smile, straight black hair, and narrow dark eyes like Max's.

"Nice to meet you," I say. "How long have you been

here?"

"Many moons longer than you." She motions to my field. "You must have just arrived."

"Yes, from Green."

"The place with the tree?"

"You know about it?"

"My first plot was closer to the tree. I could see its branches and leaves high above the wall."

"They moved you? Why?"

She shrugs casually. "Why does anything change? A force acts, and there is no greater force to resist it. So it was."

"Someone made you move?"

"Yes, I do not mind. This land is better. Just wait. You will see more of my sunflowers bloom. You will smile."

I smile already. I like her easy, cheerful way of talking. It almost makes me forget the downpour drenching us. "Do you usually work in the rain?" I ask.

"I only work in the rain! It makes the soil softer. And mud is good for your skin."

"Where were you from on Earth?" I ask.

"Straight to it!" she says with a laugh. "Most of my neighbors come to me only wanting my seeds, though they will not grow in their land."

"What do you mean?"

"Your dirt grows only your crop. My dirt grows only mine. It is the way of this place. It is a good order."

"But I planted oats. From Drew."

"So sorry, they will not grow."

Something about the way she speaks, the line of her lips opening subtly, reminds me again of Max. "So who were you?"

"Li Min," she says, "I told you."

"Tell me more."

She looks up to the sky, where the rain has just stopped. Light pierces through a few small gaps in the clouds. She takes a step closer, only a foot short of the invisible wall, and sits cross-legged in the dirt. She takes off her hat and lays it upside down on the ground beside her.

"Please," she says, motioning for me to join.

I sit in front of her and use the wall to brace myself as I lower. My hand stays there, feeling the transparent, stone-like barrier. Li Min holds up her hand and presses it to mine—only an inch away. Though our skin does not touch, a sudden shock of energy courses through me.

I jerk back instinctively. My hand feels cold. I raise it slowly. The blisters are gone.

"You healed it," I say.

"The small wounds, yes," she replies, fixing her curious eyes on mine. "But not the scar. It is deep, very deep. Who are you?"

"My name here is Cipher. I was Paul Fitzroy, an American doctor, on Earth. I began in the Blue Tower, and have since been to Red and Green. What about you?"

"Only Yellow, as far as I remember. My story from Earth—what I know of it—is not easy. Do you want to hear it?"

"Yes, please." Her words remind me of what Hank told

me once in the Red Tower. "A friend here said that telling our stories again weakens their hold over us."

She smiles and folds her hands neatly in her lap. "That sounds nice. But my story's grip is iron. Let me tell you."

It should have ended better for Li Min, because she had the perfect citizenship score: 1,000. Everyone in China started there, but few maintained it. The scores began to fall early. Eight-year-olds failed to complete their homework. Eleven-year-olds sent crude text messages—which they believed to be encrypted, but the State saw every word and pixel. Sixteen-year-olds snuck alcohol or cigarettes. Adults crossed streets when the traffic light prohibited it. People tried to avoid taxes, they failed to pay their bills on time. There were a million ways to drop from the perfect score, and few ways to get the points back.

Li Min had advantages from birth, she knew. Her father had been very rich and left her with the family fortune, though his score had fallen so low he had fled the country soon after she was born. His wealth came from shameful activities—casinos and tourist attractions that praised Western culture and did not honor Chinese heritage. She had three sisters, but by ten she had lost her entire family. Many whispered that the State had eliminated her mother and sisters as punishment, and that she was kept alive only as a hostage the State used to try to control her exiled father.

She ignored these rumors. By the age of five she had

learned the value of loyalty to the State. It became her family, and she would not squander her wealth as so many did. She used it to every advantage. She had the best computing chip installed in her brain, doubling her mental processing and memory. The best tutors left nothing to chance, ensuring she excelled in school. The best financial advisers reviewed every purchase to evaluate its impact on her score. She did nothing without thinking about her score. What to eat for breakfast? Which car to drive? Who to marry? Every decision was perfect. Li Min was perfect.

The State agreed. It honored her with titles and public attention. At sixteen, she was chosen with a dozen others for a special pilot program of China's best to serve the people as role models for the country. Cameras filmed her every move. Sensors reported every heart beat. Journalists wrote articles about the length of her hair, the shampoo she used, and the brands of shoes she wore. All were made in China. Including her husband (she doesn't remember his name, but he had a respectable score of 957). Their wedding was front-page news. State officials attended as guests of honor. She became all that China hoped a citizen could be.

Then came the pregnancy, and the miscarriage.

It changed something in Li Min. There was no penalty to her score. She had done nothing wrong, even the State recognized her ideal behavior. She ate the perfect diet, got the perfect exercise. Her husband's genes perfectly suited hers. No one could explain why the baby's heart stopped after sixteen weeks. It simply stopped, and that was that.

The country mourned with Li Min. She became an exemplar of not only success, but of proper mourning in the face of inevitable human tragedy. She moved on, as everyone must, to serve the State as she could.

But inside, the switch that had driven Li Min to perfection had been flipped off. It didn't seem to matter anymore. Nothing seemed to matter. The more the people praised her as a model, the more she drew inward, to dark and quiet places that no one could monitor.

On a Tuesday morning in February, as she took her morning walk—heart at 75 beats per minute, no more, no less—a hooded man strolled toward her on the sidewalk. It was crowded, but his eyes stood out. They were blue and gentle and fixed on her. He said not a word but slipped a paper into her hand. The way he did it, so furtive, made her wait to open it. There was a place where the cameras did not record her. It was a two-by-two water closet. There she read the note, alone, breathing steadily to keep her heart rate normal.

(She knows she read the note, she tells me, but she cannot remember what it said. She remembers only what she did.)

Five days later, on her morning walk, Li Min got into an unmarked car at a certain place and time. The driver was the man with the blue eyes. He sped away from the cameras, out of the city. An older man sat in the backseat beside her. He used a device to hack into her neuro-chip and shutdown the trackers.

Then he told her that he was her father.

Neither of them spoke until they came to a meeting in a remote farmhouse. It was a great risk. They were a rebel religious sect, opposed by the State. They were opposed to everything Li Min was. They spoke about the importance of the soul, of humility and love. She discovered a secret part of herself—as if unlocked by a special key that only her father possessed. This part of her had longed to hear words like theirs. It explained her sorrow at her loss as a mother. It comforted her in ways the State and the perfect score never could. She turned on herself, opposed to what she had become. And then she joined them, undercover.

They asked her if she could ever get close to the President and press a device to his skin and start a revolution. They said it would inject an undetectable nanotechnology that would work its way to the President's brain and neuro-chip. She agreed and took the device, no bigger than a chrome flea. She would wait for her moment when she could fight back against the State. She would use her score, her wealth, her following.

The next day, when the State inquired, she told them that she had been abducted. The news brought great media attention. The State reduced her score to 995 for not reporting the abduction immediately upon her return. She hosted an international conference on the benefits of neuro-chips in the fight against human trafficking. She got her perfect score back. And she waited, eagerly, to tear the whole thing down.

It took more than a year for the opportunity to come. The President of China invited her to an honorary dinner.

The secret group sent her a letter, in her father's hand. All was ready to hack into the President, if only she could touch his hand.

Li Min dressed in red silk. She wore the President's favorite perfume. She bowed low when he approached her. He held out his hand. She placed hers in his, and he never noticed the chrome flea that burrowed into his skin.

They next day the State's citizenship scores were wiped out. Two days later, the President grew very ill. A week later every document and scrap of data produced by the State was released to the world on the internet. Then the President died peacefully in his sleep from a neuro-chip malfunction.

Just as the revolution began, the State came for her. They had tracked the source of nanotechnology and found her and sent her (she doesn't know how) to the Yellow Tower.

Li Min rises from the ground. She gracefully dusts herself off, then extends her hand to the invisible wall between us. On her palm lies a cluster of sunflower seeds, glowing like jewels in the golden light. "Now you know what I have lost," she says. "This is why I am at peace with these. I have learned not to yearn for more. It only brings pain."

"I'm so sorry." I stand facing her, feeling for her. "You were up against great powers. But you were brave. You did the right thing. And your father…"

"No, stop. You do not understand. I was a coward."

The hurt look in her eyes tells me not to press her, and not to ask about her father yet. *But could he really be Max?* What she said reminded me of his past, as I heard it in the Red Tower. And I know it's possible, because my mother was here. I force myself to be patient. We have time.

"Okay," I say. "I'll be here if you want to talk."

"Thank you. That could be nice." She studies me quietly, then a slight smile touches her face. With a sudden motion, she tosses her handful of seeds toward me.

I catch only a few and quickly kneel to gather the rest.

"Next time you can tell me more about you," she says, "and maybe bring a little corn once it grows. It has been a long time since I have had corn."

"Sure, I'll do that." I stand with my hands full of dirt and sunflower seeds. It makes me feel a bit silly. She's content with her seeds, but I dove to the ground just to pick up another grain. Maybe I could learn something from her.

"I used to be eager like you," she says. "This place has a way of tempering us. Here you will learn your limits."

I tap my foot against the wall. "I'm starting to see why."

"Yes, well, please visit again." She eyes the seeds in my hand and grins. "And don't forget to crack the shells. The good part is inside."

9

THE SPROUTS EMERGE like brave little soldiers. I kneel to the ground and study the green shoots. Sunlight coaxes them upward through the resistant soil. Clods of dirt crumble away from the narrow cracks that permit life to pass through. The little plants have no minds or muscles, but their force is steadily and gently relentless as they push through the layers of dirt. The seed could just rest there, quiet and dark, but that is not the way of things. No matter what we do, the allure of life and light draws all of us upward. Even Sally, even Li Min, even me.

Sally has ignored me since we spoke. I've called out to her, but I have nothing ripe to trade, yet. I will try again once my corn grows. At this pace—only two days for the green shoots to rise—the harvest may come soon. None of Drew's oats grow in my plot, but in his field they rise chest high. Li Min's sunflowers are small round yellow faces, like a cheerful audience for our conversation. I tell her more about my past. She listens peacefully and we talk of the modern world we lived in, but she avoids talking about her father no matter how I pry. I still wonder if he could be

Max. I would ask him, but he hasn't appeared since our first encounter.

I rise from the ground and marvel again at the row of plants. The growth is unnaturally fast, but then, little about this place is natural. The leader of the Green Tower, Daniel, said time is different here. The suns rise and fall, but there's no way to know if that means a day or a year has passed. On my plot the rain comes most days at the same time—when the suns are halfway down the horizon. The water moistens the earth, perfect for growth, and fills the little reservoir in my hut.

The animals have come at all different times, in different shapes and sizes. Mostly cats. Sometimes birds or rabbits. Once there was a goat with an udder full of milk, and I saw a horse in the distance. The cats bring most of the gifts. Salt from one, and a small dull blade the size of my finger from another. It's perfect for slicing cornbread.

The only usual cat is mottled gray and white. I started calling him Spunky because of the way he chases my shadow and likes to surprise me by leaping through my window unannounced. He plays with Kernel when they're both around.

As much as I appreciate the animals, the days begin to feel lonely. I can talk to Drew and Li Min, but the invisible walls isolate us. I start to wonder if other plots around me are simply empty and abandoned. Some fields show sign of work, but others lay fallow. Maybe Yellow needs more people. The last time I saw the towers' numbers, Black had the most and Yellow had the least. But the plots could also be occupied by serfs who stay inside and sleep. No one, other than me, seems very interested in leaving.

I use the dull blade to draw another line in the dirt where I'll plant another row of corn. I'm not sure why, but it feels like an act of hope. The first green shoots make me want more of them—more life growing around my little domain. And maybe the sweat will bring new dreams, or at least more corn to trade.

Just as I finish placing kernels in one row and start to line up another one, someone shouts nearby. It's from the field opposite Sally's, which has been fallow and empty ever since I arrived. Now there's a large boy standing at the edge, waving toward me vigorously.

I walk toward him, shading my eyes from the suns low on the horizon, shadowing the boy's face and making his round body look like a dark blob. A small round dog sits by his side.

"Cipher!" the boy shouts. "Cipher!"

I recognize the voice before I can make out his face. The voice belongs in Red, not here, but… "Seymour?"

"Cipher! It's really you!" He presses his palms against the invisible wall and leans forward like a boy looking into an aquarium. "I can't believe it. This place sure is something. You get a hut and some grains and a dog too?"

I come to a stop in front of him, and his happy freckled face makes me smile. "Looks like that's how the Yellow Tower does it. But no one gave me a dog."

Seymour laughs and rubs the head of the squat dog beside him. It's a brown bulldog with squat legs, a round belly, and wrinkles like thick folds on its face.

"Nobody *gave* me Kraut," he says. "But he came right after the king and queen left me here last night and told me they wanted a fancy bread with nine grains. This morning I was resting and Kraut came and hopped right up on my belly. I gave him as much barley as he wanted. We emptied the whole jar and the next time I looked, the jar was full again. Amazing, right?"

"That's one way to put it."

"Same old Cipher!" he says. "What grain are you supposed to grow?"

"Corn. I planted it a couple days ago and already have a few green shoots coming up."

"So you're new like me! That's great…except I guess we're kind of stuck. What's with this wall? You think it's made of glass? Or do the collars make it work? Looks like you got one, too. But it's not like Red, because no girl has paired with me. Well, the queen—that girl with the dark hair and the mean eyes—but I don't think that counts because she hasn't commanded me to do anything. And there's no way she'd pick me, not when she's with that tall blonde king. Are they the leaders? They look too young."

"No. Her name is Joan, and he's William. I'm not bowing down to them."

"No surprise there. I didn't like them much either. They seemed…well, you know the way royalty is."

"Not really."

"Ha, right, you're American, sorry. Anyway, think you could take my collar off?"

"Not through the wall." I tap lightly against the barrier. "At least we can talk. It's good to see you, Seymour."

"Better than good, my friend!" He stands up straight and taps his thick finger against the wall, pointing it toward me. "You know this can't be a coincidence. How long's it been? A year? A century? I got wiped a few times. But hey, here I am with my memories back. And you're the boy with the wind! You brought back a dragon's tooth! You were the Alpha! So…can't you blow down this wall or something?"

"Sorry, I've tried. The power doesn't work."

"Well at least you still got it, right? Everybody in Red was worried. They said you got caught by Green…how'd that go? And how on earth did you end up here? Me, sure, nobody's surprised when the first time I finally make it to the Scouring—paired with my sister, remember her, she got pretty powerful with the flames—and well, my first time I get caught by Yellow. It figures. But you! You're Cipher, the Alpha, the chosen one. How'd you get caught?"

I look down and kick at the dirt. "I let myself. It was a trade. Emma wanted to come here, but she…"

"Emma! I remember her! She paired with you, lucky guy. She sure is cute. Always made me think of a princess with her golden hair. You two made quite a pair in Red. Did she go to Green with you? What happened?"

I sit down and motion for him to do the same. We face each other and, for once, he stays mostly quiet as I tell him about how I was captured by Green and killed and wiped twice in the tribal fighting, but then got my memories back and grew stronger and worked with others to rule the tribes and bring peace to the forest. Until I was traded to Yellow, and collared.

"I don't think I'd like Green," he says.

"How did you feel about money?"

He smiles and shakes his head. "I couldn't care less about it. I love food! And I loved that girl I told you about from my past, Frau Manziarly. I learned a lot more about her…hard things. But none of it had to do with money. Does that mean I won't have to go to Green?"

"Sounds like it. Why do you think you came here?"

"Yellow caught me, duh! But I know what you mean. Rahab says it all happens for a reason, that we have to be scoured of our past stains, and all that. So what's Yellow for, other than growing grains and baking bread? Well, I don't know…you've been here longer than I have. This is, what, your fourth tower? You're becoming a professional scourer. You might as well make it five towers, right? First you can become king here instead of that other boy with the crown, and then you can go ahead and take over Black. Then we'll pronounce you ruler of the universe and you can put an end to all this silly Scouring business!"

I can't help but laugh. "We have to get past this wall first."

"No problem, right? Just grow some grain and bake the royals their yummy bread. Except…" His green eyes blink as he looks around us, at some fallow fields and others fully grown, but with no one else in sight. "How are we supposed to get nine grains?"

"I think we have to trade for them. The land is a grid, so you have eight others around you. We just have to convince them to trade with us. Counting you, I have four grains so far."

"Hey, no sweat. I'll talk them out of their grains, or I'll bake something so delicious they have to trade!"

"With barley?"

Seymour laughs. "Barley and corn and salt and milk and baking powder. Surely there are eggs around here, too. What fields have you ever seen without eggs? Just you wait. Seymour will teach you everything you need to know about bread, maybe even cakes." He sighs, and smiles down at the bulldog by his feet. "I was born for this. I feel like Yellow and I are going to get along just fine. Aren't we, Kraut?"

The dog barks happily. I'm not so easily convinced.

"If Red was about passion," I say, "what do you think Yellow's about?"

"You ask me like you already know the answer. Why don't you tell me, oh great ruler of the tower universe."

I smile but inside the question troubles me. I have been avoiding it. Drew, Li Min, and me. As different as our stories are, they all have a similar torment. We were afraid of something, and it made us regret not doing what we thought we should have done. Drew even named his fears as a spirit, Napalm.

"Fear," I say. "Everyone here was afraid of something."

Seymour shakes his head. "No, that can't be it. Fear's

not a stain. You really think I'm here because I'm afraid of the dark, and you because you're afraid of heights? How are we supposed to be scoured of that?"

Heights, I think, amused as I remember my fear. There are no heights here in Yellow, and it's definitely something more important than that. *Even fear serves a purpose.*

"You're right," I say. "It can't be fear by itself. Fear only matters if we let it twist us or stop us, if we don't have courage."

"Like how you scrambled on your hands and knees over the bridge away from the Red Tower?"

"Yes," I admit. "But you know, after we lost you to the dragon, I walked straight over that bridge when I came back. I was still afraid of the height, of falling, but all of life seemed more fragile. Losing you put it in context."

"Hey, I came back!" Seymour says. "It took a while, but the memories came back, too. So…what were you afraid of on Earth? Did you have courage?"

The simple question carries me like a leaf in the wind, falling, rising, spinning. My son, Benjamin, had been sick. I was a doctor, trained to face that. When he had the seizures, I had been ready to diagnosis and treat him, but I had failed. I couldn't save Benjamin. He died and could speak no more. I'd given up everything and moved to Washington to research a cure, to fight back against what had taken my son and what, ultimately, would take all of us in a thousand different ways.

"Death," I say. "I was afraid of…mortality."

Seymour slaps his knees with both hands. "Ooh, big

deal! Afraid to die, no way! Come on, Cipher, who wasn't?"

I meet his green eyes and don't know what to say. It was different. It was not just fear of death. It drove everything I did. After I'd let go of the desire for Samantha and the thirst for wealth, there had been only one thing motivating me. I tried to call it "saving kids like Benjamin," but it was still mostly about myself. *We could be gods*, I had thought, *if only our brains could survive.* I was trying dangerous things, experimenting on brains, to fight against death. Was that courage?

"What if…" I pause, trying to find the right words. "What if I feared death so much that I transplanted a brain?"

"Alright, now that sounds pretty bad, or maybe just crazy. But what if I feared rejection by Frau Manziarly so much that I agreed to cook for mass murderers?"

"That sounds bad, too."

"No kidding! But enough of all this death and fear talk. We're back together. Let's make the most of this Yellow Tower and its dirt and dogs and grains."

"How do we make the most of it when we're trapped?"

"We bake a cake!"

10

MY PALMS SWEAT, my heart races. I'm wearing my best navy suit and red tie, sitting in the oval office, before the President of the United States. The sky is blue, tips of roses showing, outside the immense windows. The President's chief of staff and my lead researcher sit beside me. The researcher's hands fidget in his lap as he tells them what we've discovered—it really could be the cure for cancer.

"But you tested this on *people?*" the President asks, turning to me, man to man. "And one *died?*"

"Yes, but they all volunteered freely, and four were healed." My voice is surprisingly steady. "The possibilities are far greater than this."

"This isn't about possibilities," the President says. "You've seen the press."

The chief of staff holds up the newspaper, with the front-page headline that makes me cringe.

Victim sues after rogue NIH program proves lethal.

"Perhaps you failed to realize," the chief of staff says, "this is an election year. You are supposed to generate good news, not *this.*"

The President leans forward with his hands folded on the desk, a red phone within reach. "I will accept your resignation."

Resign?

My throat tightens. I can't do that. Not after how far we've come. But my back is against the wall. I force myself to breathe, glancing at the chief of staff, then back at the President.

"What if I could deliver you a breakthrough that would change everything?" I say.

The President's face is stoney. "The other option, of course, is to fire you."

"There's another program you might not know about."

"Another reason to fire you," he replies.

"We've successfully transplanted a brain."

The President's perfect brow rises slightly. "A brain?"

"Yes, I formed a special team of researchers, including two from your classified defense agency. Only five of us know about it. And now you." He doesn't stop me, so I rush into the details, telling him about how their science on neuro-chip implants for injured soldiers met ours and sparked, how we used the nanotechnology to splice synapses. I do not tell him that all our experiments were on pigs. If it works on a pig, it's only a matter of time before it will work on humans.

"This won't make good news…" the chief of staff says when I finish. "You know what the base thinks about this sort of thing."

"The public cannot know about this," the President

replies. His eyes level with mine.

"Yes, Mr. President."

"You were right to keep this secret," he says. "It could prove most useful…"

"I'm not sure about this," the chief of staff says.

"We have to take risks to win." The President stands, and we all stand. "This will be Dr. Fitzroy's last day with NIH. We will release this news to the press." He comes around the desk and faces me. "You will continue the research with the defense agency, in complete secrecy. The objective is to serve our soldiers, and our national security. You will report directly to me. Are we agreed?"

"Yes, Mr. President."

I sit up on the pallet of straw and find Kernel by my side, licking at my hand. I shake my head, trying to come to. A chirp draws my gaze to the table. A bird is there. It looks like the wren I healed, and it has something like a twig in its mouth.

Still in a daze, I hurry to my feet and approach it. Its beady eyes study me. When I'm almost within reach, it drops the twig and flies out.

I peer closer at what it dropped. It's a tightly rolled piece of paper. I unroll it carefully. The handwriting is unfamiliar.

The king compliments you on your first healing. Work harder, serve the Yellow Tower well, and you will grow in courage and power. Six more grains and you may rise from Serf and have the honor of

The note is not signed. It has no further instructions.

This confirms Emma's warning. The king sees everything that happens in the light. How else could he know that I healed the bird, or that I need six more grains? I suddenly feel uneasy, like someone is behind me. I turn but no one is there. The feeling hovers like a dense fog over my thoughts. The king is watching.

I toss the note onto the warm coals in the hearth and step outside. The suns are just beginning to rise. A huge flock of birds flies in harmony, swooping and rising as if sharing one mind. My healed wren, my messenger, could be among them.

A distant squawking sound draws my attention. Kernel wags his tail and bounds past me, then pauses to look back, like he wants me to follow.

"What is it boy?"

The dog barks again and races toward the squawking sound. I follow after him. The warmth of the three suns feels good on my face. The corn stalks rise to my waist as I walk between them, feeling the tender leaves graze under my palms.

Kernel stops by the edge of the invisible wall. Past him, the source of the squawking becomes clear. Two people stand near the corner of my plot, and one of them—a tall boy I haven't seen yet—holds a chicken up with both hands. The other is Sally, standing with her arms crossed and saying something I can't hear over the chicken's constant caw, cluck, and cry. Kernel glances back at me, wagging his tail eagerly.

"Now look what you've done," Sally says loudly, casting an annoyed glance in my direction. "Brought out the neighbors again."

The boy turns to me and bows, even as he clutches the squawking, frantic chicken in his hands. The bird's white wings stay clamped down under the boy's slender hands. A wide smile spreads across his tanned face. His happy formality while clutching the desperate chicken makes me laugh.

"I love all my neighbors," the boy says, rising from his bow. "My name is Simeon. Who are you?"

"He's Cipher," Sally says before I can. "And he's got nothing to trade. And neither do you. So take your chicken on back to your hut and let me work in peace!"

The boy ignores her. He looks past me and motions—with the chicken—to my field. "I see you have planted. This is a good thing, a good work indeed. Let me guess: corn?"

"Yes, it's growing fast," I say. "It's been only a few days since I planted."

"Ah, the blessings of the Yellow Tower. We have good soil, good rain, and lots of light." His voice is deep and dignified, like someone accustomed to speaking before kings, and not at all like a skinny boy with a chicken in his hands. He glances down at the hen, which has gone quiet with its beady eyes on me. "May I make a proposal?"

"Oh, don't try with the chicken again," Sally groans.

"What do you mean?" I ask, looking between them.

"I offer you this fine bird," the boy says.

The chicken's beady eyes shift with each sudden bob and turn of its head, so that they stay fixed on me. It weirds me out.

"Why would I want it?" I ask.

"See now, the hen calms with your presence, as if its destiny lies in your hands. It is a plump hen, a source of life. Do you not know where eggs come from?"

"Of course." Eggs would be a nice change. Seymour could even bake with them. "What do you want for it?"

The boy smiles. "In exchange for the chicken, you give me two dozen ears of freshly-picked corn."

"But they're not grown yet."

"I ask only for your first two dozen ears," he says. "I can wait if you will promise this. We can be honorable, can we not?" He looks to Sally. "Neighbors must trust each other."

Sally's arms stay crossed as she stares at me. "Don't do it."

"Why not?"

"Simeon's always offering something useless," she says. "A chicken, a fork, a spot of salt. You know how this silly game works. Grain is the only thing we need. Go ahead, ask him to trade his and see what happens."

Past the tall boy, there are only a few short and scattered grassy plants. Most of his field lies dormant. And yet, the hut in the center looks better than any others I've seen. The roof is made of tile rather than thatch. A rocking chair sits outside the front door, and there are flowers around it.

"What are you growing?" I ask him.

"I cultivate goodwill," he says.

Sally groans again. "He means, what *grain*?"

Simeon keeps his eyes on me. "Flax is my allotted grain. But I see no reason for us to be limited by such. There's more to life than the growth of a single grain." He strokes the chicken gently. "So, Cipher, what shall it be? Two dozens ears of corn from your first harvest for this fine hen?"

This is the first chicken I've seen. Maybe there will be more, but there will certainly be more corn. It seems like a fair deal, except Sally has me worried. She still hasn't traded me her grain, either. I will need hers as well as his.

"Would you toss in a handful of flaxseeds?" I ask.

Simeon blinks as if offended, then he motions—again with the chicken—toward his field. "You see my poor crop. I'm afraid I do not have enough to trade."

"See…" Sally says. "Simeon and I have been neighbors for a million sunrises, and guess how many flaxseeds he's traded me?"

"None?"

"None!" She stomps the ground emphatically. "He sleeps for a week straight and plants nothing!"

"Ah, but many things I *have* traded you," Simeon says. "Your life is better thanks to me, yes?"

"You and your lazy bones…" Sally shakes her head.

Simeon turns to me, undeterred and smiling. "Do not heed our lovely neighbor," he says. "Her dreams make her restless, but we must learn to be patient here, eh? A time to plant, a time to uproot. A time to kill, a time to heal. But I'll tell you, a fine hen like this comes along only once a moon. You'll get no better offer. What will it be, Cipher?"

Sally stares at Simeon, arms crossed and head shaking. But I'm looking at the silent chicken. It can't be so hard. Take the chicken, feed it some corn, and collect eggs. It's worth trying for Seymour, if nothing else.

"Okay, I'll trade the corn for the chicken."

"Your first two dozen ears?"

"Yes."

"Let's spit on it."

"On what?"

Simeon laughs. "It was a custom of my people. The water of the body is a blessing. We spit to seal the agreement."

With that, he spits to the ground by his side, and I do the same. Sally sighs in disgust. Simeon takes a step forward, clutching the chicken. The invisible wall is between us. As he draws the chicken back, it looks like he's ready to throw it across the barrier. I tense, ready to catch it.

But Simeon suddenly grips the chicken by the neck, his slender fingers holding tight as wings flap wildly and the chicken squawks. With a quick flick of his wrist, Simeon snaps the neck and in one smooth motion tosses the chicken toward me, sailing through the wall.

My hands catch it instinctively. But the helter skelter jerking of wing and foot and body make me screech and leap away. The creature drops and lays helpless on the dirt, flapping up little clouds of dust. Its talons draw lines in the ground. There's no more squawking. No chance of healing.

Above the last shuffles of the dying bird, Simeon and Sally begin to laugh, louder and louder. My heart pounds, blood rushes to my cheeks. I rush to the barrier and press my hands against it. Simeon is only a few feet away. Without thinking I summon the wind, which whips furiously around me.

"You lied!" I shout.

Simeon quiets quickly. He holds up a finger to me. "No, not at all, my neighbor. I offered you the chicken. I gave you the chicken."

"You killed it!"

"We did not specify a required condition. The deal was the chicken for your first two dozen ears of corn, yes?" He looks to Sally, who is still bent over laughing.

She meets his eyes and nods. "That's the deal." Turning to me, her laughter and smile wipe away and she adds, "I warned you. *Don't do it*, I said. But who ever listens to Sally?"

"It is still a good deal," Simeon says, turning to go. "I look forward to your corn."

As they walk away, I release the wind and gaze down at the motionless chicken. Kernel nuzzles up to my leg and barks. He looks from the bird to me to the hut and back.

"Alright, boy, we might as well cook it."

Wagging his tail, he scoops up the bird delicately in his mouth and trots off toward the hut.

11

WHAT I REMEMBER of chicken matches nothing of the bloody, feathery mess at my hands. Chicken is a tender, white meat that comes in plastic wrap and tastes best right off the grill. Those who prefer a wilder experience buy the whole, plucked bird, ready to slide into the oven. Then all you need is a fork.

But I have no plastic wrap, grill, or fork. I pull another handful of feathers from Simeon's dead chicken and my stomach churns. I step away, take a breath, and remind myself of the flavor of chicken. I pull more feathers, but it hardly makes a dent.

I look down at Kernel by my side. "Any ideas, boy?"

He hops up with his front paws on the table, eyeing the chicken curiously. Then he hops down and sniffs at the ground where a few drops of blood have fallen to the dirt. His tail suddenly wags and he goes to the door.

I don't hear anything unusual. I walk to the door and see nothing outside. Kneeling down and rubbing his soft brown fur, I ask, "What is it, Kernel?"

Tail wagging, tongue lolling, he returns to the table and

takes the barely plucked chicken in his mouth again. He trots past me out the door, glancing back to make sure I'm following. He heads straight to Seymour's field. The suns hang high in the sky, like two oranges and a lemon.

We reach the edge of Seymour's plot. A few green sprouts have emerged in his field. He is nowhere in sight.

Kernel sets down the bird and starts to bark, loud and sharp. He keeps at it until Seymour's bulldog, Kraut, shuffles out of the hut with Seymour close behind. They see us and approach, the master and pet both with a lazy waddle to their steps.

Kraut reaches us first and plops down on the dirt. Kernel rushes through the invisible wall and pounces him. They growl and roll and play along the ground, stirring up dirt and getting filthy. I reach out, ever hopeful, but the barrier stops my hand as firm as stone.

"Hey Cipher, still a wall, huh?" Seymour eyes the chicken on the ground by my feet. "What's that?"

"It's a dead chicken. I traded for it."

"A chicken! That's great!" Seymour's green eyes flood with excitement. "I'll admit, I'm getting kind of tired of the barley. Even mixed the corn and salt, it's kind of bland. And it takes a lot to fill a belly like mine. But hey, a chicken! So there's a chance of eggs, must be. How'd you find it? Just wander onto your land?"

I tell him about Simeon and the trade, and how Sally warned me and laughed about the whole thing. Seymour agrees it was a raw deal, the way Simeon tricked me. He tells me not to worry about it. "Some lessons have to be learned the hard way," he says. "But this lesson proves it: we can get eggs someday! We just need a live one. Until then, we've still got this to eat!"

Seymour's enthusiasm makes me smile. Kernel and Kraut lay still, panting and looking up at me. I'm glad that Kernel dragged me here, instead of letting me try to handle the chicken myself. It would have taken all night.

"I wanted to cook it and bring it as a surprise," I say, "but…I'm not much of a chef."

"You have to pluck it!"

"I figured that. I started…"

"Well, give it here and I'll do the rest in no time. The hearth's already burning. We can coat it in some powder and fry it in the pan." Seymour licks his lips. "I can taste it already!"

Not me. I bend down to pick up the chicken. Taking it by the scaly feet, I hurl it toward Seymour. It sails smoothly through the wall. Seymour catches it and cradles it close like a precious bundle. I'm glad to be rid of it.

Seymour tells me it will be ready in a couple hours, then he waddles off with Kernel and Kraut by his side. I turn back for my hut to get my jar of milk and my pan to use as a plate. The fields are quiet around me. The afternoon heat makes the air heavy.

Inside the hut the mottled cat, Spunky, lays curled up in his usual spot in front of my hearth. He rises and stretches gracefully.

"Ever tried fried chicken?" I ask.

Spunky responds by rubbing his cheek against my hand

and purring. It makes me sleepy. There's time for a nap, so I lay on the pallet and close my eyes. I dream about a research lab with animals in it. Mostly white mice in little cages. But a loud squawking enters the lab and a pecking hen suddenly stands over a cage of mice, flapping her wings. The chicken consumes a mouse with each peck, growing and growing until it pecks at me and swallows me in my white coat.

I wake up sweating. It doesn't take long to realize this dream isn't like the others. It wasn't real. I almost wish the others could be shrugged off so easily.

Outside, the suns are low on the horizon. I head toward Seymour's plot, with Spunky following and pouncing at my long shadow as it glides over the ridges of dirt. We wait together by the invisible wall. The yellowish-white sun in the center remains higher and larger than the two orange suns flanking it. The round white orb reminds me of the Scouring and the White Tower. My goal has not changed: to get out of this place. But now a loaf of bread and a crazy boy-king stand in my way. It shouldn't be harder than defeating Baron in the Green Tower's forest, except that here there's no Jubilee to get the collar off my neck. Maybe the collar is what creates the wall—to enforce the command that I stay on this acre of dirt. Emma's note said I had to get the nine grains. I will find a way.

Seymour comes out just after the suns have touched the horizon, painting the sky red and orange and purple. He uses both hands to hold a pan in front of him, with steam and the fragrance of fried meat drifting into the early evening air.

"Smells good!" I call out.

"Oh it is!" he says. "I mean, *if* I'd tried some already. I quartered it and made a brand new batter and fried it real quick. The batter's got three grains. Barley, corn, and quinoa. The quinoa gives it a little extra crunch and smooths out the nutty taste from the barley. I guess I could have just used cornmeal, but what's the fun in that?" He stops in front of me, breathing heavily as he holds out the pan. "Which one you want?"

I point to one of the drumsticks. "That one. The leg."

"Good choice. A leg *and* a thigh. Very tender, juicy. You're going to love it." He lifts it carefully from the pan. "Ready?"

I nod and he tosses it. For a moment, eyeing the leg in midair, my breath freezes. This is Seymour's work. I can't drop it. My fingers close around the drumstick and clutch it tight. Some of the flaky crust crumbles off to the ground. Spunky licks at the crumbs beside me.

"Go on, try it!" Seymour says.

I take a bite and smile at the taste of the tender meat. Seymour may not be able to fight dragons, but give him a few ingredients, and he can cook for a king.

"Amazing," I say, mouth still stuffed.

He laughs and digs into the other drumstick. Kraut barks up at him until Seymour tosses down a few other bits—probably the innards. The two dogs eat happily beside each other, even allowing Spunky to come over and have a bite. The animals in this place live so peacefully. No dogs I remembered would have let a cat that close, much less to share a meal of fried chicken.

I finish chewing and study the flaky crust in my hand. "You mentioned quinoa," I say. "How'd you get it?"

Seymour wipes his mouth and points with his drumstick to his left. "That girl over there grows it. She traded me some."

"When? I've never seen her."

"A couple nights ago when we had that full moon. She says she only works at night, under a full moon. How loony is that? Her name is Itzel. She used to live in the mountains and prefers the cold. She wouldn't take my barley by itself, so I offered one of my little cakes. No eggs, no yeast, but I still know how to bring the flavor out. After she tried a bite, she gave me a little quinoa. I've used it, but maybe we could get more. She said she's also trying to collect some honey from a beehive on her land. Nice girl, if a little crazy. You should meet her." He looks down at the chicken, still steaming, in his hand. "Now, can we let the chef eat?"

"You're the one talking."

Seymour laughs and I laugh and we both take bites. We eat together as the last light of the day fades. With the help of Kernel, Kraut, and Spunky, we finish the whole chicken without leaving a scrap.

12

THE NEIGHBORS TAKE notice of my growing corn. Drew hollers out to me that it's looking good. Simeon asks when he'll get his two dozen ears. Even Sally says she'll be expecting a trade offer soon. The green stalks rise so tall that I can't see past them from the hut. Their golden tassels rise above my head as I walk along the rows, checking the ripening ears. The bounty fills me with surprising pride. I planted the kernels. I grew this. And now with this crop I should be able to trade for more grains. I just have to figure out how to convince Max to play along, or to find another grower of rye, so I can get out of this agrarian cage.

One day Seymour and I stroll along the invisible wall, with Kraut and Kernel ahead of us, playfully dashing back and forth between the fields. Seymour tells me he got his first egg from a neighbor on the opposite side. The only thing the neighbor would accept in trade was a drink that Seymour brewed with his barley. Seymour says everyone around has started offering better and better things for a jar of the drink. The ingredients have opened up a world of opportunities for Seymour. With the egg he baked a delicious pastry.

"Sorry," he says, grinning. "There weren't any leftovers."

I laugh and tell him not to worry. It's good to see him happy. Like the others around my plot, he hardly even minds the walls around him.

"Safer this way," he says.

Maybe it's because of the Green Tower, or my life on Earth, but I'd rather have freedom than safety.

A dog's deep bark interrupts Seymour as he tells me all about what he'll do with the next egg. Kernel and Kraut race ahead of us toward a white puffy dog in the distance. A girl walks toward the dogs, and us.

She reaches the corner of the fields before us and stands there with a hand on her hip. As I approach I realize she's about as pretty as a girl can be, with long black hair and bronzed skin. In the wind, the light fabric of her white tunic hugs tight to her tall, slender frame. She looks like a model on vacation, not a farmer stuck in the Yellow Tower. The land behind her is plain, sandy dirt.

"Hello!" Seymour greets, waving eagerly as the three dogs get acquainted. "I'm Seymour. This is—"

"My name is Cipher."

"I am Camille," she says, with a rich, lilting accent. "This is my first day back. You will want my millet, no? All the people want my millet."

"Back from where?" Seymour asks. "And what millet are you talking about? All I see is dirt. Oh, the grain! You are going to plant it. Yes, I'd love some of your millet. I will bake you a cake! Do you have any eggs?"

A playful smirk settles on Camille's lips. She looks to me. "This friend is forward, no?"

"He's just friendly…and talks a lot," I say. "He's also an excellent chef. You really should try something he cooks."

"A chef, yes, I can see that," Camille says, eyeing Seymour up and down. "You want my millet, so you bake me a macaron. Then we trade, yes?"

"A macaron! Yes! Oh, I love those!" Seymour bounces from foot to foot with excitement. "Let's see…it's been a while, but I'll need…"

He suddenly kneels and starts drawing with his finger on the dirt, listing ingredients and saying them half under his breath, as if forgetting that we're there. Camille waves and turns to go.

"Wait, please," I say. "You said this was your first day back. From where?"

"From the tower…" She sighs. "I baked my loaf and joined the artists there. But I did not last long with them. It was not worth the effort. I was wiped and sent back here to start over again. This is what my dreams show me so far."

"Who are the artists?" Seymour asks, rising from his drawing in the dirt and stepping closer to the intersection of our walls. "You mean like painters? That doesn't sound so bad. Why didn't you last long? What's the tower like?"

"Trust me, it is more peaceful here," Camille says. "But if someday you must see, then you will learn that it is good to be as far away from the king as you can be. Paint something he does not like and you are wiped. Bake something he does not like and you are wiped. I prefer life out here." She looks to me. "Sorry to say it, but the tower will not be kind to you."

"Why?" I ask.

"I see in you what I've seen in me. It is plain in your eyes. You want people to love you, no? To adore, to praise, to desire."

"Maybe in the past…"

"Ah, yes, so I have heard."

"From who?"

"Emma, of course. She misses you, you know. You really ought to get the nine grains, but for the right reason. Not for your own desire, but for her. Do it for Emma. Ah, we go to such lengths for the adoration of others…" Camille runs a hand through her long hair.

"So you will help me?" I ask.

"I will trade, yes."

I point past her, to the field at the far corner of hers. "That plot over there should have rye. Have you seen anyone there?"

"Not a soul," Camille says, "but I will watch."

"If you get some rye, will you trade it to me, too?" Seymour asks. "Imagine the bread I could make with it!"

"I would rather taste than imagine," she says, smiling at him. "Will you share?"

"Oh, yes! It would be my pleasure." Seymour's cheeks redden. "I mean, every true chef loves to share. What's the point of creating if it is not shared?"

Camille's smile falters. "Creation meant fame and wealth for me. All my country, maybe the world, came to see me on the screen. But it all twisted into fear—fear of losing what will certainly be lost with time. Such is the way of beauty. We should never fear what is unavoidable. It will make you run from even yourself. But enough of this. Ta ta!"

She blows a kiss and strides away without pausing or glancing back. All three dogs follow as if compelled by her magnetic pull.

Seymour looks up from his writing in the dirt. "Kraut!" he shouts. "Get back here!"

The bulldog stops, glances back, then continues ahead with Kernel and the white puffy dog, following Camille all the way to her hut.

"Don't worry," I tell Seymour. "They'll come back."

"Well, there's only one thing to do," he says. "Time to bake macarons! Bye Cipher!"

He leaves and I go back to my hut and find the mottled cat, Spunky, with a rabbit. The meat roasts over the fire as the suns beat down on the land outside. The meal is filling. Kernel returns and gnaws the bone as we sit by the hearth. The heat and the words from Camille lay over me like a blanket. The king is a tyrant. The fields are peaceful. This explains why my neighbors are in no rush, why some of them sleep rather than work their fields, why some will not trade. They do not want a loaf of nine grains. They fear the king. They would rather be serfs than face him.

I almost wish it were the same for me.

But that's not who I am. I'm Paul Fitzroy, and I'm Cipher, the marked boy. I'm unable to be still, to have peace. And it's not just for me. Emma needs me. So I must continue seeking the grains, even if I can't make the corn grow any faster.

Two nights later the moon is full. I decide to wait for Itzel, the girl whose plot is at the corner of mine, bordering Drew and Seymour. Seymour has already traded for her grain, quinoa, but he used it up. She has planted her field in stages, with part of it fallow, part with small green shoots, and part with grown plants bearing lush reddish purple clusters of grain at the top. I'll offer her corn in exchange for it.

The night air turns so cold I can see my breath. The only warmth comes from Kernel, who sleeps by my side on the dirt. He sleeps a lot. Life's easier that way. His chestnut fur presses against my back like a pillow as we wait. And wait.

It remains quiet. There's no sign of Itzel or anyone else braving the cold night. Stars move across the sky in a steady, slow march, faintly lighting the cloud that spills out of my lips with each breath. One of the stars shines brighter than most, twinkling and holding my gaze.

Emma?

There is only silence.

My eyelids grow heavy, my breathing settles into the same steady rhythm as Kernel's. I sleep and dream that Emma and I are wrens soaring together over the Five

Towers. The dream swells like a balloon in my mind, so full and buoyant that it takes me away. When I first hear the scratching sound, it takes me a moment to realize it is not a dream.

In the darkness there is a darker spot, a figure. She wields a hoe and moves methodically between two rows of small green shoots, swinging the tool down, lifting, swinging.

I call out to her, "Itzel."

The night seems to swallow my voice, but a moment later she turns. The hoe drags behind her as she approaches. Straight black hair sways with each step. She comes to the corner, just across from me, and sits cross-legged on the dirt. Her large round eyes are like black holes in the night. She doesn't speak.

"Hi, Itzel. Our neighbor, Seymour, told me your name. I'm Cipher."

"I knew a boy who looked like you." Her voice is soft, weary.

"Here?"

"No. In the past."

"Maybe our paths crossed," I say. "I lived in America. I was a doctor named Paul Fitzroy."

"Drew has told me about your people," she replies, with an edge to her voice. "They sound like conquerors. My people fought against conquerors. You look like one of them."

"Probably a coincidence." I shrug innocently, feeling defensive but curious. "Who was he?"

"He lived in the mission. His people captured my family, all of us. They told us stories about a man who died and lived again. They told us to believe the stories. My father said we would and so we agreed to live with them. A woman wore a white hood and tried to teach me. She hit me when I spoke their foreign words the wrong way. The boy laughed at me, but he always stared. He thought I didn't know. This was the same with his people and mine—the staring of a boy at a girl. He visited me after each day's lessons. I told him our stories, and how I believed that his stories and ours could both be true—the sacrifice of innocent blood for the atonement of evil. He called me a savage, but still he stared. His gaze felt like ants crawling over my skin. After my father left on a ship, I decided to leave, too. It was night, a night like this, when I ran."

"Where was this?"

"We called the land Yucatan. I went back to my people, the Maya, deeper in the jungle, safer, they thought. I tried to warn them. We had a few years of peace before they came with weapons that blew holes into us. There was a fight. The boy, taller by then, saw me. *Itzel*, he said, with a look in his eyes that I have tried to forget. This time I tried to fight him with my spear, but a bullet hit me in the back. The pain was like nothing I'd ever felt. The boy held me and told me he loved me as my life poured out on the stairs of our temple. He pressed his hand to my forehead and blessed me while all around my people raised their spears against white beasts like him, and like you."

Through the whole story her voice has remained soft, and now as she finishes the night is quiet. Her dark eyes study me, waiting, accusing. Her accusation somehow blends with Camille's words from earlier.

"You are brave to tell me this," I say.

"Brave? I ran from the mission, from the boy. I fought only when I had to. Even as I laid there on the steps of my temple, life pouring out, I felt the terror grab me and shake me like an angry giant."

"Anyone would have felt that way."

"Would any boy have done what *he* did? Would you?"

"No…" But I hesitate. How could I know what I would have done in that other boy's shoes, or in hers. "I hope not, anyway."

"You're all the same," she sighs. "The last boy on that field said he was sorry. He got my grain."

"I'm sorry for a lot of things, but I'm not the boy from your past."

"What are you sorry for then?"

I take a deep breath and tell her. It's easier now than it used to be. My name was Paul Fitzroy, a neurosurgeon who thought he was God's gift to humanity, who lied and cheated, who married for money, who spent a fortune, whose son died because I couldn't save him. Then I poured everything I had into research about the brain—trying to unravel its secrets and stop its diseases and make it live forever. I tell her I don't know how my story ended, only that I woke up here, in the Blue Tower.

She listens quietly and when I finish, she speaks softly:

"Maybe you're not a beast… I've grown this crop a million times now. I've seen people come and go. I've looked into my past and gone over it again and again. We're all guilty of something."

"That may be true," I say, "but we don't have to carry the guilt forever. The leaders of the towers say we will be scoured."

"I'll believe it when I see it." She looks down and reaches for something. In the dark I can barely see what she's doing. "So you want to trade grains?"

I nod, suddenly hopeful. "It's the only way out."

"Hold out your hands. All the way against the wall."

When I do as she says, she tosses a scoop of grains through the invisible wall and into my hands. Only a few of the dark beady grains fall to the ground.

"Thank you," I say. "I'll bring you my grain soon."

"I don't care much about the grain." She gazes up at the night sky. "But if you find a way to shed this guilt, I'd like to know."

13

THE SUNS CROSS the sky by day, stars by night, and the land heats and cools and yields its bounty. Simeon gets the first twenty-four ears of corn. Sally sees me deliver it, and when I propose to trade a dozen ears for an armful of wheat, she agrees. Later that day, Simeon calls to me and says he'll give me a handful of flaxseeds for a dozen more ears. We spit on the ground and make the trade then and there.

The handful of flaxseed joins the other grains on the table in my hut. Barley from Seymour, quinoa from Itzel, oats from Drew, wheat from Sally, sunflower seeds from Li Min, millet from Camille. That's seven, plus my corn.

There's only one short of nine: rye…from Max.

He has avoided me. His field remains mostly barren. The only growth on his land is a vine that climbs the side of his hut. The few times I've seen him he retreats into his hut, doesn't answer when I call out. The two neighbors we share, Sally and Drew, say he won't talk to them either.

Drew promises he'll keep an eye out for Max. "Eight grains!" he says. "I can't believe ya already got eight grains.

Sure, I'll give a holler if I see the grumpy rye boy."

I ask Li Min, as I did with Camille, if she has a neighbor on the far side who grows rye. She tells me the plot has been dormant ever since she arrived. I also ask her about Max. She says she knows nothing about him. I tell her what I learned in the Red Tower—how he was a wealthy Chinese businessman with four daughters and casinos and even a replica of the Roman Colosseum.

A shadow crosses her face. "My father once owned casinos."

"It could be him. You look like him."

She shakes her head. "I do not know what happened to him. I know only what I told you, about he found me and led me to the resistance."

I don't believe her uncertainty. The more I study her face, the more I see Max. "Does he have any idea you are here?" I ask.

"He shouldn't. Probably better that way."

"No, that's not true. I found my mother here, in the Red Tower, and she revealed so much. You should at least talk with him. To find out."

"Even if it is him, what could I say?"

"Tell him something only he would know, and then you can find out if he was really your father."

She falls quiet, looking down. When her gaze meets mine again, tears moisten her eyes. "I need some time," she says, turning away.

I watch her leave in silence, then I go to my field and gather an armful of fresh corn. I return and toss it gently over onto her land. I don't ask for anything. I do the same an hour later, and a third time. The pile of fresh ears of corn rises to my knees. The next time I come, she is waiting.

"You dishonor me," she says. "I do not deserve this."

"If you help me reach Max, you will deserve it."

She looks down at her clasped hands. The word comes out as the faintest whisper: "He called me Lily."

I study her, questioning it. "Not a Chinese name?"

"My father turned his back on our homeland. The State called him a traitor. In the secret messages I received from him, through the rebel group I told you about, he always called me Lily."

"Thank you for telling me." I add the armful of corn to the pile. "I promise, this will be worth it. He will want to know about you."

"I shamed him. I put the State—and my perfect score—before him."

"But you told me you changed, and worked with him, right? There must be more to it…"

She shrugs. "Perhaps. I do not know how his story ended."

"I will talk to Max and tell you what I learn."

We part and I get to work with my plan. No more shouting or calling out. This time I'll set up something harder for Max to ignore. I flip over the table in my hut and use ashes from the hearth, mixed with water, to write a message in big block letters:

LILY LOVES YOU

Kernel prances around wagging his tail while I work, no doubt confused about why I'm vandalizing the table where we eat our meals. Once it's done, I use the wind to haul the table outside—it feels good to use it for something more than moving dirt and seeds—and set it down so that the message will face Max every time he looks my way. It's not perfect, but it's the best idea I've come up with.

I set up a vigil by the overturned table. Kernel and Spunky come and go, as if checking in on me. Once Kernel returns with a fresh container of milk, lets me take it, then plops down beside me for a nap. Spunky brings a capsule of salt. I use the wind to harvest a few fresh ears of corn and eat them salted, raw. Night falls and I try to stay awake but Kernel's warmth and heavy breathing lulls me to sleep by his side.

The voice that wakes me is harsh. "What do you want?"

I hurry to my feet and face Max, who glares at the message on the table, scowling. Even in the pale starlight, the strain on his face is plain—dark bags under the eyes, gaunt cheeks. Mist blows from his mouth with each breath in the cold air.

"Rye," I say.

Max does not look up from the message. "You found her?"

"Yes, just over there." I point to her plot of land behind me.

His gaze lifts. He stares at me in quiet. "If you want rye, tell her something for me."

"What is it?"

"She made up for everything. What she did changed the world. I'm proud of her. I love her."

His mouth opens, but closes again. It is so quiet that I can hear the purring of a black cat as it rubs against Max's ankle.

"Anything else?" I ask.

"She will understand…if it's really her." He turns and walks to his hut with the cat following close.

I run with excitement to Li Min's land, like a messenger entrusted with priceless words. She changed the world. And Max…he loved her—even cold, hard Max felt this for his daughter.

When I reach the invisible wall, it's still dark and no one is in sight. Fighting the urge to shout to wake Li Min, I look up to the stars and guess it's only halfway through the night. It can wait. Better to sleep on straw in a warm hut than out here.

I wake at first light, eat stale cornbread, and rush outside. Kernel bounds behind me, sensing my excitement. Li Min is already outside, working near her hut. When I call to her, she comes gracefully toward me. Not hurrying— whether from reluctance or calm, it's hard to tell.

"Your father gave me a message," I say.

"What did you tell him?" she asks. "I saw the table. You wrote something?"

"That you love him."

Li Min closes her eyes, doesn't reply.

"He came to me in the night," I say. "I've tried

everything to speak with him, and this is the only thing that has drawn him out. He told me to tell you: You made up for everything. What you did changed the world. He's proud of you. He loves you."

She stares at me, motionless. A slight shudder courses through her like a little shock wave transmitted from the earth up through her legs and body. The next shudder is harder, and then there are tears. Her face falls into her hands and she cries.

Kernel goes to her, but I can only sit and be there, on the other side of the wall. Kernel sniffs at the tears as they fall to the dirt. He presses close and gently licks at her hands. She pets him, looks into his friendly white and chestnut face.

Eventually her shudders slow and stop. She looks up to me and tells me what happened. The State had been searching for her father. She said they pressured her, threatened to reduce her score. *But I haven't seen him in many years*, she told them. They wouldn't believe her. But it was true, until that day when the rebel group had taken her. Her father had been one of them. He had given her the nanotechnology. Then, after the invitation to join the President's dinner had come, the letter from her father followed. The chrome flea that infected the President was inside the envelope. But the words mattered more to her. In the letter her father said that he was sorry for living like a crafty fox, and that she would be brave to carry on as he had.

The State knew what the note said, of course. All of

China did, because they were spectators of every aspect of Li Min's life. But only she knew what it meant. The words were from a bedtime story her father had told her, when she was only a little girl with a perfect score, and before his exile. It was a story about a fox who disguised itself in sheep's wool. She knew immediately what it meant: she would be the fox who would wear red silk and touch the President's hand and start a revolution.

"I made him proud," she says.

"Why did he want a revolution?" I ask, realizing that Max must have known the danger and guessed how it could end for her. He sacrificed his daughter for this.

"I do not know the details," she says. "His group had a secret project with the Americans. They were doing research about this nanotechnology and neuro-chips."

A shiver runs down my spine. It is too much for coincidence. My research connected to Max's and Li Min's lives? Did we know each other? It's too much to explain, too much to wrap my mind around.

"What's wrong?" Li Min asks, studying me.

"Nothing," I say. "Was it worth it? Playing the fox?"

"I hope so. Will you tell my father something for me?"

"Of course."

"Tell him thank you, that I would like to see him. Ask him what it all means. I don't know what happened after he came. The bedtime story he read to me ends with the fox in sheep's wool getting caught because it tries to steal away too many sheep. Maybe that's what happened to me. Is that what happened to him, too? Please, ask him that."

We say goodbye and I set up another vigil at the corner of my land beside Max's. He peeks out of his door only once during the day, but spots me and ducks back inside. I try a new message in block letters on the table.

MESSAGE FROM LILY

He comes again in the middle of the night, waking me as he did before, asking about the message. This time he holds a handful of rye. The slender seeds look silver in the starlight.

I tell him exactly what Li Min said. At first the words soften the hard edges of his eyes and lips. But at the words *steal too many sheep*, he frowns. All the hardness returns and settles like concrete by the time I finish.

"Too many sheep…you mean the State caught her?"

"Yes, she said they came just as the revolution began."

"I was the leader! No one told me!" Max clenches his fist around the rye, and spins away.

"Hey!" I shout. "We had a deal!"

He stops, turns. Breath fogs his face in the cold night.

"I delivered your message. I brought one back."

"All you brought back is pain." His voice is eerily quiet.

"Please, I could give another message to Lily. I want to help."

"You only want my rye." He lets the grains fall to the dirt by his feet, and stalks off into the darkness.

14

THE FOLLOWING DAYS blur uneventfully. I try different messages on the table, but Max does not come out again. Seymour tells me to give up. He says it's a waste of time, that Max was never the trading type.

"You remember how he was in Red," he says. "He wasn't Max there. He was Axe. He was a fighter, that was about it. Hard to imagine him going any softer after the Black Tower."

I know now that Max is more complex than that, but I admit Seymour is right—there's little hope of Max giving me his grain. Seymour says he would trade a whole cake for a single rye seed if anyone was on the rye plot neighboring Camille's, but it has remained empty.

When I tell Li Min what happened, she says she is sorry, that she should have expected it. Her father was a vengeful man, and he may not have known what happened to her. He spent a lifetime working against the State. But that did not mean he was prepared to lose her in the fight.

"Perhaps the revolution failed," she says, gazing past me toward Max's fields. "I am sorry about my father. You have given me much. I will try to help you get rye."

"How?"

"A new neighbor could come."

"Thank you," I say politely, but my hopes are low. Yellow would have to capture or trade for someone new in the Scouring, or shuffle people around to new plots. There has been no change in the fields so far. The only thing to do is plant more corn, and wait.

I could use the wind, but instead I sweat. It makes my dreams better. One day a cow came to my hut with a hoe strapped to its back. I wield the tool and swing it over and over into the dirt, taking out my frustration and anger. I clear out the old crop of harvested corn and gather it into a large pile. Then I plant more seeds in straight lines. The cat, Spunky, follows me as I work, chasing my shadow and keeping me company. By the end of the day, blisters cover my hands.

I try healing the wounds, closing my eyes and searching for the yellow threads, but the power will not work. Spunky purrs by my side. I try sending the weaves into the cat, and it works. I search its small feline body and find a small cut in one of its paws. I prod around the wound, then meld the golden weaves and seal the crack. Spunky hops into my lap and curls up and sleeps contentedly.

The next day I visit Li Min. She heals the blisters. She tells me there is no new neighbor, no other way to get rye. I thank her and plant more corn. Once the pile of dead corn stalks rises as tall as I am, I take a hot coal from my hearth and set it on fire. I sit on the dirt and watch the blaze rise.

It is somehow very satisfying, like a flash of passion from the Red Tower.

As the fire burns low, the sky grows ominous. Huge dark clouds billow up like mushrooms and block the light from the setting suns, making it almost as dark as night. This is not the gentle drizzle that comes most afternoons. Wind and rain sweep across the yellow plain. The first drops of rain fall to the dirt around me, making tiny dark spots. Then the drops come faster, heavier. Spunky and I take shelter in the hut.

The rain reminds me of the deluges in Green's jungle, the storm over Blue's sea. Wind whips against the rugged shelter. Water drips from little gaps in the thatch roof. I hunker down, planning to sleep through it. Kernel comes in, soaking wet, and barks at me.

"I know, boy. It's a storm. Lay down here."

But Kernel keeps on barking until I stand, and then he points his nose at the place where I had made neat little piles of the different types of grain. The wind—gusting through the open window—has begun to scatter it.

Kernel was warning me.

"That's a good boy." I cover the grains.

The blowing wind tickles at my skin, like a faint electric current. I go outside, where dark clouds rise in stacks. A gust of air fills my lungs. I focus and channel the blue threads coursing around me.

It starts small. The weaves expand into a shield like a bubble overhead, enclosing the hut and me, blocking the rain and the wind. The shield pulses with glowing veins of the power. The energy of the storm courses through me. The rain comes down in sheets. Lightning strikes in the distance.

These forces tingle at my fingertips, drawing my hands up to the sky, palms open. More and more of the blue threads connect with mine, like creeks flowing into a swelling, racing, intoxicating river. I expand the shield up and out, spreading to the edges of my field, pressing against the invisible walls. The walls do not give, but they shake as if affected by my power.

Kernel barks at the open door into the hut. Inside the jar of corn rests on the table, an endless supply that needs to be planted again and again. I've done the work, sweated through the day, collected the blisters. What good has it done other than a few dreams? I've learned nothing new in days. I want to be finished and move on, to find Emma.

Threads of wind pull the kernels out in straight lines, hovering and streaming out of the hut. In long, smooth motions I drag the ribbons of power across the dirt and drop the kernels down in perfectly parallel lines—the rest of my field planted in minutes, without a crumb of dirt on my hands.

I feel exultant as I draw in a deep breath and expand my lungs, flexing and pushing the power out against the walls. And there, gazing out at my little domain, I spot Max's hut in the distance and something turns in me. Anger, then fear. As long as Max is here, refusing to trade, I will never leave this place. I can't let him control my fate.

My power meets the emotion like a chemical reaction.

The threads weave tighter and tighter, gathering streams of yellow and green and funneling into a shape like a drill aimed at the corner of my land, at Max. Spinning and pressing with everything I have, the clouds roiling above, I feel the wall shake more and more and I give it all I have until the pressure between the two forces is too much—straining and straining and…bursting.

The blast knocks all the threads away.

I collapse to my knees, hands still raised to the sky. The darkness spins above—grey and black, black and grey—coiling as it begins to descend. Slowly at first, the whole sky seems to lower, but then it comes fast, twisting like a vicious corkscrew until a full grey cyclone strikes the ground. The tornado starts at the corner of my land, right where my power had pressed, and it ziz-zags along the ground, tearing up dirt and whipping all the fields around. It takes only seconds. The funnel races straight toward Max's hut and passes over it and then there is nothing left. The tornado lifts and hides innocently in the roiling clouds above.

I'm still on my knees, soaking wet, palms in the mud, when I realize the sun is shining down on my back. The storm left as quickly as it came.

"Hey, did you see that?" It's Sally, yelling the question from the edge of her field. "Cipher! You hear me? You okay?"

I stand and don't bother brushing the mud off as I approach her. I look to the left, blink, then look again, hoping to see something, but nothing changes. There's no hut, no Max.

"Boy, you look like you got a flock of crows perched on your shoulders," she says. "That storm mess you up? Ain't no need to worry. They roll through here time to time."

Her expression is friendly, gentle, but I can't keep my eyes away from Max's empty land. "Has *that*…happened before?" I ask.

"Sometimes. But that's the biggest twister I've seen."

"It took Max."

"You act like that's a bad thing!" she says with a laugh. "That boy wasn't growing any rye, now was he? Maybe we'll get a better neighbor."

"But he—" I think, somehow, that I might have done it.

"Don't you worry your little self about him." Sally waves off the concern like it's a gnat. "You know he can't die. Can't get out of here, neither. He'll be back. I bet ole Elijah just wanted him in a new plot." She laughs again. "That's one way to move 'em!"

"Elijah?"

"The leader," she says, suddenly serious. "They say he picks everyone's plot, that it's all carefully arranged, for some grand design. But I'll tell you—" her voice drops to a whisper, though no one is remotely close to hearing us— "no one's seen the old man in ages. Now I saw him long ago. He used to walk these lands, come up and wave all friendly like, even give out little gifts. But he ain't been seen in a long, long time. I wonder if he's gone."

"Gone where?"

"I was hoping you'd tell me that," she says, glancing down at my hands. "I saw what happened with your corn…when you held those scarred hands up to the storm. You're something special, aren't you boy?"

I look away, back to Max's empty plot. "I don't know."

"Well then, you better find Elijah and ask him!"

That night a nightmare wakes me. It begins in the clouds—dark and swirling like the storm from the day, except this time the tornado touches down directly in my mind. I see neurons carrying thoughts, spinning up and up in the chaos—and the thoughts are from earth—they are Dr. Fitzroy's thoughts, eager, striving, seeking to find some cure. But all of the effort is ejected into the sky by the storm and left to come crashing down like meteors, burning through the atmosphere and landing as harmless bits of dust on a hospital bed.

Benjamin is on the hospital bed. His monitor shows a flatline, but his eyes are open, fixed on mine.

"Don't worry about me," he says. "I'm right where I'm supposed to be. But I'm worried about you, Dad. What would you believe if you were on this bed instead of me?"

His question, said so innocently, haunts me more than any ghost. If I were on the hospital bed, I would believe the world conspired against me. I would be furious. I would be a great man assaulted by the horrors of existence, because existence fears me. It knows I save lives. It knows that it must eliminate me, because I am a threat to death.

"You know how weak I look?" my son asks softly.

I nod, but I don't understand how he is speaking. His body has no pulse.

He says, "I have light in me that is more powerful than the whole world."

"How, Benjamin?" I ask, shaking my head, afraid.

"When I die, I know where I'm going. Do you?"

"Into the earth. *If* I die."

He smiles, but tears are in his eyes. "I want you to be with me."

"I want that, too," I say.

"Then you have to change."

15

"I HAVE RYE!"

Li Min holds a fistful of grain stalks with ripe, golden straw at the top. She's smiling, as excited as I've seen her. I didn't come for the rye. I came to tell her that I might have accidentally, or not so accidentally, created a tornado that destroyed her father, Max. Temporarily.

"You didn't need my corn?" I ask.

"He didn't want any grain at all," Li Min says. "Once I told him I wanted rye for my neighbor, Cipher, he lit up like a lantern. He told me that if I delivered a message to you, he'd give me a lifetime supply of rye."

"What's the message?"

"First, he says his name is Hank, and that you'll know him."

"Hank! Incredible! How did he get here?"

Li Min smiles. "He told me you'd ask that, and he already gave me his answer for you. Here's the whole story, sorry if I get any little bits wrong, but there was a lot."

The message from Hank is that he asked to be traded to Yellow. He figures he followed me from Blue to Red, then I followed him from Red to Green, so it's about time he followed me again from Green to Yellow. He says it's a pattern. The terms of the trade were two from Yellow for Seneca and him. They've decided to stick together, but he hasn't seen her since arriving at his plot. He got the same task of baking a bread of nine grains, and he insists that I bake mine right away. He says that he refuses to send me another message because that will only make me delay (but Li Min doesn't believe him; she has realized he likes to talk). He says he wants me to go ahead. He's doing this for me. I'll owe him one.

"How did you get a friend like him?" Li Min asks.

"I don't know," I say, thinking of how I met Hank in Blue, and how he helped me there and in Red and in Green. "Ever since I met him, he has been on my side, making my goal his own. I haven't done much to deserve it."

"Friends are not something to be earned, but gifts. The likeness of heart and mind, united in a cause, comes about as often as opposed wills make enemies. Both friends and enemies can grow or wither, like tender plants needing water."

Her words make me think of Max. "I will try to return the favor to Hank, but I have to tell you something. Your father has sort of been my nemesis here. And well…I was the one who wiped out his hut, with my power."

"Don't be silly," she says. "You didn't do it. Nothing we do passes through these walls. It must have been Elijah's doing."

"The leader? Sally said he's been missing."

"I don't need to see Elijah to trust him. He has been very kind to me."

"What do you mean?"

"He gave me my memories back."

"How?"

"In my dreams, of course. Do you not see things in your dreams?"

"Sometimes…" The visions from recent nights stream through my mind. Dr. Fitzroy's research on the brain, his meeting with the President, and just last night, the tornado taking Dr. Fitzroy's thoughts and spitting them up into a roiling storm. "Many of my dreams are nightmares."

"But were they real?" she asks, and her question is innocent. "I have seen many dreams, especially after I have used the power to heal or to speak to others. I believe they reveal the past. Even the nightmares tell something of my inner state."

"I'm not sure. Some of them could be meaningless. On Earth dreams were only the mind's way to process information, to *store* long-term memories, not to reveal them."

She smiles. "You know this is not Earth, Cipher."

"Yes, and your father will come back. But I'm sorry."

"Your life and his and mine are connected. I hope you will learn more and tell me. All can be forgiven. All can be healed. Elijah told me that long ago. When you get to the Yellow Tower, please remember me."

"Wait, let me trade you a little of all the other grains for this rye. I couldn't have nine grains without you. You could come to the tower, too."

"That is a kind offer, but no."

"Why not?"

She glances back over her field, toward her hut. "I've settled here. It is a fine plot."

"But how will you ever leave?"

"Why would I want to?" she asks solemnly. "I don't want to fight anymore."

I don't understand, but I don't press her further. She tosses me a handful of the rye, which I clutch like a treasure.

"Thank you, Li Min. I will repay this somehow."

She bows formally and we part. I walk away amazed by her serenity. Maybe her time in these fields has given her this calm. Part of me wishes it had done the same for me. But it did not. I don't belong out here. And now that I have enough rye, I want more than ever to move on from this stifling prison. I want to find Emma and get out. First the Yellow Tower, then White.

I hurry to Seymour and, as promised, give him a few pinches of the rye. He lights up like it's candy. He tells me how we should bake it all. Smash the nine grains and mix them together in a pan, with milk and butter and salt and baking powder. Set the pan into the hearth and watch it rise. As the top becomes golden brown, pull out the pan and...wait for whatever is supposed to happen.

I follow his instructions as well as I can. The proportions of each grain are roughly the same. The mixture looks like a yellow soup, but in the hearth the smell is that of bread, delicious bread. When I retrieve the pan from the fire and place it on the table, a shadow darkens the doorway behind me.

"Well done," says a familiar voice.

16

THE GIRL-QUEEN, Joan, stands at the door of my hut looking completely out of place. She wears a silver crown, a yellow silk gown, and a smile as radiant as the sun. Her presence makes me shy at my own squalor. The dirt floors, the grubby clothes.

She glides to the bread, golden and steaming in the pan. She leans over it and takes a sniff. Her hand hovers over the loaf as if she plans to pinch off a bite, but instead she pulls her hand away and looks to me.

"Do you wish to advance?" she asks.

I say yes and she tells me to bring the bread and walks out. Kernel watches me with dark brown eyes as I take the pan and look around the hut one last time. There isn't much else to bring. But it's harder than expected, leaving this little place. Maybe I won't have to leave all of it. I pat Kernel's head. "Come on, boy."

His tail wags and he follows me out. Ahead, Joan has mounted a large white horse. Her silken dress spills over the horse's flanks, glimmering and flickering like a candle flame over the dull landscape. Kernel and I hurry to catch up with her. She rides straight toward Seymour's hut.

"We have one more stop," she says as we come to her side. The horse's back is level with the top of my head.

"How did you know to come?"

She glances down, eyes knowing. "Your emotions told me."

My fingers go to the collar. I'm still her servant. It's enough to quiet my questions and focus on staying calm.

When we reach the line between my field and Seymour's, she rides over it without hesitation. I stop.

"Do not worry," she says. "You may pass now. My command has lifted."

I move my foot forward tentatively, expecting to meet the invisible wall. But the barrier is gone. I cross over onto Seymour's field like it's foreign territory. I'm free. I'm tempted to run.

"Feeling excited?" She grins down at me. "Remember, you are still my serf."

There have been no commands in so long that it was easy to forget the collar. But I've worn one in Red, and in Green. I don't need a reminder of how completely she can control me. The last thing I want is to give her a reason to use this.

"I understand."

She nods and continues riding toward Seymour's hut, with me following by foot. When we reach the door, she dismounts and enters first and begins to laugh. Inside, Seymour stands with crumbs on his shirt and his mouth full of bread. The bulldog, Kraut, is cradled in his arms licking at the crumbs. The hut is identical to mine, except that Seymour has made a mess of it. There are powders and vials and ingredients scattered everywhere, like the laboratory of a mad scientist.

"Sorry…your highness…" Seymour mumbles through the mouthful, then gulps it down with a tremendous swallow. "It looked so good! I couldn't wait to try it. Who thought of using nine grains? They really are delicious together. A touch dry, but if I had some proper yeast, your mouth would be watering. Is there any yeast here? Oh, hi Cipher!"

"Hey Seymour."

"Wait, how did you…?"

"That is quite enough," Joan says. "Bring your bread, what's left of it, and come with me."

"Yes, your highness. I'll just need—"

"Silence." She holds up her hand. "Do not test my patience."

We leave together without a moment's pause. Seymour and I trail after the horseback girl-queen, each holding our pan of bread. Kernel and Kraut trail after us. The expression on Seymour's face is a blend of excitement, hunger, frustration, and curiosity. For once I wish he could ask all the questions on his mind. The girl surely has answers.

The fields around us look like the ones we left behind. They spread in a gridded, patchwork pattern. Some have golden grains ready for harvest. Many are dormant. It is impossible to tell whether the dormant ones are empty plots or lazy tenants. The huts look almost identical from a distance.

Only one change marks the landscape as we follow Joan—the tower ahead of us. It grows larger, more detailed, more like a fairytale castle. Turrets shimmer in the sunlight, with the bright reflection of glass. The central tower has a golden pennant streaming against the blue sky—and on the pennant there's a symbol of a single sun.

The plots of land just beneath the tower have cottages rather than huts, with stables adjacent to them. A boy approaches us and takes the reins of the white horse. He wears nicer clothes—clean linen pants, a silken yellow vest—but the collar at his neck marks him as one of us, servants. Joan dismounts and thanks him. He bows and leads the horse away, while Joan leads Seymour and me by foot to the tower.

There is no moat or wall. The castle rises before us as towers stacked on towers, turrets on turrets. Upper turrets jut out from the side of the central spire, with only blue sky beneath them. The whole structure looks counterweighted and precarious, like a stalk of corn that would fall if one ear of corn were moved to the other side. The many pinnacles of the tower are glass or crystal, reflecting the light of the setting suns.

We move into the tower's shadow as we would into a canyon. Kernel and Kraut sit and watch us advance, as if they've gone as far as they'd like. Ahead a line of six guards waits before an immense open door. They are radiant and commanding in golden armor that covers them from head to toe. Tall yellow plumes rise from their gleaming helms, and they grip long pikes in front of them. It makes no sense. Where did the armor and weapons come from? If Yellow had this all along, why didn't they wear it into the Scouring?

Joan stops in front of them. They do not bow or even register her presence. Maybe there are boys inside the armor, but they look like men looming over a little princess—not servants standing before their queen.

"We bring bread," Joan says formally, motioning to the pans that Seymour and I hold. The bread has long since grown cold. "These two serfs are ready to meet the king."

A guard in the center steps forward. "And do the suns shine upon you?" The question emerges from the slits of the visor like a squeak. The boy inside the golden armor can't be much older than I am.

"The suns shine first on the king," Joan answers with a bow.

The guard who spoke taps his pike twice on the ground, and the group forms into two lines of three, making way for us to pass through them. Joan leads the way, her silken dress sweeping back and forth with each step.

We enter a hallway three times as high as it is long. Pale yellow stone pillars stand like giant legs to our sides. Above, light pours through a mosaic of crystal shards—a thousand hues of yellow, some milky and others vivid as orange—forming a sunburst that makes the room dizzying. Maybe it was meant to be brilliant and dazzling and impressive, but the barrage of yellow makes me squint and feel sick to my stomach. Seymour pulls at my arm to keep us moving.

We follow Joan down the hall, past doors, to a broad, central staircase at the end. The sandstone stairs rise and then turn left and right, climbing up and up. A maze of stairs and dazzling hallways follows. Seymour pants loudly by the time we come to a large door of golden painted wood.

"Steady yourselves," Joan says. "Stay still and silent by my side. King Chamberlain will decide your fate."

She knocks firmly against the wood, and the door groans open. She leads us into a round room with a round table in the center. The floor is a mosaic of tiles, matching the one in the larger hallway at the bottom of the tower. A glass spire rises in steep lines above us, reaching a point a hundred feet up.

"Two at once?" asks the boy-king, William. He sits on a chair across the round table from us. Six more guards in golden plate-mail sit to either side of him. They look just like the six guards at the entrance, except that these do not wear helmets. Three of them are girls.

And one is Emma.

She looks straight at me, no trace of emotion in her steady blue eyes. Her golden ringlets spill on the heavy armor around her shoulders, making it look dull. I try to open my mouth to speak, but Joan's command still holds.

"They worked together," Joan says. "They can part here."

"Hmm, yes…" the boy-king says with contempt, eyeing me, then Seymour. "I suppose they will. You have a recommendation?"

"This one has a way with cooking." Joan looks to Seymour, whose hands tremble so much that the bread almost spills out of his pan. "He would do well with the bakers or the managers."

"Warm it," the king says. "I will taste and decide."

Joan takes the pan from Seymour's quivering hands and places it in front of the king. She then lifts her hands again, as she did outside, and gazes up to the glass turret. The three girl guards do the same, and faint threads of yellow descend into the room like smoke. They swirl toward the pan of half-eaten bread and concentrate there for a moment, then disappear. Steam now drifts from the bread, drifting up in the same way that the yellow threads had drifted down.

The boy-king pinches off a piece and drops it into his mouth. He chews thoughtfully, looking from the pan to Seymour.

"It's good," he says. "Did you eat the other half?"

Seymour nods.

The king laughs. "The kitchens would tempt you…What did you fear on earth, boy?"

Seymour looks to Joan, who nods for him to speak.

"The Nazis," he says.

"Ah, we've heard about these people," the king says, turning to one of the guards—a stern-faced boy with roguish dark hair. "What do you say, Neville, baker or manager?"

The boy studies Seymour for a long moment. Ten breaths pass. Sweat beads glisten on Seymour's forehead.

"He has already been a baker," the boy says. "Let him manage now."

"Manager it is," the king replies. "Take him, Neville, and see that some of his fear—such moist fear—is scoured."

The guard rises in his golden armor and moves to Seymour. He and Joan meet each other's eyes, and something seems to pass between them. Maybe she gave him control of Seymour through the link.

As the two boys are leaving, the king says, "And what of the other one?" His eyes are fixed on me. "Now I will try your bread."

Joan takes the pan from me and sets it on the table. She and the other guards warm it with the golden threads. The king tastes it. All goes as it did with Seymour, until the king chews, pauses, face twisting, and spits out everything in his mouth.

"Not a baker," he says. "Recommendation?"

"He fears not being in control," Joan answers. "But he is powerful, as promised. I recommend him for the guards."

"High praise!" the king says. "What say you, guards? Whose place would he take? Or should he start with the archers? Or…" The king eyes me up and down again. "He is rather small. Maybe the artists would be more suitable."

"There is much tile to be laid," a guard says.

"If he controls the air as they say," adds another guard, "then his arrows will hit the mark."

"Vincent has wanted a painting apprentice."

"The air could help place tiles."

The king looks from guard to guard as they offer more ideas about my fate. Apparently wherever I go I'll be an apprentice to someone else. Arranging tiles or painting sounds about as boring as growing grains in a field. Archer wouldn't be so bad. I could do a lot while patrolling the walls, maybe even get revenge for the ones who shot me when Emma and I first visited this place.

"And what of you, daughter?" The king has turned to Emma. "You know him best. Surely you have a recommendation."

Her face remains serene, unreadable. "You know my recommendation," Emma says.

The king smiles. "Ah, but do your comrades in arms?"

"They've seen what he can do," Emma replies.

"And yet none of you is willing to give up your position?" The king sounds amused, looking from guard to guard. "It almost seems that you are…afraid. But no, surely not."

The guards shake their heads in unison. They look unnerved, even in their armor and seats of honor.

"Why then, there is nothing to fear." The king turns to me. "Boy, would you serve me honorably?"

"What's the alternative?" I say.

An urgent command comes from Joan: *Manners, he is the king!*

So I add, stiffly, "Your highness."

"There is no alternative," he says.

"Then why did you ask?"

"Ha! I like this boy. We shall have a competition at sunrise, and perhaps a new guard." The king stands, and the five remaining guards quickly rise to their feet around him in a clanking of metal armor. Emma does not look anywhere near my direction.

"Joan, stay," the king orders. "Anna, show our potential guard to his room. The rest of you are dismissed."

17

THE GUARD NAMED Anna leads me away from the king and the throne room. As we leave, she takes a golden helmet and lowers it over her straight brown hair, making her look just like the other golden guards, like Emma. The same Emma who followed me to the Red Tower, who fought with me in Green, who has been my friend every step of the way. She must have a plan.

Anna goes back the way Joan and I came, winding down flight after flight of stairs, until we reach the grand hallway at the base of the tower. We move through one of the doorways to the side, which leads to another set of stairs. It is hard to track where we are going, constantly climbing up and turning and turning again. The tower has a maze-quality, almost like the Red Tower, except here everything is geometric yellow stone—as if determined by a grand math equation.

I follow Anna up a narrow spiral staircase, thinking it must be inside a turret. A plush yellow carpet runs up the stairs, softening the sound of our steps. It is hard to hear anything beyond the clinking and echoing of the golden armor. I do not even hear the wall begin to open beside me. I glimpse it from the corner of my eye, and then someone grabs my arm and yanks me inside.

The wall closes, shutting out all the light.

I twist and grope around, trying to figure out where I am, when I trip over something or someone and send us both falling to the ground. Metal clanks loudly. A hand presses hard over my mouth. I still can't see anything.

I try ask a question, but it is muffled.

"Quiet. Follow me."

The voice is Emma's. My mouth spreads into a smile under her hand. Through the metal and dust smell comes lavender, soap.

When I nod, she uncovers my mouth, takes my hand, and leads me into the blackness. From the sounds of our footsteps, it's a hallway, long and narrow with a slight incline. We stop at the end. There's a slight sound of Emma moving, the soft clink of metal.

The stone wall swings open into a small room with light diffused behind heavy curtains over the window. The room has a simple bed, desk, and chair. It reminds me of my first room in the Blue Tower, except this one has a few nicer touches—a soft yellow rug in the center, a candelabra with three half-burnt candles, and a large oak wardrobe.

Emma moves to the door and checks the lock. Her movements are elegant as ever, even in the armor. It must be her room; she seems comfortable.

She motions to the chair. "Please, sit."

She sits on the bed across from me. The bed bends

deeply under the weight of her armor. We are quiet for a moment. She is the same Emma, beautiful and radiant as ever. She was my first capture in Blue, my partner in Red and in Green. Now we are together in our fourth tower. *This was the only way*, she said as Joan put the collar around my neck in the Scouring. Emma's note, the one that came on a cat's collar, warned of the darkness around her father. She said we would defeat him, and yet she seemed loyal. As I look into the depths of her blue eyes, I don't know where to start with my questions.

"Curious as ever," she says serenely.

"How do you know?"

"Touch your collar."

Before I can say anything, my hand goes to the collar. "Wait, *you* have command?"

"Anna gave it to me. Just for now, so she can rest easier while you're in here. She'll take control back as soon as she leaves."

Her explanation doesn't make sense. Anna could have kept control while Emma and I talked, but there is something like fear in her voice. "Do you still trust me?" I ask.

"Yes, of course," she says. "But I understand why you might be…upset with me, after what happened. I needed to take every precaution. We must be united. We face a very powerful enemy here."

"Who?"

"My father, or the darkness that clouds him."

"Your note said that. What kind of darkness is it?"

"Did you destroy the note?"

"Yes."

Her shoulders relax, but her face remains intense and her voice lowers. "I think it comes from the Colorless One. My father is not...himself."

"What do you mean?"

"Yellow's leaders, Elijah and the Widow, are missing. Without their oversight, my father has not ruled us well. He has grown complacent and even cowardly. He no longer cares about the Scouring or Yellow's numbers. All that matters to him is maintaining his own power. He has ruled here a long, long time."

"It sounds like you want that to change."

"We are planning a rebellion."

"Against your own father?"

"I know how it sounds. But I have also learned more of what happened on Earth. You remember what my son, Oliver, helped me see in Green?"

"Oliver said your father knew you were planning to marry a poor servant and leave the family estate, but he did not reveal that he knew this. He let you go. And then you lost your husband, your child, everything."

"Precisely. Now I know why my father did it." She takes a deep breath, but her fists remain clinched. "My father had a son, a bastard son, with a servant he had sent away to another noble family. The son was nearly my age, my half-brother. I knew none of this. My father planned to give the entire family estate to his son instead of to me. That is why he sent me away, allowing me to marry in the belief that it was my secret decision." She stays composed as she says this, but the normally gentle and delicate lines of her face are tense, severe. This has hurt her deeply.

"I'm sorry, Emma. How did you learn all this?"

"My powers have grown. I can see and hear through the light of the suns. Just as I've watched you, I've watched him. I wanted to see how he was leading the tower, but I saw far more than that. He has been searching for his son. This is why he has traded away Yellow's people so freely with other towers. Whenever there is a report of a boy who faintly resembles his memory of his son, he trades for the boy. That is why he traded for you. Now he wants to trade for Oliver. I've told him nothing."

"Is this why you let them collar me?"

"Part of it, yes. I needed to appear neutral about you. My father does not know how powerful we are together. If he did, we would be in more danger than we already are. He would have greatly doubted my intentions if you had received special treatment. It is the way of the Yellow Tower to begin in the fields, just as new arrivals in Blue begin in the first level classroom. I started in a field as you did. I knew you would work your way out."

"You're more confident than I was…"

She smiles. "I saw what you did. Few have advanced so quickly. I'm proud of how you worked with others. You've come a long way, you know."

"Thanks, I guess. I couldn't convince Max. You saw that, too?"

"We managed to get around that."

"We?"

"Joan is also on my side. She has grown tired of so many rules, so little change. It has been suffocating. She let the command through your collar lift for a moment when that storm came. You must have wondered how your power converted into a tornado that took Max away."

"I felt sort of bad."

"Don't. Max is fine, on a new plot. Joan and I helped place Hank on the rye field near yours. You did the rest, and now you are here. Do you understand now?"

"Most of it."

"But you are still angry about being captured and collared?"

The metal link at my neck tells her exactly how I feel, so I do not deny the simmering anger that remains. I try to let it go. She was doing her best. "I'm sorry. I still trust you. We're on the same side, right?"

"Yes, and I need your help." She pulls off her gauntlet and holds her hand over mine. The criss-cross scar is the only blemish on her smooth skin. "We are marked. We are meant to work together. If we can get the towers to equilibrium, I think we can put an end to this place."

"How?"

"Remember what Daniel said in Green. Five marked ones, five towers. If we can find the fifth person, and arrange the towers to have one hundred forty-four each, something will happen. Maybe everyone can go to the White Tower then."

"I doubt it will be that easy."

"I did not say easy, only possible. But first, we must take control of Yellow. I believe that is the only way to build its numbers."

"And to get revenge against your father?"

She shakes her head, solemn. "To heal him. He has much to be scoured still. As do I. As do you. This place is changing, Cipher. We may be running out of time."

"How is that possible?"

"Come, I need to show you something."

I obey, as commanded, and we move to the window together. She pulls the curtains open a crack. We have to stand close beside each other to see out. The hard golden metal of her armor presses against me. Outside, I see a stone arch slanting down to a slender turret nearby. The arch must hold the secret path Emma led me through to get here. Other turrets rise above, all connected by arches and leading to glassy spires that shimmer with reflected light. It is beautiful.

"Do you see that?" she points away from the other turrets, toward the Scouring beneath us.

From this angle, the Red and Black towers are visible in the distance. Blue is obscured by clouds. All appears as I remember it. I don't see anything unusual.

"Look at the center," she says.

My gaze shifts to the center of vast grey stone battleground and my chest clenches. It is where the white circle should be. It is where the White Tower blazed in a beacon of light and took my mother up and away. But now the circle is black.

My throat tightens. "What happened?"

"I do not know. I first noticed it in the last Scouring. The circle was dark as soon as we entered."

"What does it mean?"

She steps away from the window and lets the curtains fall closed. No more light enters the room from outside. "I hope you can help me figure that out," she says. "Here is what happened. We traded for a boy from the Black Tower, and—"

"Wait, you traded with *Black*? Did they not fight?"

"Not for long. It was very odd." Emma looks down at her golden armor. "They came straight to us at the Yellow gate. We drew our weapons. They drew theirs. We clashed violently, but they could not dent our armor. One of their girls sent the smoke, but it did not stop my power. I think the armor somehow stopped it. I still don't know how my father got it. The gold wasn't here in Yellow before. I asked him, and he told me this was not my concern. It's yet another reason why I fear he has been twisted. But I cannot deny the power of the armor. Without the smoke stopping me, I knocked the whole Black team to its knees. They held out their spears in immediate surrender."

"Incredible!" I say. "But then…why did you trade? Why not take all of them?"

"My father had commanded me not to. I had to obey. I told the Black team that our king proposed a trade. We offered one suit of the armor for one of their boys."

"That's a terrible deal, if this armor does what you say it does."

"I know. I had no choice. They accepted, and one of our guards stripped out of his armor. We took a boy named Neville. He was related to my father and me, descended far down our family line. The Black team took the armor and raced away across the Scouring. That's when I saw it. Red attacked them in full force. Black held them back, and in the onslaught, a boy from Red was pushed into the center of the Scouring. This time he did not stand there, held by a vision. He fell, Cipher. It is a hole."

"But, the only thing down there is…"

"The pit," she says. "So now this boy from Red could be trapped. So could others."

"What should we do about it?"

"If you win the competition tomorrow, you will become a guard, and get the armor, like me. We will be free to go into the Scouring, and maybe to explore this hole."

Daniel's warning comes to me. Rahab let us go through the pit to reach Black's land, but Daniel said she shouldn't have. He said not even the leaders should go there. "Why would we want to go there?"

"It is not what we want, but what we must do." She takes my hand and runs her fingers over the scar. "We are going to fight the Colorless One and find the way out of the Five Towers. For everyone."

18

THE COURTYARD SPREADS like a perfect grid in the grey light, surrounded by the tall turrets and spires of the Yellow Tower. Each square of the courtyard has a different shade of yellow. The pattern has rows of three by three, nine colors total, repeated in the same geometric mosaic until the courtyard reaches the wall of the Scouring.

I follow Anna in her golden armor, back in her command through the collar at my neck. I begin to understand the courtyard's pattern. Some of the squares have a neatly written letter in the center, as if the whole courtyard is a map of the Yellow Tower's land. Maybe even a command center, deciding where to put us. I step over an L in a square that is the brightest of the yellow colors—Li Min—then over a square with a greenish yellow hue and a smudged letter that looks like a C that has been erased— my plot, but no more. Beside it is a brownish yellow square with an erased S. Seymour's plot. There's still D for Drew, I for Itzel, C for Camille, and on and on. Many of the squares have no letter. Many plots are vacant.

At the end of the grid, the boy-king, girl-queen, and

their guards wait. Behind them is the large gate in the wall that separates us from the Scouring.

"Kneel before them, still and silent," Anna commands.

I approach and kneel. Six guards, wearing golden armor and helmets, stand to each side of the king and queen. The gate looms behind them. It is so unlike the gates in the other towers, which were hidden, even underground. This gate is on broad display, like a centerpiece of the courtyard with the tower rising around us.

To the sides of the courtyard, but not standing on any block representing the fields, there are short lines of others—about ten to each side. One of them is Seymour, dressed in a silken yellow vest like the boy who took Joan's horse. He, too, stands among the observers. They must be the ones who have advanced beyond the fields. Managers, bakers, archers, and whatever else. Whoever they are, they add to the perfect order of the courtyard. There's no sign of disobedience, no air of rebellion. All stand at attention, looking toward me, kneeling before the king in the center.

The first ray of sunlight streams through the tower spires and shines brilliantly on the king and the queen and the golden gate behind them. I keep my eyes ahead, but I can tell when the other two suns rise, adding two layers of light to the first. The golden gate reflects the dazzling light. The guards' golden armor does the same. I have to shade my eyes.

The king raises his arms and lifts his crown high above his head, catching the light. "Behold, the suns rise again on the Yellow Tower. This is day 59,666 of my reign, and day

843 since we have seen our leaders. Today we do again what we must, until we all become pure as the sunlight. *Who* do you serve?"

"King Chamberlain!" the crowd answers in unison.

"*Why* do you serve?"

"To sweat away fear!"

The king lowers the crown back to his head, then turns to his right. "Neville, come with me."

One of the golden-plated guards steps forward and joins the king as the two of them step toward me.

"Helmet off," the king says, and Neville lifts the golden helm and holds it curled under his arm. His dark hair and stern eyes are familiar. Other than the color of his hair, he looks like he could be the king's brother.

"My guards fought in the Scouring," the king says, turning and speaking to the crowd around the courtyard. "Most of them defended valiantly, as they must. They evaded attention. None were caught. A trade was successfully made. But the light revealed to me a defect. One of the guards tried to take someone I had not commanded."

A gasp ripples through the crowd.

"Sire, please," Neville says, "it was only this once. I thought I—"

The king cuts him off. "Remove your armor."

Neville falls to his knees, with gauntleted fists pleading. "No, sire, please…"

"Remove it," the king demands.

Neville rises slowly and turns away from the king. He

reaches to his wrist, as if to unclasp something, but then suddenly spins around. He fist flashes like a golden blur at the king.

But it hits something and cracks. Neville shouts out in pain, clutching his hand.

"So it comes to this," the king mutters, just before he raises his leg and kicks hard at Neville's armored chest.

Neville falls flat on his back.

The king stands over him, with his sword suddenly drawn. "What would you rather lose, memories or a hand?"

"No…" Neville whimpers. "I can't—"

"If you don't choose, I will." The king raises his sword. "Both!"

Neville tries to scurry back. The boy-king shouts out as he lunges forward and swings his sword down in a violent arc. It slices through Neville's wrist.

Neville screams in pain.

"Heal him," the king says.

Emma rushes forward and takes Neville's arm between her hands. The bleeding and the screams stop.

"Remove his armor," the king commands.

A half dozen guards rush forward. Together they pull away Neville's golden plate mail, leaving it on the ground like a turtle's empty shell.

The king kneels beside Neville. He draws a round golden disc from his pocket and presses it against Neville's temple. Neville's face goes pale, then blank. I don't know how the king did it, but I've seen it before. Neville was wiped clean.

"Rise, Neville," the king says.

Neville obeys, his face still blank. But his fist—the one that remains—clenches tightly. He must not need memories to be on edge before the king. Emma healed the stub of his arm, but he doesn't remember that. He disobeyed the king, but he doesn't remember that either. All he knows is that he appeared in this sunny palace courtyard, surrounded by guards in golden armor.

The king turns to me, and I take a step back.

"What, are you afraid?" he asks.

"No, your highness."

He lifts an eyebrow.

"Okay, a little," I admit, glancing at Neville.

"Fear is an evil that must be purged from us all," the king says. "But all can be healed here. Sweat away the fear and learn to obey. Dream well and you will learn the past."

The king lifts the golden disc that he held to Neville's temple. It looks like a large coin, the size of his hand. He holds it high, glinting in the light. There is a lion engraved on it, on hind legs with paws ready to strike boldly.

"The two of you will search for the matching coin. I have hidden it personally within the Yellow Tower's domain. Whoever finds it first will join my elite guards. Whoever does not will return to the fields, wiped clean again. Am I understood?"

"Yes, your highness," I say.

But Neville says, "No. I do not understand at all. Who are you? What is this place?"

The king clasps his shoulder, like they are old friends.

"To make this fair, Neville, I will take you to a place where special memories await. Then you will understand."

Neville shakes his head in dismay, but does not reply. I want to ask about this place that shows special memories. I want to tell Neville not to trust the king. But the king turns to me and the wild look in his eyes stops my words. At least I manage not to cower back. I need to appear brave.

"Cipher," the king says, "you will have a room provided for you here in the tower, as will Neville. You may both go and search wherever you please. You both have the honor of competing to be my twelfth guard. It is only fitting that the loser will lose everything. Now, listen carefully, here is your only hint to find the coin: *the one who sweats the least fears the most.*" The king flashes a bright smile. "Let the competition begin!"

19

THE KING DISMISSES the morning meeting in the courtyard, and the crowd disperses in orderly fashion. Two guards join the king in escorting Neville away. The other guards trail after Joan, the girl-queen. The servants enter various doorways into the Yellow Tower.

I stand still on the mosaic of stones, thinking of what to do, of where to go. The grid beneath my feet shows dozens of plots of land, countless places where a coin could be hidden. Or it could be right here in the tower, where the king watches everything. This king is not to be messed with, and yet Emma is plotting a rebellion. I begin to sweat, but it does not make the fear go away, despite what the king said.

Anna approaches me. Without a word she reaches behind my neck. I suck in a deep breath, then gasp as she unclasps the collar. My hands go to my neck. The skin is bare and tender to the touch. I am free.

I take a step back, eyeing Anna cautiously.

"King's orders," she says. "You can go where you please, but it's easy to get lost here. If you're smart, you'll follow me."

She turns to leave. The collar hangs from her hand, clinking against her golden armor as she walks. Emma told me that Anna was on her side. And now she's set me free.

I follow her.

We go through the main hallway and up the same spiral staircase as the day before. This time we stop at the door to the secret passage, where Emma took me. Anna presses her hand against the stone wall—with no trace of a trigger or switch—and closes her eyes in concentration. A moment later the door opens and we slip inside. I glimpse Emma waiting in the narrow, windowless hallway. Then the door closes and all is pitch black.

Clinking metal approaches. Then a small flame springs to life. It hovers above Emma's hand.

"Enjoying freedom?" she asks.

I rub again at the ring of chafed skin around my neck. "Yes, but I'd rather keep my hands."

"You see what my father has become? I think he suspected Neville. He was on our side. *And* he is descended from my father, and me. We must be very careful."

"What should I do?"

"Find the coin," Emma says. "My father will expect you to make every effort, and so you must. As will Neville. Remember, anything under the suns or stars can be seen. We can only talk safely in places such as this."

"And even here, only briefly," Anna says. "Last night the king asked me about Cipher. I think he suspects that you spoke with him, Emma."

"It would have been more suspicious if I had not," Emma says. "He has learned of how we worked together in other towers."

"What does he want?" I ask.

"To preserve his power, above all." A tinge of sadness touches Emma's voice. "He fears what would happen if he were not king."

"If he's afraid, does that mean he has the coin? His clue was that the one who sweats the least still fears the most."

Emma is silent, as if considering it. "No, it is possible, but he cannot see his own fear, not fully. You should search for someone else—whoever does the least work. My father detests laziness."

"Okay, I will try. Any ideas?"

"Start here, in the tower. Ask among the servants. If they appear busy and give no clues, move to the fields. It would not surprise me if my father hid the coin in a dormant plot."

"What, like buried under the dirt?"

She shrugs. "Perhaps."

"This could take forever…any chance you have a metal detector I could borrow?"

"What's a metal detector?"

I laugh, remembering how different things had been when Emma lived on Earth. "Never mind," I say. "Is there anything you can do to help?"

"I will do what I can, but we must be careful. My father will be watching you closely. I also need to figure out where my father is taking Neville. I have spent a great deal of time in the Yellow Tower, yet I have never heard of this place that reveals special memories. It must be new, and hidden. Or it could be the pit. It makes me very concerned."

"Cipher and I should go now," Anna whispers urgently.

"Yes, yes," Emma says. "Just one more thing. Cipher, even with your power, I fear it will be difficult to take control. Many guards remain loyal to my father, and the golden armor is immune to our powers. The rebellion must be a surprise, done quickly, with limited fighting. Your search for the coin will distract my father while I gather more support. Then, if you can find the coin, he will summon everyone together again. We will be ready."

I gaze at the flame hovering above her hand, then meet her blue eyes. She sounds confident in her plan, but there's fear and uncertainty in her eyes. It doesn't make sense. Together we have risen to the top of three towers already. Why not Yellow? There's not even a leader to hold us back.

"You really think the golden armor is so strong?" I ask. "If we attack together, we could beat your father and his guards."

She reaches out and touches my cheek softly. "I fear there are greater threats than my father. We must be cautious, Cipher."

"Aren't we supposed to get over our fears here?"

"If only it were so simple. I will try to learn more about the pit and my father. You try to find the coin, okay?"

"Needle in a haystack. No sweat."

She smiles. "Good luck, Cipher."

Her flame blinks out and her armor clinks lightly as she moves away down through the darkness.

"This way," Anna says, taking my hand. "And, once we are in the light, act as if this meeting never happened."

The doorway opens and Anna leads me up the spiral staircase to my room. A fresh loaf of bread sits on the small desk, and a clean set of clothes is laid out on the bed. She tells me that I am free to come and go, but that I should sleep here each night.

"Why?" I ask, with my skepticism only half-pretended.

"Servants will bring you food," she says. "The king would not want his competitors for the coin to go without adequate sleep and nourishment."

She bows formally and leaves me alone.

I go to the slender window, considering what to do next. It's still hard to believe I'm free of the collar. I gaze out over the fields, spreading in the grid pattern of grains and huts. The threads of air beckon to be used, and I harness them and send blasts coursing over the distant grains. There is nothing to stop or diminish it, but wind will be little help finding a hidden coin. The view down from the turret brings back a painful memory of falling out of a tree and off a cliff—so much falling in Green. Here things seems to grow, not fall. Drew thinks the place is heaven. He does not sweat much. Could the coin be hidden with him? Or maybe with the tower servants? There was a group of artists. How much could they sweat from painting?

"Impressive," says a voice behind me.

I turn away from the window and swallow. The king stands in front of me, with a hand resting lightly on the hilt of the sword at his side. He wears gleaming, golden armor.

Not knowing what else to do, I bow. But I do not release my hold over the wind.

The king smiles. "Do you intend to uproot all of my fields?"

"No, sorry. I was just…"

"Testing, yes, I know. It feels good to use our powers at times. But we must not rush. Better to start slow. Beginnings are always most delicate. I saw how you planted your field with the wind. Very fast, impressive indeed. But wind without light is a blind force. It takes courage to see."

"To see what?"

"Use your fingers to make a number behind your back."

Intrigued, I hold out all five fingers so that he cannot see them. "Okay, how many?"

"Five. Very clever."

I close my fist, extending only one finger.

"And now one."

I switch them three more times, and he tells me the moment each time it changes—perfectly accurate.

"How do you do that?"

He holds up the golden coin from before, the one he pressed against Neville's temple. It somehow wiped him. "This allows me to see what the light sees, and more. How would you like to have such power?"

"Where did you get it? From Yellow's leaders?"

His eyes narrow. "That is not your concern. We no longer need the leaders here. With this, I have all the power I need." He casually flips the coin up into the air.

I react instantly, summoning the wind. The coin is here. The king is alone. I blast the air at him to knock him back and take the coin. His hair blows, but he does not budge. I shift the air to coil it tightly around him, but nothing happens. The threads whip past him harmlessly, like a river around a boulder.

"Do you think me so stupid?" the king asks, amused as he catches the coin, pockets it, and runs a hand through his blonde hair. "My daughter says you are very powerful, but inside you there's only the power of a storm. Storms come and go, but the light remains. Let me show you. Hold out your hand."

I hesitate, eyeing his sword, thinking of Neville. The king cannot be pleased with my failed attack, and I would rather keep my hand.

"Come now," the king insists. "I will not hurt you. The competition has begun, has it not? And I prefer a fair competition. I have shown Neville this, so I will show you as well. Now, your hand please."

As my hand extends, I weave the air around it, forming a dense shield of air—hopefully enough to block a swinging sword.

The king holds his hand over mine, eyeing my criss-cross scar curiously. "I will need to clasp it."

I fold back a small gap in the shield, ready to restore it

instantly if he moves fast. "Okay."

He takes my hand in his. We do not move, but suddenly we are soaring. My vision blurs and races out the window along a single bright yellow thread among countless millions of identical threads. We dance from thread to thread until coming to a pause above galloping horse and rider. The horse crosses a field and comes to a hut. The rider dismounts using one hand, as the other is only a stump. He must be Neville. He goes inside the hut. Suddenly we are racing again, down and through the hut's window. A person sits at a table, talking. I cannot hear the words, and I can see only a blurred figure on the other side of the table, in the shadow. Then, in a flash, my vision races back through the sky and into the room and the king is in front of me, standing just as he was, smiling.

"Amazing," I say.

"Humans were made to work together." He releases my hand and grips his sword hilt again. "Some were made to serve and some to lead. You began in Blue. The Genius operates in individual minds. It may give you the power of a storm, but I have the power of order. The Healer shows those who serve the most in Yellow how to heal, and those who lead the most how to see. We must see before we can heal, yes?"

I nod, playing along, though his words confuse me and my thoughts churn at the threat. In the hut there was darkness, in the secret corridor was darkness. Yet the towers have glass spires, windows everywhere. Few places will be safe from his sight.

He suddenly produces a dazzling gemstone, the largest and clearest diamond I have ever seen. It occupies almost his entire palm, and its facets generate a thousand flecks of light in the little room. "Here, I want you to take this."

I stare at it, mesmerized. "Where did you get this?"

"I am the king. And you ask too many questions. The people in my domain know the diamond is mine. Show it to others and they will obey, for you have my support. Please, take it, as a gift."

Hesitantly, I pick up the diamond and hold it between my hands. The prism reflects countless flecks of color.

"What do you want from me?" I ask.

"Loyalty, Cipher. To me, and not to anyone else, not even my own kin."

"I can be loyal."

He smiles again. "So can Neville. So can Emma. Good luck."

20

WHEN I LEAVE the room, the diamond protrudes like a rock from the pocket of my yellow silk vest. The king will expect me to have it. And if the fear the king has given me is any indication, showing this jewel to anyone else could come in handy.

The king showed me Neville riding in the fields, searching for the coin. But it could be anywhere. There are so many plots out there, spread across such a vast expanse. The servants are more concentrated in the tower. That's where I will start.

I make my way through the great hall to the courtyard. Voices come from the base of a small turret. Inside, I find Seymour and five others sitting around a large rectangular table with papers sprawled across it. Chalkboards full of words cover the walls. Words like rye, salt, rain, and milk.

Seymour spots me in the doorway and introduces me to the group. The same dog, Kraut, is by his side, wagging its tail.

"Cipher!" Seymour says. "Listen everyone, this is Cipher. He's amazing. I met him in the Red Tower. He became the Alpha. You should see him with the wind. Why, there was one time when we were—"

"That's enough," one of the girls says, cutting Seymour off. She has wide shoulders and a serious-looking face. She turns to me. "We are busy. What do you want?"

"I'm looking for a golden coin."

"It's not here. We are the managers, and we have much work to do. So if you don't mind…" She points to the door.

After I hold up the diamond, casting dazzling light around the room and telling them that I have the king's support, the girl begrudgingly lets me ask a few questions. I learn that each of these managers is responsible for a block of nine plots and their tenants. The head girl oversees the other managers. They are responsible for provisions to the farmers—sending out the capsules of salt and baking powder and the jars of milk with various animals. It is a mild disappointment. I preferred to think of Kernel, Spunky, and the others deciding on their own when and where to make the special deliveries.

After a while, the lead girl refuses to answer more of my questions, and she won't let Seymour or any of the others talk. "You know what's at stake," she tells me. "The greatest managers become guards, and I won't let anyone—not even you and your diamond—get in the way of that. Go ask the bakers. They're never as productive as we are."

The only thing I extract before leaving is the girl's agreement to let me know if they see a coin, but I have my doubts. At least Seymour will know to keep an eye out for it.

Following the girl's directions, I make my way to a long low building that borders the wall to the Scouring. A dozen different stone chimneys rise from a steeply pitched, thatch roof. The smell makes my mouth water.

A wave of warmth greets me when I open the door. Inside is a single, large room. Seven boys and girls scurry around, tending to various ovens no doubt cooking bread and other delicious things inside. One of the chefs, a rotund boy with rosy cheeks and sweat beaded on his forehead greets me. This time, when I reveal the king's diamond, the boy's face lights up and he announces that there will be an impromptu taste test.

"I just want to know if you've seen the coin," I say.

The boy shakes his head. "You are a new palate. We talk after you taste."

The other chefs each bring one of their creations to a table. They insist I try every one and announce the best, but they make me close my eyes and shuffle the treats around so that I won't know who cooked each one.

The first is a raspberry tart with a creamy, yellow custard inside. It's very good, but a touch too sweet for my taste. Next is a dark, thick toast covered in butter. By the end of the seven tastes, my stomach is full and the winner is clear. It is a dried fruit, something like a fig, wrapped in bacon and drizzled with a savory sweet sauce that reminds me of blackberries.

"You see?" the head chef says, proudly tapping his

rotund chest. "A cook knows his eater. I thought of serving my tart, but no, this boy has bacon and blackberry written all over him."

I ask the group about the coin, but none of them has any idea about it. They are at least more friendly about it, telling me that they will keep an eye out for it in the kitchen and that I should come back any time I am hungry. The head chef urges me to check with the artists next and tells me the way.

I approach a tall, freestanding tower and climb its spiral staircase to a round room surrounded by glass. Four people are there, painting. One of them approaches me and tells me that I'm not to distract their work. It's a boy with dark eyes and a floppy, funny looking hat on his head. When I show him the diamond, he hardly seems to care.

"Your work is no more important than ours. We create beauty."

I ask him about the coin, but he only laughs and tells me that such things are a distraction from the artist's way. The other three people have all turned to us, and when the leader sees them, he snaps that they must continue.

"Be gone," he says to me.

"Are they painting the Green Tower?" I ask, glancing around at the tree-like shapes on each person's canvas.

"This is not your concern."

"But why paint another tower?"

He looks annoyed but answers, "The king wishes to know his opponents."

"I've been in Green. I could help."

The instructor's brow furrows as he eyes me up and down. "I doubt you could survive it."

"I didn't say I survived." But I don't need to convince him with words. I still have Green's power, though I've hardly given that a thought. There was no need to go invisible on my plot of land. I think of content memories. Susan's touch as we left the mansion. Sitting by seashore with Emma, talking of the past. I focus on the light. It begins to bend around me.

"Whoa…" someone says.

"He's gone!"

"You may come back now," the instructor says.

I release the power and appear again in the room. "Now, may I help?"

"Hm, yes." He chews at the wooden end of his paintbrush. "If you have ideas for the painting, make it quick."

I move to one of the painters, the leader staying close by my side, and offer a few suggestions. The trunk is wider. Most of the buildings in the tree cannot be seen from outside, but the platform is noticeable. It rests at the point where the trunk divides into a dozen branches. When I've shared these thoughts with the other painters, the leader asks me to comment on his.

"Yours is the best," I say studying it. The painting is a masterpiece—almost familiar in the style of blurred but moving reality. "Have you been there?"

"Many times…there and back to here, and again, and again. The king toys with me. He trades me, then yearns for another work and gets me back."

His words and tone swell with sadness. I gaze at the painting again and notice a signature in the bottom right. It is a gentle cursive form of the name Vincent.

I turn to him, realizing he could be one of the most famous painters of all time. "Are you Vincent van Gogh?"

He waves dismissively, but there is a bead of sweat on his forehead. "I am the leader of the artists, and you have been here quite long enough. Go on, find your coin, and leave us to our work."

All the servants—managers, bakers, artists—sweat in their work for the king. They are not likely to be the ones who "sweat the least," as the king said in his hint. So maybe the coin will not be in the tower. I leave the studio and head to the fields to search for a golden coin.

21

I KICK AT the dirt as I walk away from the Yellow Tower. Clouds of dust rise behind me. The patchwork fields are no longer the mystery they were when I arrived in Yellow. I have baked my bread and moved on. I have seen the map in the tower's courtyard. And now I know that the fields are like a tapestry of people and huts and dirt—with a billion places where a coin could hide. It could be buried like a seed for all I know. Except the seeds we plant show signs of life, but gold stays dead forever under the soil. No glimmer of it appears from my kicking.

The three suns beat down on my shoulders. I envision the fields from above, as if looking down at the grid pattern in the courtyard, where the king sliced off Neville's hand and sent us off on this quest. It seems best to start with people I know, so I head toward my old plot.

With my collar off, the invisible walls no longer stop me. The bare ring of pale skin around my neck will probably redden with sunburn. A boy farmer works close to me as I pass, head down, hoe in the ground, up, down, up, down. His field is impressive. He sweats heavily. *The one*

153

The farmer spots me and calls out. He leans on his hoe and rubs at his forehead, smearing a dark streak of dirt through the sweat. He tells me he has seven grains and that he just needs two more but that one plot beside his is empty and another is unworked.

"Tell the king, will ya? It ain't fair."

I say that I will and I produce the diamond. He stares at it wide-eyed. But when I ask about the coin, he looks at me like I'm crazy.

"A coin out here?" he says. "Might as well try to find a needle in the haystack."

"The king told me to find the one who sweats the least."

The boy spits on the dirt, then points to a plot beside his. "Talk to Yeats. That boy don't work a lick. Worst farmer ya ever lay eyes on."

I thank him and walk to Yeats' plot. It looks worse than the ones Max and Simeon had—almost completely barren. Around the hut there is a small patch of green growing, the way it would if someone just threw out a handful of seed and left it to fare on its own. I knock on the wooden door of the hut. When there's no sound from inside, I knock again. He could have been assigned to a different plot without the other boy knowing it. I knock a third time and start to leave when I hear a faint sound inside.

The door opens to a lanky boy with no shirt or shoes and a mop of hair hanging past his shoulders. He rubs the back of his collared neck and yawns. He should be surprised to have a visitor, but instead he steps past me as if I'm not even there. He stretches his arms overhead while gazing out at the sky. He runs his hand over a vine that grows wildly up the side of his hut and mumbles, "The mist-drops hung on the fragrant trees, and in the blossoms hung the bees."

"I'm on a quest for the king," I say, showing the diamond. "Have you seen a golden coin? It has a lion on it."

The boy glances at the brilliant stone, then motions vaguely toward the sky. "Three coins up there."

"A real coin," I say. "The kind you can hold. I need to bring it to the king. Have you seen it?"

He eyes me curiously. "The best lack all conviction, while the worst are full of passionate intensity."

"What are you trying to say?" I ask. "Is this about the Red Tower?"

He smiles as he shakes his head. "I have not seen your coin."

I'm not surprised, but I'll take any clue I can get. "The king says someone who sweats the least will have it. Any ideas?"

"The world is full of magic things, patiently waiting for our senses to grow sharper."

"Which means…what?"

"What can be explained is not poetry," he says, flashing a friendly grin. "You look like you need a rest, not a coin. Good luck."

He steps lazily back into his hut. He doesn't bother closing the door. I peer inside as he lays on a pallet beside a large shaggy dog that snores. The hut is bare as mine once was—a table, a hearth, and a jar of grain. The boy is odd, but he doesn't seem the type to keep a golden coin hidden.

I move on. It won't be easy to talk to every serf across Yellow's vast land, and maybe not worth it. They can live peacefully like Yeats, eating, sleeping, and spouting poetry. They don't need to care about my question, regardless of the king's diamond. And even if some of them did care, it would take days to canvas all of them. Already the suns have fallen halfway down toward the horizon.

I pass several plots without stopping and approach my old field. I see Drew working his field. He waves and rushes to me, hoe in hand. He stops at the invisible wall. His shirt is drenched in sweat—not a good sign for a golden coin.

After we exchange hellos, he wants to know what happened. I tell him about the bread of nine grains, the tower, and the king's quest.

"I knew ya was special," he says. "How can I help?"

"So you haven't seen a coin?"

"Not here, nothin' like it. But there's one I seen in my dreams. It was in a big glass box where I used to work, in the Treasury Department. Every day as I mopped down the hall and passed it I'd stop and just stare. A mighty big coin it was."

I ask him more and learn that it was some sort of rare golden coin kept on display, with a large eagle imprinted on it. Drew thinks the coin was worth lots of money, because the government kept a satin red rope around the case, keeping anyone from getting too close. He tells me that one time he saw a smudge on the glass case and tried to scrub it off—"that bein' my job and all"—until a guard saw him and drew a gun and told him to back away. He never got close to the coin after that.

"But I'll keep an eye out for ya!" he says.

As we part, I start to wonder if the king's golden coin is even real. It could be a metaphor, some kind of hint about memories or treasures in people's minds. I walk across my former plot, which sits empty, and come to Sally's. She sits on a rocking chair outside her hut.

"Well look who it is," she says.

"Nice chair. Mind if I join you?"

She tells me that a new neighbor built the chair, mostly out of vines, and she traded a whole crop of wheat for it. When I ask her about the coin, she tells me that she hasn't seen anything like that in her many days in the Yellow Tower. I also ask whether she has any memories about a gold coin, and she tells me that her old master gave one to each of her sons—their sons—when they were freed.

"It wasn't much compared to freedom," she says, "but better to go with a little gold than bare-handed."

"What did the coins look like?"

"Like any other, but real shiny, with an eagle on them."

I thank her and visit next with Simeon and Li Min. Little has changed on their plots. They continue growing their grains, trading here and there. Neither one has seen a coin. But they both have memories of them. Simeon says he was the treasurer for his queen in Africa. He often journeyed with a chest of coins. It made him a very important man.

Li Min says she has not seen her father, Max, since my power funneled into a tornado that swept him away.

"How about the past?" I ask. "Was there anything in your life, or his, about a coin?"

"Oh yes. My father loved to collect coins."

"Really? Golden ones?"

"Mostly gold, some silver. Part of the fortune he left for me was a safety deposit box full of coins. I have seen another thing in a dream. After telling my story to you, more details came. In the meeting with the rebel group, my father mentioned the name Dr. Fitzroy."

A chill runs down my spine. "Not every dream here is real."

"Yes, it was very real. Did you develop the technology that I used against the State?"

"Maybe…I don't know all the ways it was used." I tuck this part of her story away, somehow knowing it will come back to me—whether through Max or my own dreams. "What about the coins?" I ask. "Did they mean something?"

"Oh, I don't think so. When I opened the box, being recorded as I always was, I knew there was only one thing to do: to give the coins to the state, to be distributed however the state thought best. This made my citizenship score rise."

By the time we finish talking, the suns hover just above the horizon, making the farmland ripple in golden light. I begin making my way back to the tower. Better to sleep there than on the ground. The suns descend among the glassy spires and I realize it will be dark by the time I make it back. I keep plodding forward.

The clap of hooves comes up from behind me. It's Neville, riding toward the tower, with his good hand holding the reins. He draws up beside me and rides slowly at my pace.

"How goes it?" he asks, friendly.

"I haven't won yet."

He laughs. "I suppose neither of us has. It may take a year at this pace, but I have found some clues."

"Oh?"

"Ah, but a gentleman does not share his secrets. That would spoil the fun, wouldn't it old chap?"

I eye the stump at the end of his arm. "You think this is fun?"

"Why, I suppose so. I had the most awful dream last night of a place called Earth, and I must say, this is far better!"

He taps his heels against the horse and canters ahead, leaving me in a cloud of golden dust as the suns set. I stalk after him, legs aching, wishing I had a horse.

It is dark when I reach the tower. The guards let me pass without a word. I pass no one else as I climb the turret to my room. I don't bother undressing before falling into bed. Too tired. Too spent. Too hopeless.

*** ***

The dream pounces on me like a lion. The executive office has marble floors and a stunning view of the San Francisco skyline. A man sits behind the desk, and though he is grown into middle age, I recognize him. It's Max.

"I will fund everything, Dr. Fitzroy," he's saying. "Whatever staff, whatever budget. But you must promise, bring me back to life as soon as it's ready."

My head spins at his offer. But we are not ready to deliver what he wants. Not yet.

"This isn't the same as the nanotechnology," I say. "This isn't just hacking or controlling the mind."

"Yes, of course. But if you can do those things—and you certainly have, just look at our little revolution in China—then enhancing the mind to sustain its life is possible. You have admitted it. I believe in this. The brain is remarkable, amazing."

"This is true…" The brain is worth everything I have, and words like remarkable and amazing do not do it justice. The brain is godlike. Just days after conception a fetus's neural plate forms, the linchpin of life, growing and folding onto itself, folding again, and again, until the neural tube closes and the weeks-old baby fires neurons that move the body, that spark the first synapses. Since life starts so early and vibrant, no good God would have made it so vulnerable. He should have made brains impenetrable. Only then would we be made in the image of a god. As long as cancers and tumors and toxins prowl around like a lion, death will come and gods will be no more. This is what I will do. But only with funding.

Max's offer is the only way forward. The government says it's too risky. Most investors have abandoned us. My own fortune—even Susan's—has dwindled, but not the memory of Benjamin. This is for him, and for everyone like him.

I shake Max's hand. "Deal."

22

A CHEF COMES to my door at dawn. She wears a yellow hat and apron and holds a tray full of golden bread, butter, and jam. There's even a large jar of milk.

I rub the sleep from my eyes. "All that for me?"

"King Chamberlain thought you'd be hungry," she says. "Is it not to your liking?"

"No, I mean, it looks delicious."

"Nine grains, the best we have. Go on, try it."

She waits in the doorway. I slather butter on a loaf and take a bite and tell her I like it, to give my compliments to the chef. She bows with a smile and leaves.

I eat half of it, watching the suns rise over the golden fields, and think that maybe Yellow's not so bad. Delicious food, art, music. Even the visions of the past seem easier in the form of dreams—gentler than Blue's Sieve, Red's flames, and Green's sap. If only this place didn't have an insane king, who happened to be the father of Emma.

I bring the leftover food with me as I descend the spiral staircase for another day of searching. I'm halfway down when I hear a whisper.

"Cipher."

It comes from a crack in the wall. A golden gauntlet slips through the opening and pulls me into the secret corridor. The door closes making it pitch black.

"It's me," Emma says softly. A flame flickers into life, casting her face in reddish light. "Any luck with the search?"

"Not really. No one has seen a coin, except in their memories."

"It could be a clue," Emma says. "You must keep searching. I have learned something very disturbing. The guard who was helping us, Anna, she's…gone."

"What happened?"

"She followed my father. I have long thought there could be some secret place he went. It's the only way to explain the golden armor, the coins. Anna found it—a hidden passage at the base of the tallest turret. She saw my father enter it with Neville. She said that it went down, and that it was very dark inside. When she tried to go after them, moving silently down stairs that seemed to have no end, she began to feel a force pushing against her. She glimpsed something bright, maybe even golden, in the distance, but fear overcame her. She fled and hurried to tell me this. I asked her to watch discretely for my father's return, from outside the hidden passageway. When my father came back, the first thing he did was order his other guards to seize Anna and strip her armor. No one has seen her since…"

"Not good." Anna gone. The king a tyrant. Emma at

risk. "Where do you think your father went? What about Neville?"

"The way Anna spoke of the darkness makes me think it is connected to the pit. But there must be more to it. The golden light. I think it could be some sort of underground mine, or prison. Yellow's leaders could be there. Or…"

Fear seems to choke the words before they can leave Emma's lips. I finish for her: "The Colorless One."

She nods. "Sometimes I feel…well, there is a darkness even here, in the Yellow Tower. And my latest dreams have revealed new things about the past—saturated in shame and fear. You know how I told you before, in Green, about how my father knew I planned to run away, and didn't stop me?"

"Yes, that's why you wanted to come to Yellow."

"I have now seen more. My father was a coward for what he did, but I was not innocent, either. There was one time, before I ran away from the estate, when my father asked me about John. I looked him straight in the face and I lied. I was afraid of what he would do, but now I know that he only wanted me to tell the truth. I was a coward, too. I fled rather than tell him. You know the harm that caused, but it was not even the half of it. This fear, this cowardice, it did not die with my father and me. It passed through Oliver to his son, and his grandson, Neville Chamberlain."

"The same one who is searching for the coin?"

"Precisely. My father learned about his past before wiping him. He forced him to say everything. Neville was the leader of England at a time when the clouds of war loomed darkly. He sought peace, but in doing so he was driven by fear. He would not confront the truth, that a terrible enemy grew in power. His cowardice—the same cowardice that descended from my father, and through me—led to war and atrocities beyond compare. He let an evil man murder millions of innocent people. This is all so bad, I know, but it has not ended. The darkness that rises here—from the Colorless One—it exploits the very same weakness and frailties from the past. It threatens to hold us here forever."

"How is this all connected?" I ask.

She takes my hand, her gauntlet now off. Her fingers gently trace over my scars. "I wish I knew for sure, but I think my father has become twisted by some darkness, maybe even by the Colorless One. I believe he has helped keep Yellow's leaders locked away so that he can hunt for the fifth marked one, just as we are. If the marked ones all have connected pasts, as we think, then he may have picked you to search for the coin in hopes that you will find this marked one for him. What better way to force you to talk to everyone in Yellow?"

"If that's true, then why pick Neville instead of you as my competitor?"

"He wiped Neville." Emma's voice sounds haunted. "But then he took him into the darkness. Neville is from our family, but he may now be corrupted as my father is. They will be watching you. You must keep them convinced that you are trying. But I fear the coin is a diversion from the real threat."

"I can do that," I say, "but if your father locked Anna away…or worse…and he let Neville be corrupted, what makes you think you'll be safe? Shouldn't we stay together?"

"I am his daughter. I will be safe."

"That's not much hope…"

"Even a little hope can defeat fear," she says. "Keep speaking with others. Find the common thread connecting the gold coins in the past and follow it to the coin."

"I'll do my best."

"That has always been enough for you here," she says. "But this time, move a little faster. Take a horse."

We embrace and say goodbye. She opens the secret corridor's door, careful to avoid the slender beam of sunlight that shines in, then closes it as soon as I'm in the stairway again. As I descend, the significance of Emma's behavior grips me. She has always been so calm and steady, dignified despite all the towers have thrown at her. Now she resorts to shadows and whispers. Her secrecy speaks louder than her words about the urgency of finding this golden coin.

I leave the tower alone and go straight to the stables. Before the stableboy notices me, I watch him tending to the horses. He rubs the velvet of their noses and looks them close in the eye. He talks to them, feeds them.

When he notices me, I tell him I'd like to take one of the horses out for the day. He says that anyone on the king's business may ride them. He measures me and asks me questions, like he's a tailor sizing me up for a suit. He leads me to a chestnut mare. My head just reaches the height of the grand horse's back.

"This is Serenity," the boy says. "She's not the fastest, but sounds like you need reliability more than speed."

I thank him and, before leaving, ask if he's seen a golden coin, either here or in his memories. Not here, he tells me, but in his dreams he sees a man coming to his town with a sack full of gleaming coins. The man brought them from California, and said gold was coming out of the hills there. Only nineteen at the time, the boy was engaged to be married in a month. His fiancée was seventeen years old and five months pregnant. It was an accident. His parents said they'd help them, give them a good plot of land. But fear of commitment drove the boy wild. He felt like a fenced-in stallion. He stole his parents' horse and rode west. He crossed mountains and plains. He traveled for years and became a man the hard way. He eventually found his own share of gold and even bought a nice ranch like the one where he'd grown up.

"But it wasn't the same," the boy says. "Gold taunted me, made me feel brave to ride off hunting for it, but I was gutless and yellow-bellied. Try as I might, I could never buy back what I'd run away from. My family. My home. I should have stayed. I should have worked my own land, loved my wife, and loved my child. I never should've been so scared…"

His story stays with me as I ride away on Serenity. The horse trots calmly, needing little guidance from me. We ride past the hut where I lived before, past Drew and Sally and the others. Emma was right about the speed. Riding fills me with hope about the ground I can cover. The yellow-grey dirt kicks up behind us in a cloud. We reach the wall bordering Yellow's land before the suns have reached their peak. Serenity and I rest in the shadow of the wall, sharing food I'd brought from the tower.

We ride along the plots of land by the wall, where most of the dirt lays dormant. Only a few scattered plants grow in these plots. I speak to many boys and girls along the way, each time dismounting at their huts and producing the diamond to show my mission from the king. They all say they've talked to Neville already. They already told him: no gold coins that they've seen.

But I ask about their pasts, hoping to find a common thread. Their stories are as different as lives could be on Earth. One was a hermit in the Australian Outback, afraid of needing anyone's help. The only gold he remembers was in a tooth that he sold to a man for a sack of grain. "Tooth wouldn't do any good if I was dead, now would it?" he asks.

Another boy does not rise when I knock on his door, but he tells me to come inside. I find him laying soft and still as a pillow on his pallet. He tells me he no longer leaves the bed. Why would he do such a thing when he has everything he could need? A fat cat brings him a fresh jar of milk every day. He says that, on Earth, he worked a short time as a software engineer until one day he sold his company and became a billionaire. He doesn't remember doing any real work after that. He worried nothing would ever live up to his first success. "No use trying," he says.

Later I come to the hut of a girl who sits on a bench combing her hair, which falls all the way to the ground. She tells me she was a geisha in Japan. Her mission was always to make men completely relaxed, to use music and art and beauty to make them feel on top of the world. "Silk," she says, "my life was silk."

I ask her about gold but she remembers only one man who once held out a golden ring to her and asked her to marry him. He was a good man, but a peasant farmer. She feared a life with more dirt than silk, so she told him no. And, like the others, she tells me she has seen no sign of a golden coin here.

Next I talk to a boy who was a security guard from Canada, another who was a priest from Argentina, and then a coder from Korea. Their stories all have memories of gold, and it always represented something to them. Gold meant wealth, but that was not what they cared most about. What they craved was a life of ease and freedom from fear.

Suddenly I see the irony, and the pattern. The more dormant the plot of land, the more clues. The boys and girls on these plots do not sweat. They take inaction to impressive levels, as if they do not even want to advance to the Yellow Tower, much less to the Scouring. They would rather coast without work, without resistance, than strive for anything. Fear has petrified them, and time has ground them down into cowardly dust.

The suns fall and shadows stretch over the farmland between the tower and me. I decide to try one more plot, before calling it a day and riding back. This last plot is a dormant field at the far corner of Yellow's land. It has no wall, but cliffs border it. I ride past the quiet and dark hut to the edge of the field, where steep cliffs drop as far as I can see to the left, and down and down until they reach the wall to the right.

Clouds billow up from the dark, turbulent sea and block the view of the Blue Tower. But it must be close. This is so unlike the other parts of Yellow's lands. It seems as much blue as it is yellow, with its gusts of winds and hovering grey. I lose myself in the thoughts of when I first saw these cliffs, when Emma and I sailed past on our journey from the Blue Tower to here. There is comfort in the blue threads, in the sound of waves crashing against the rocks far below. I watch their white spray as the light retreats and night advances.

Serenity neighs faintly. I hear a quick motion behind me.

I start to spin around just as an arm grabs me tight and a sharp point touches my throat.

"Don't move," a boy commands.

I stay still as a statue. The boy's breath smells of musk and cloves. The crashing waves hid the sound of his approach. But he still doesn't have a chance.

I summon the air. In a blink the swirls tighten into a powerful thread. I use the woven air like a rope, pulling the sharp point away from my neck and lifting the boy like a fly in a spider's web.

I spin and see his face. Max. Again.

I squeeze the wrap of air until his eyes bulge. I step toward him, tempted to throw him off the cliff. He snuck up on me. He could have killed me. He's in my way again, like he was in Blue and Red and before in Yellow. And apparently on Earth.

"Do you know who Dr. Fitzroy is?" I demand.

He shakes his head, then he manages to breathe out: "No clue. But…the coin…I know where it is."

23

"WHERE'S THE COIN?" I demand.

Max smiles, sneering at me, even as the threads squeeze tighter. My power may not be able to control his face muscles, but I will wipe away his smug grin.

I swing him out over the cliff. There's nothing between him and the waves crashing into jagged black rocks below. Nothing except me. His face goes pale.

"Where is it?" I say again.

"Let…me…down…safely." The words escape like drops of juice from a squeezed lemon. "Please."

I'll give him one chance. I set him down on the land, five feet from me, and loosen the web of air.

He stands slowly, tucks his blade into his pants, and raises his hands innocently. "Don't look at me like that. I could have killed you…but didn't."

I shake my head, but I know it's true. He could have just stabbed instead of talked. I didn't hear him approach because of the roaring wind and waves. But I could have tossed him off the cliff. We're even now.

"Where is it?"

"It's not so simple," Max says. "You'll have to hear my story to understand. Come, we can talk in my hut."

He walks off. The wind blows his tunic so that it hugs his left side and billows out like a sail to his right. The dust of his field swirls up in little cyclones. He does not look back.

I'm tempted again to grab him with the wind, harness the blue threads swirling around me, but he has acquired something I want. Unless he's lying. He may know nothing about the golden coin, except that I seek it. Neville could have told him. I've asked so many people already and found nothing. It's also possible Max is telling the truth, and that's enough to make me follow him.

I pass Serenity, still calmly munching at the ground, and pat her velvety nose as I take the reins. "You saw him coming, didn't you?" I ask. "You could have given me more warning."

Serenity eyes me innocently, then shakes her mane.

I sigh and lead her toward Max's ramshackle hut. He has already gone inside. I tie the reins to a post outside. "Be ready," I whisper to the horse. "I may need to leave in a hurry."

Serenity nuzzles my shoulder, as if fondly urging me on.

The door creaks as it opens. Dust lays heavy in the dim room. There's a half-empty jar of milk on the table. No animals are in sight. Max takes a handful of grains from his clay pot and offers them to me. I say no. He closes his fist over the grains, then kneels by the straw pallet at the side of the room. His fingers run along the wooden floorboards. My old hut had the same simple layout, with the reservoir of water pooling under the boards. Max wedges a finger between the wood and pulls two planks away.

"Listen," he says.

He holds out his handful of grain and drops it. There is no splash or sound. His finger is raised, his head cocked to hear.

I lean closer and hear a faint, distant splash.

"What's down there?" I ask.

"Come and see."

He climbs down a ladder, and I follow, staying on guard with a steady weave of air. The smell is earthy, but a briny breeze rushes up through the chute. When the ladder meets a landing, it is almost completely dark. Max tells me to keep my hand on a wall and follow him down. The stone is moist underfoot. I tap my toes from the wall and only two feet away the floor is gone. A pebble kicks loose and falls and falls before there is the bouncing thud of stone against stone far below.

"Stay close to the wall," Max mutters, farther ahead.

I press tight to it and go after him. My eyes begin to adjust. The outline of the ledge separates us from a vast openness—a cavern. We climb down until we reach the cavern's sandy floor, squishing wetly under my toes. Crashing waves echo from outside the cavern. Moonlight glows through an opening, reflecting off a pool of tranquil water. A dark shape is silhouetted on the calm, silvery pool—a hull, a mast.

A word slips out of my lips in a whisper, "Boat."

"Thought you'd like it," Max says.

"Why are you showing me this?"

"You think you're the only one with a chance to be a king's guard?"

"No, Neville has a chance."

"So do I."

"But you never advanced from the fields."

Max laughs, and the harshness of it reminds me of when he led the Red Tower as Axe, and led a fief of the Black Tower as Lord. "You are too linear, Cipher. The king sees what I'm capable of. He assigned me to this plot, with this hidden cavern and boat. I can't get nine grains when the cliffs and the sea are my only neighbors on two sides. But I can still serve."

"What does he want from you?"

"Captives."

"And you plan to use the boat to get them?"

"No, that's what you're going to do. For me."

Now I laugh, an angry laugh, as I whip the threads into a cord that tightens around Max and lifts him off the ground. "Have you forgotten so soon? I will not serve you."

He does not fight against the invisible binding. His eyes blaze, his lips snarl. "Then you won't get the coin."

"Why should I trust you?"

"You have no other choice."

"There are more places to search. I don't need you."

"I have the coin." His voice is steady, confident. He is the same boy who fought me in the Blue and Red Towers, who tried to kill Emma and me when we went to the Black Tower, and who refused to trade his rye to me. I can't trust him. But I can use other means to get at the truth.

I shift the air and flip him upside down and dunk his head into the pool. Ripples spread like silver circles in the water. I lift him enough so that he can breathe, but his dark hair stays submerged.

"Where is the coin?" I demand.

"I'm not afraid of you," he says, spitting water. "We both know death is only a temporary here. And you need me."

"Where is it?" I demand.

"The king showed me," he gasps. "Bring me Kiyo."

"What?" It's the last thing I expect him to say.

"Kiyo. She should be in Blue. Go there, bring her back, and I'll give you the coin."

"You have it?"

"I know where it is."

"Why do you want Kiyo?"

"I was going to tell you, before you dunked me."

I draw him back to the sandy shore and release him. He drops to the ground and heaves great breaths in and out.

Eventually he rises to his knees. "Can I talk now?"

"I'm listening."

"Kiyo is my ancestor. A great-great grandmother, many generations back. I thought she had betrayed me, but I have come to see that she helped me escape from Black, only to let herself get caught again by Blue. She has gone between those towers more times than we know, Blue to Black and Black to Blue. She hurts, Cipher. She bears wounds from this struggle. Bring her here. Maybe she can be healed."

He sounds genuine. And I do care about Kiyo. She was the first person I met in this place, who became my first friend in the Blue Tower. We were in the Scouring together when Black caught her the first time.

"What kind of wounds?" I ask.

"A scar like yours. On her hand."

Is this true? Could she be the fifth marked one? Max could be lying. He could know my interest in the scars, and the king's. He could be working for Emma's father.

"Why should I trust you?" I ask again.

"Because I could have killed you, but didn't," Max says. "Bring her and I'll give you the coin. Simple as that."

"Nothing is ever simple here."

He grins and takes a step toward me. "Can I show you something?"

I hold the wind ready. "Go on."

He comes within arm's reach.

"That's close enough," I warn.

He raises his hand, palm open with a golden coin on it. The lion image is a perfect match. As the reality of this hits me, I summon the wind. At the same moment Max flips the coin high in the air, a golden blur in the dark cave.

I focus on it and snatch it with the air.

Just as I look down, Max is coming at me. A flash of

metal streaks down and stabs into my foot. He yanks the blade out.

The pain is instant and terrible. I crumple over, fighting to hold onto the air. Max snatches the coin and swings again. The blade pierces into my side, an instant before my blast of air flings him back into the rock wall. The dagger drops to the sand beside him. I fall to my knees and the pain overwhelms me. I can't find the blue threads. The power is gone. I finger the wound and watch a dark splotch spread on yellow silk.

24

CRAWLING HURTS TERRIBLY, but it's the only way to move. On all fours, squishy sand beneath me, crashing waves echoing in the cavern, I make my way to Max. He hasn't budged since he slammed into the wall. His blade glints on the ground beside him.

The options are not good. Even if I take the coin and leave Max here, it's doubtful I'd make it out. I'm losing a lot of blood. My head spins, the pain makes me woozy. Maybe I could climb out. Maybe I could steady myself enough to use the wind. But then I'd have to mount Serenity and ride through the night to get back to the Yellow Tower. Or hope to find someone who could heal me. A slim hope.

I could take the boat. Maybe I could get Max on it. We could sail to the gentler beach along Yellow's coast. The archers would be there. I could show them the king's diamond and get inside. Or I could lose consciousness on the boat and crash against the rocks. No, not the boat. Max will have to stay.

His body lays in my path to the incline out of the

cavern. I watch and listen closely as I approach. He doesn't budge. He breathes as if he's unconscious. His head must have hit the rock wall. I stop beside him. His fist is closed. I put my hand over it. Still no movement. I pry open the fingers gently, one by one, and still Max does not move.

I take the coin, small and golden and useless for this dilemma. As I move around Max, a new level of pain erupts from my wound. Max's eyes are wide open, staring at me, as he presses hard against the wound at my side.

A rush of cold pours over me like an avalanche. The shock makes me collapse. I shake violently, curling up for warmth. The pain at my side is gone. The pain at my foot still burns through the cold.

"This could have gone better," Max pants out. He takes the coin back.

I open my mouth but shaking chokes the words. It's so cold.

He leans back against the cave wall and studies the blade. Then, in one fluid motion, he flings it into the darkness. It splashes far from us.

He turns to me, then sighs. "That's twice now. Maybe I should have just killed you. But look at me, a changed boy, healing you instead. Think about that while you go after Kiyo in Blue. You'll get your coin when you bring her back to me. Maybe then you'll trust me. And don't bother trying to take the coin. I'll hide it where only I can find it. I'll also be pulling the ladder up. You can take the boat. See ya, Cipher."

He leaves me there alone, still shivering uncontrollably

on the muddy ground. The sound of waves outside masks his footsteps as he takes the path up and away.

The diagnosis is shock, extreme shock. Partly from blood loss, partly from whatever Max did to heal the wound at my side. I focus on my breathing, trying to steady it, slow it. My eyes grow heavy. It is easier to sleep than think.

I dream that I am a microscopic golden particle traveling through a brain, down from the cerebral cortex through the hypothalamus, passing electric currents and flashes of light as synapses connect. I float onward, riding the waves of thought to the brain stem, at the connection to the spinal cord. Millions of other golden particles gather there and work like little robots, fusing nerves like a welder fuses metal. One of the particles comes to me and introduces himself as Max. He says thank you for gathering so many helpers in his brain.

Something wet wakes me up. My back is soaked. I have no clue how long it's been, but it's still dark. I shake away the dream—surely too surreal to be real—and sit up and see the pool of water has risen. The tide is coming in. Tiny waves roll up the sandy ground and tickle my toes. The salt will be good for the wound on my foot.

I rise slowly and limp out into the pool, toward the boat. It is a simple craft, even smaller than the ones we learned to sail in Blue. The hull is about fifteen feet long and shallow, with no supplies in sight. There is a single mast and a triangular sail. The opening at the end of the pool seems barely wide enough to fit the boat. But if it got in here, then it can get out.

As I draw the sail up, I begin to see more. Dawn lets grey light into the cavern. The sandy shore where I bled and shook has been covered in water. There is no trace of the blood or the fight with Max. Above, the path we took down leads to a dead end. The ladder that we climbed down is nowhere in sight. Max must have taken it away, as he promised. He stabbed me, then healed and abandoned me. He's more of a mess than I am. I won't play by his or the king's games.

With the sail raised, I sit by the rudder and summon a small wind. The boat turns gently, slicing through the shallow pool of water. A glint of light catches my eye. The blade.

I channel the air toward it and pluck it out of the pool and drop it in my hand. A keepsake.

The boat fits easier than I'd thought through the cave opening, but the exit is like a birth. Inside was still and quiet and dark, with only the echo of the sea. Outside, immense waves batter at an immense rock, thundering loudly and spraying salty mist. After each wave comes a dramatic suck of water, followed by the rushing pour of frothy white rapids with the next wave. The timing has to be perfect to get out without hitting the rocks.

I ready the wind. Water sucks out, races back, and then I funnel everything I have into the sail, riding the water out through the narrow chute. The next wave comes at the boat like a monster, pushing it up and up as my wind tilts it hard forward.

There's a moment of perfect balance as the hull rises to the crest. It's a coin flip of whether I crash back and drown or glide harmlessly down the wave's other side into the open sea. I lunge to the front of the boat, blasting all the wind I can into the sail and praying the mast won't snap.

Then the boat glides down. The wave crashes violently behind me. The boat rises and falls smoothly over the next incoming wave, and the next. I sail a hundred yards out before I look back. The cavern opening is completely hidden behind the giant craggy stone rising from the turbulent sea like a fist. How could anyone find that cavern, much less sail this boat into it? But now I know that this huge stone marks the spot.

The open sea stretches in a wide, liberating arc. A sense of freedom washes over me. I could go almost anywhere—to Blue to try to find Kiyo, back to Yellow's gentle shore, or to the edge of the horizon. They say the Five Towers are on an island, but what if there's more beyond this sea? It's tempting to try to find out, but I'm not ready. I have no supplies, no food. And my foot still hurts terribly.

I gaze down at the wound, beside the scar on my other foot. It's a bloody sore now, and I have a feeling it's going to leave a mark—probably a criss-cross, super-important, save-the-five-towers kind of mark. Maybe I should be glad. It could be a fourth scar. It could be progress. But why does everything in this blasted place have to hurt so bad?

Through the pain comes a new hope, a direction.

Emma. If anyone could heal this, she could. And she wants my help. I can't leave her. I will tell her about the coin and the boat. She'll know what to do next.

I adjust the wind to veer right, away from Max and Blue and through the open sea along the same path that she and I sailed ages ago to the shore of the Yellow Tower.

25

THE GOLDEN COAST gleams like a sickle, extending from the sheer cliffs to the right, where this boat had been hidden, to a sandy beach. The suns are still behind me, rising lazily with the morning, when I reach the gentle shore. The water glints like a turquoise jewel. The boat carves into the sand. I give it an extra gust of wind to pull it further up the beach. Better to have an escape route if things go bad.

I climb off the boat and curl my toes into the sand. The gritty particles shift and play on my feet. A gentle wave washes over the wound. It still stings, but the salt is good for it. The sea heals. It restores. Wet, warm, salty.

I limp up the beach and across the sandy dunes. They rise and fall like delicate little mountains, sand scattering with each limping step. Reeds sway around me in the breeze. Small, almost translucent crabs scurry away.

A dark figure stands motionless on the wall in the distance. The memory comes at me like a bowshot— arrows raining down, cracking my shield, stabbing into my thigh, Emma healing, and us fleeing together. This time I'm wearing Yellow's garb instead of Blue's robe, but I'm still not taking any chances. I summon the air and draw it into a dense bubble overhead. I'm stronger now. I remember more.

Another figure joins the first, then another. The three of them watch me approach until I'm directly underneath. No one takes a shot. Their bows stay at their backs.

"How'd you get out there?" one of them shouts down.

"By boat. One of our people had hidden it there." I point to the right, where the rocky cliffs loom in the distance. With my other hand, I hold up the diamond.

They suddenly duck behind the parapet, out of sight.

"Hey, I serve the king!" I shout. "Where can I get in?"

"Put the rock down, against the wall," one of them shouts.

"You mean the diamond? Why?"

"Put it down!"

I see no harm in it, so I set the dazzling jewel down on the dirt, against the stone wall.

"Now cover it in dirt!" one the archers shouts.

I stare down at the diamond. What are they worried about?

"Cover it!" an archer shouts.

I kick a pile of dirt over the diamond so that it is completely buried. "Okay, happy now?" I call up.

They do not answer, but one of the figures rises with a rope in hand. The three of them lower a large basket down the side of the wall.

"Hop in. We'll pull you up."

Their bows are still at their backs. I climb into the basket, keeping the wind ready. They haul me up foot by foot until I reach the top and step onto the wall beside them.

"Thanks," I say. "Why did you make me bury the diamond?"

"Can't talk here," an archer replies. "I'll lead you back."

I look past them to the tower and its glimmering turrets in the distance. "I know the way."

"Someone wants you."

"Who?"

The archer glances up at the suns, shades his eyes, then shakes his head. "You're being watched. Your diamond proves that, even if it can't be used now."

The king must have been using it somehow. Emma warned me that anything in the sunlight could be seen. Maybe the diamond added to that power. It means the king, her father, might know I've come from Max, hurt and needing help.

"Alright," I say, "lead on."

The archer guides me along the wall until we reach a stairwell leading to the ground. We walk across fallow yellow-grey fields. We pass many abandoned huts. The suns begin to lower in the sky.

My foot throbs worse with each step. "How much farther?"

"It's close," the archer says.

"Have you seen a golden coin?"

The archer shakes his head. "Not here."

"In your past?"

"Aye, there was one. I wore it. Hollowed out in the center. Called it a wedding ring."

"Care to tell me about it?"

The archer talks as we walk. He tells me that he was a famous football player in Europe. He says he was very good, one of the world's best, known for his golden feet. But he doesn't talk much about that. He says it wasn't that important. It was just work to him. What he mostly sees in his past is a single day, replayed over and over in his dreams. It was the day when he did the most courageous thing in his life. He promised to love his bride for the rest of their lives, until death do them part. Now that death has done them part, he explains that his life after that day was one long slide away from courage. He traveled for games. He feared the opinions of his teammates, who went out in clubs wherever they traveled. He joined them. He stopped wearing his golden ring.

"It was cowardice," he says. "But she was so brave."

When I ask what he means, I hear much of my own story in his. He explains that his wife did not leave him. She knew about his unfaithful ways. She could have left with half his fortune or more. But she stayed, and he retired. Then slowly, slowly, he came back to her. The wounds remained but scarred over.

The archer stops before a hut. "This is it. I'll wait here."

I tell him thanks and approach the little building. It is in disrepair like all the others. It looks like it hasn't been occupied in a hundred years.

Parting cobwebs over the door, I step inside. The window has been boarded up, leaving the room dark and musty. A sole figure sits still as a statue at the table. She has wide-set eyes, long dark hair, and a silver crown. Joan, the girl-queen.

"Sit," she commands.

I stay standing. "Why are you here?"

"I thought a servant never forgot his prior master…" There's a touch of amusement in her voice. "Sit, please?"

I sit across from her, out of reach. Emma said Joan was on her side, but I'm not convinced. I keep the wind ready in case she tries to spring at me and slap a collar around my neck again.

She leans down and studies my foot. Then she kneels, the yellow silk of her dress pressing against the dirt floor. Her hands run over the wound. Her eyes close and a rush of cold enters me through her hands. It does not spread much above my knee, but the wound is healed. The scar remains.

"Thank you," I say.

"It's strange. I couldn't fully heal it." She sounds tired as she returns to her chair. "The wound left something."

"My fourth mark," I say. "Courtesy of Max."

"Does it still hurt?"

"No, the pain is gone, thanks to you."

"Good," she says, smiling. "There were more cures than we knew in the natural world."

"We invented cures," I say. "I was a doctor, a

researcher."

"Invented? But you used only what you found in nature, yes?"

"I guess that's true," I admit. Even the golden nanoparticles that I invented were manufactured from compounds and molecules that already existed. "But why does that matter?"

"The Healer made the world with all the elements needed to bind up pain. Even inside us the spirit rises and knits scars over wounds."

"Those are called platelets."

"Call it what you like, the Healer is the only true source of restoration." She leans back with her hands clasped. "Did you enjoy your sail?" Her tone is knowing, taunting.

"What do you want?" I ask.

"The king saw you enter Max's hut. He saw you sail away, alone. He believes you have the coin now. Is this true?"

"Why should I trust you?"

"So you don't—" Joan begins, but then turns sharply, listening. There's a distant sound of horses, approaching.

"Guards," she whispers. "We don't have time, Cipher. The king traded Emma away. I will help you find her."

"*Traded?*" My mouth gapes open. This can't be true.

"Yes, and I think I know where she is. We must go." She rises quickly and moves to the corner of the room. She pulls away wooden boards from the floor, just as Max had done, revealing a hole.

"Hurry," she says. "You first."

I gaze at the hole, remembering what happened last time I went down. I meet Joan's eyes, as the heavy thud of hooves makes the ground tremble beneath our feet.

"I'm not afraid of the guards." But even as I say it, I remember their armor and how my wind swept past the armored boy-king like a river around a boulder. "What do they want?"

"To collar you!" she whispers urgently. "If you want to get Emma back, we must go."

Horses come to a stop outside. There's a clanking of metal, then a murmur of hard voices.

"Now!" Joan's face shows fear as she points to the opening in the floor.

Emma said Joan was on her side. The same Joan who collared me in the Scouring, but also who healed me. The clank of metal armor rings out by the door. The guards. My power won't work against them. I look at Joan again and her fear seals my choice.

I spring forward and scramble down the ladder. Joan hurries after me. She pulls the boards back into place, enclosing us in complete darkness.

26

FOOTSTEPS THUD LOUDLY in the hut above. Metal armor clanks. An angry voice demands: "Where is he?"

"He must be in here!"

I back away from the voices but can't see anything in the darkness. I bump into Joan. Her hand covers my mouth and she whispers in my ear: "Keep up."

She takes my hand and pulls me forward, striding quickly and silently away from the voices. The ground beneath our feet feels like hard-packed dirt. We race ahead in the pitch black. No turns. No hills. No sounds behind us.

By the time Joan stops, I'm covered in a sheen of sweat. I listen and hear nothing except our breathing.

"Where are we?" I whisper.

She is quiet for a moment, then answers: "The tunnels."

A candle-sized flame flashes into life. It flickers above Joan's palm and makes the long lines of her face look severe and dangerous.

I take a step back from her. "You were in Red?"

"Long ago," she says.

She lifts her flame higher, lighting the area around us. We stand at a crossing. Tunnels go right and left and behind us, in the direction we've come. All three tunnels stretch as far as I can see, with stone frames supporting the earthen walls and ceiling every twenty paces or so. I suddenly feel very small, and vulnerable. I have no idea how to get out of here without her help. I do not want to be trapped underground.

I take a deep breath, trying to steady myself. "Thank you for helping me," I say, as pleasantly as I can. "Now can you tell me what's going on? And what happened to Emma?"

"Yes, there is much you should know. But we have little time. The king expects me back soon. So…where to start…" She rubs her chin as if in thought.

"How about with Emma," I suggest. "Where is she?"

"Yes, this is the heart of the matter. She's in the Blue Tower."

"Blue!" My hopes rise. I expected much worse—the Black Tower, or even the pit. "How did this happen?"

"It's a long story," Joan says. "After Anna disappeared, Emma followed her father into the tunnels. Not even I would dare follow the king here, and he trusts me…at least I think he does. But Emma is brave. Down and down she followed him until she discovered the source of the gold, in a mine deep beneath the ground. She told me that she sensed a power, a dark force, there—and that it was somehow connected to the pit and the circle in the

Scouring that has turned from white to black. She saw boys and girls, too, collared and slaving away in the mine, digging out gold. She even thought she saw one of the leaders, Elijah, but she had to flee. Her father almost saw her. She told me she had to go again, to find out what was happening. I warned her not to go. I told her it was too dangerous. The king could be setting a trap. Unfortunately, I was right. The second time Emma followed him, she came back as the king's captive, collared. He took her armor. He announced the sentence before everyone in the courtyard. She would be traded."

"But why?" I ask. "He could have kept her collared. Or wiped her and sent her to the fields."

"I wish I knew," Joan says. "I think the king must have discovered that she was plotting against him. But he could also have learned that many were loyal to her, so instead of keeping her here, he made arrangements to trade her. Their relationship is…complicated."

"How do you know she's in Blue?" I ask.

"I was in the Scouring when the king traded her. We brought back four captives back from Blue, and here's the strangest thing: I have not seen a single one of them since. Not in the fields. Not anywhere. Based on what Emma saw, I think they might be enslaved in the mine, digging for more gold. The material is not natural—the way it blocks the power, shapes the mind. I wore it once. But ever since rising to queen, I've refused to wear it again. It is tainted, I feel sure of it."

I study Joan's pretty but stern face. Some parts of her

story don't add up. Like why the king trusts her, why she's helping me, and why she gets a place of honor even though she refuses to wear the armor. Everyone else has to obey the king. Completely.

"How did you become queen?" I ask.

"The king chose me."

"Why?"

She hesitates, then looks down. The flame above her palm flickers and almost goes out. "Emma said I could trust you."

"She said the same about you," I reply.

Joan's gaze lifts slowly. Her eyes do not quite look as stern. "You understand that people can change? Even here?"

"Yes, I know that very well. The leaders say we are supposed to change, that we *have to* change before we can leave this place."

"Right. And I have changed. A lot."

She still hasn't answered my question. "Why did the king choose you to be queen?" I ask.

Her voice comes out very faint: "I kept his secret."

"What secret?"

"I didn't know it would happen like this. The king and I were guards. We fought in the Scouring together. I trusted him. He was only William Chamberlain back then. One night when I was on watch duty, I saw him with the leaders, Elijah and the Widow. They moved under the cloak of darkness. There was glint of gold. I hurried to inspect and discovered that he had bound the leaders with golden shackles around their wrists and was leading them into a dark stairwell beneath the Yellow Tower. I ordered him to stop. I demanded to know what he was doing. He told me he had found a hidden place beneath the Yellow Tower. He showed me. It was the mine, with rich veins of gold on the rock walls. You could *feel* the gold's power. He had been experimenting with it and learned that it would block other powers here. He told me that the leaders had known about this, but kept it hidden. He had found a golden coin that showed him the truth. The leaders were slowing us down, he said. They kept the Yellow Tower from progress. They were the reason boys and girls here were so lazy and rarely advanced. He told me he could change things if only I let him go. He promised he would not hurt them. I looked to them. Their faces were blank. It was surreal. They didn't even resist him. It was the last time I saw them. I promised William I would tell no one. He named himself king, and me queen. But I felt terrible. I could barely get out of bed. The king began producing the armor. I don't really know how. I didn't ask. I became numb to it all. It was easy, comfortable, being queen. I kept this secret for so long. But then Emma came back. I told her everything. I confessed, and she welcomed me to her side. So here I am."

Joan's shoulders slump, like someone who has carried a great weight for too long. The silver crown over her straight black hair looks different in the firelight. If this is all true—and my gut tells me it is—it explains so much. This is why she and the king argued when they first left me in my hut, and why she is helping me now. But a question gnaws at me.

"I'm glad you told me this," I say. "Of all people, I understand joining Emma. But you had already chosen the king's side. Why did you risk switching against him?"

"King Chamberlain has now ruled the Yellow Tower across many Scourings. Before he became king, he was different, gentler, kinder. I believe he is corrupted by the power or the gold or both. I believe he would rule this place forever, as a tyrant. I once thought the leaders were tyrants..."

"What were they like?"

"They were very patient. They talked often of the Healer. They knew that boys and girls in the fields could dwindle into shadows of what they once were."

"Why does this happen in Yellow?"

"It was not always this way," she says. "We once had more order, with each person having a chance to rise. Now King Chamberlain gathers more and more of the power, and those furthest from him lose hope of ever advancing."

"I think I saw that in the fields. They are afraid."

She nods somberly. "Fear destroys hope. Fear saps the strength of virtues. Without hope, the serfs cannot reach the Scouring, they cannot leave. Fear is a dreadful trap."

"Why haven't you done more?" I ask. "You were the queen. I still don't understand how you could betray the leaders, and now betray the king."

"There is something in me, in my past, that loathes all tyrants. I was once known for great courage against those in power."

"On Earth? Who were you?"

"This is not the time," she says. "We have already talked for too long. The king expects me back soon. You must go after Emma in Blue. I believe she is destined to rule here, the right way. She needs your help to reach the throne."

"Can I get to Blue through these tunnels?"

"Yes, they weave underneath all of Yellow's land. Only a few huts have entrances. We use them strategically. That's how we were able to meet without the king knowing."

"But he sent his guards…"

"After you, not me. He didn't know I was there, because I came by tunnel."

"Why did he send guards after me?"

"He knows you are on Emma's side."

"But he's known that all along. He could have captured me and wiped me when I first arrived here. Instead he sent me to a hut and then gave me this quest for the golden coin. Same as Neville."

"The quest was rigged from the start," Joan says. "The king saw what you did to Max when you were a serf, blasting him away with the tornado. After that, Max told the king he could convince you to bring back the fifth marked one. The king planted the coin with Max so he could bait you. But fortunately for us, you and Max went underground, where the king could not watch. He does not know what you and Max spoke about. Unless Max tells Neville…"

She pauses, as if wanting me to reveal what happened between Max and me. Max wanted me to bring him Kiyo. She could be the fifth marked one, who the king wants to find. Max said she's in the Blue Tower. And now I know Emma is there, too. There's no doubt now, I will go after them both. I've had enough of Yellow and its king. I may never come back. I belong in Blue.

"Thank you for telling me all this," I say.

"It is my duty to Emma. Do not come into Yellow's light until you have her. The king is watching for you. His guards are watching for you. You know the power of their armor. They will overpower you and collar you the moment they get the chance. You cannot risk that."

"I know. I need to find Emma before I worry about that." I don't mention that I have no plans of coming back. Joan doesn't need to know.

"Here's how you get to Blue." She points down one of the tunnels. "Start this way, then take the first two rights and then a left. It will be a long way, so do not worry about the distance. This will lead you to the border of the pit. You cross it to get to Blue."

The pit…the place Daniel told me to never go again, where there's some path to the mine and Yellow's captive leaders. I take a deep breath. "Is there any other way?"

"No. And it is too dangerous alone. I will send one of my servants with you, one you already know. His name is Hank."

I smile and breathe easier. "How will we find him?"

"Follow me. He is not far from here."

27

A DOOR OPENS in the tunnel's ceiling. Pale light streams down, showing motes of dust in the air. Hank drops down, closes the gap above him, and stands at attention before Joan. His collar glows orange in the flickering light. She must have summoned him through the link.

"Cipher, Hank," she says, as if introducing us.

Hank rushes to me and sweeps me into a hug just as he did in Green, and in Red before that. He smells like grain, dust, and sweat.

"Boy, it's been a while," he says, releasing me. "I sure do have some stories since we talked."

"It's good to see you."

"You'll have time to catch up on the way," Joan says to us. "I will cover for you with the king."

"Thank you," I say.

"Just doing my part," Joan replies. "Now go and bring back Emma. Yellow needs her." She turns and strides down the opposite tunnel from the one we'll take. Her flame goes out, leaving us in complete darkness. The sound of her footsteps fades.

"I can't see a thing," Hank says. "Hope you know the way…"

"Yes, but…" I listen until I'm sure I no longer hear Joan's footsteps. "What commands has she given you?"

"She told me to bake a loaf of bread with nine grains. Then just a minute ago she ordered me to come down here. That's it."

"Did she tell you there was anything to keep from me?"

"No…except, well you know collars better than I do. If she'd ordered me not to say something, would I be able to tell you that?"

I laugh. "Fair point. I'm glad you're here, Hank."

"More exciting than a little plot of dirt, that's for sure!"

"I hope it's not too exciting. Changing towers never seems easy. You remember how you and Emma came after me in Red?"

"Oh yeah," he laughs. "One of Red's fighters hit me in the Scouring with a mighty blow to the head. Knocked a few screws loose. But hey, I survived, memories intact."

"And then you helped me rise to Alpha," I say. "Now it's our turn to help Emma."

"Lead on, my friend!"

I lead us down the tunnel Joan indicated, keeping a hand on the wall to feel the way forward. There is comfort in the stone support frames at regular intervals, and in Hank's company.

He stays close behind me and talks steadily and quietly. He tells me that, in the Green Tower, he and Seneca learned all about their shared past. He was hard up when he stumbled on her home by the shore of a big lake in New York. These were the days just after the war, when America won her freedom from the Red Coats. The frontier was a constant struggle. Hank had been on his preaching mission, but a native tribe had not been receptive to his message. They'd taken his horse and his gun and his boots, leaving him with nothing but the clothes on his back and his large black book. Seneca found him like that and nursed him back to health. She was like a mother to him. He helped her with chopping wood and a little hunting. It didn't hurt that she had a daughter with eyes like galaxies. Her daughter went by a native name that meant Tender Twig.

Together the three of them had gotten through that first winter, but the next winter, after Hank had married the daughter and welcomed a baby girl into the world, raiders came. They took almost all the food stored for the winter—roots from the cellar, cider, lard, even their chickens. Something new had taken over Hank after that. He was scared to death, he said, not for himself, but for his daughter. He'd sworn that he'd never get stolen from again, that he'd be stronger. The next year he traded for a shotgun and a pistol. He kept them loaded and ready. When the raiders came the next time, he'd fought them.

"Killed a good number," he says, "but they got one, too. My Tender Twig."

This was the last thing Hank had seen from the sap in the Green Tower. After that he and Seneca had agreed to be traded to Yellow. He didn't mind the square plot of land too much.

"It's easy farming," he says. "No raiders, and plenty of grain."

He tells me that dreams have filled in a thousand gaps in his memories. They've shown him mundane little things. Days spent chopping wood and stacking it so high he couldn't see over it. Days spent in the forest, hunting game. Days spent sitting by the lake, fishing with Tender Twig by his side. They're good memories, Hank tells me, but not much action. Kind of like life in the Yellow Tower.

As Hank tells me all this, I remember how much it helps just to have someone listen. Sharing stories from the past unites us. Hundreds of years and infinite circumstances make us different, but we've had similar struggles and successes. And now we relive them here. We scour them, seeing the facets of Genius, Passion, Provider, and Healer.

Eventually the wall gives way on the right, so we turn that way. We keep up the long, dark march until the next right. Then left. I've lost all sense of where we are under Yellow's lands, but hold some hope that I could get back to Hank's old hut if it came to that.

The air suddenly changes. It stirs and blows gently, with a heavier feel. I move forward more cautiously. Soon the wall to the right ends. I reach to the left and feel no wall there, either.

"Man, you sure about this?" Hank asks. "It feels weird in here."

His voice sounds faint, even though he's only a few feet behind me. The darkness swallows it. I step forward and an object clatters at my feet.

The bones. This is the pit.

I take a step back. "Every tower connects here," I say. "Blue should be the first right."

"*Should be?*" Hank asks. His low voice is very close now, maybe a foot or two away.

"That's how it worked going from Red to Black."

"Man, I don't like this. Something about the air. It's not right."

"Just don't use any powers." I try to sound confident, but he's right. The air moves in strange patterns around us. It feels like invisible fingers prodding me as we move back to the wall.

"Let's stay quiet from here, but close," I say.

"Lead on."

I move along the wall to the right, to Blue, I hope. My fingers brush lightly against the rough and dry stone. The air spins and prods as we advance. The sound of Hank's breathing stays close. It's not far until bones clatter again at my feet.

We know what to do. I've told Hank what I learned last time Emma and I went this way. Stay quiet. Keep moving. Slow and steady. Still it makes my skin crawl. The air pulls goosebumps out of my flesh. The bones make every step terrifying.

These are people who never were.

They can't hurt us. They never lived. But can they haunt us?

There's a sudden crash behind me. Hank gasps. Bones

clatter and clink all around us. But then the clattering stops and echoes through the cavern, making me feel tiny and exposed.

"Hank?" I whisper through clenched teeth.

"I'm okay. Just tripped."

Something touches my hand, making me jump.

"It's me," Hank says, his hand closing around mine. "Maybe, um, if it's alright with you, we could hold on until we're out?"

The warmth from his hand feels good in this cold place. "Yeah, okay."

"Good. Now hurry, man. I want out of here."

We move faster. It's easier to keep our balance with hands clasped. Hank's strong grip and heavy breathing make the clattering bones seem further away and…less haunting. Twenty steps later the wall opens up.

Just as we turn out of the cavern, a gust of wind rushes over us from the pit. It smells like death, and the darkness grows darker. The void of color sucks me in like a black hole.

This was to be, says a booming voice, *but for you.*

28

THE YOUNG WOMAN on the park bench glows. She is pulling juice boxes from a plastic bag and setting them in a line on the bench beside her. It is such a simple thing, so normal, but the way the light touches her honey brown curls makes me wonder if she is an angel.

A child rushes up to her. He looks just like her, with the gentlest, most innocent brown eyes.

"Mommy, juice?" he says.

She strokes his cheek. "Of course, here darling."

He takes one of the boxes and sucks on the straw. She laughs and says, "Not so fast, Fitzy!"

Before he finishes, a graceful older woman approaches the bench with two other kids. Their cheeks are flushed with playful energy as they claim their own juice boxes. The three of them look so much alike. Two brothers and a sister.

The little boy finishes his juice and turns to the older woman. "Nana, what's your real name?"

The woman beams down at the boy. "Susan Fitzroy."

"Is that why my name is Fitzy?" the boy asks.

"You are named after your grandfather," she says. "He was a great man. Just as you will be someday."

"Nana, what's your favorite color?" the little girl asks.

"Purple, my dear."

"Fitzy, Johnny, let's go find a purple flower for Nana!"

The three kids bound off. The youngest, Fitzy, wobbles adorably as he chases the older two.

The younger woman sighs as she retrieves the scattered remains of juice boxes and straws. The older woman turns to her, smiling warmly.

"You're doing a great job with them," she says.

"Thanks, Mom. It's been really hard. Charles has only a few months left of residency. It should get better after that. One of his interviews is with a small practice out of the city. The hours wouldn't be so bad. We might actually see him sometimes."

"What about his interview here?" the older woman asks, gazing up at the skyscrapers that surround the park.

"It went very well," the younger woman says dourly. "It's very prestigious. He would work even more. Save a bunch of lives…and never see us."

"Your father faced a choice like that."

"Yeah, I know. He worked hard, very famous, and all that."

"Only to a point," the older woman says. "When we lost Benjamin, he changed. He had an offer to become the head of the National Institutes of Health. He turned it down. It wasn't long after that when I became pregnant with you."

The younger woman smiles, and her radiance makes everything else look black and white. "I'm glad he did."

"So was he. He had no idea how little time he had left to live. If he'd taken the job, we probably wouldn't have had you."

"I miss him. Life can be so short. I've told Charles that, but he seems set on taking this job. If only I could convince him that we need him more than his patients do."

"You can't change a man like that."

"So how did Daddy change?"

"Hmm, such a good question. I wish I really knew. Do you know the difference between humility and fear?"

The younger woman shrugs. "Enlighten me."

"Fear affects all of us. We are afraid to die, to fail, to disappoint. You name it. We fear it. What matters is how we respond to fear. Most people, like your father at first, try to take control of all the factors around the fear. When Benjamin died, Paul was more terrified of death than ever. His first instinct was to tackle the fear head on, as if he could defeat it through his own abilities. But somehow—I really wish I knew how—he came to let go of this desire for control. He opened himself to the fear and conceded that, ultimately, the biggest things were outside his control. Life and death. Success and failure. All he could control were the little decisions before him each moment. And when we accepted that truth, he started making different decisions. Humble decisions. Can you imagine the courage it took for him to want another baby after what happened to Benjamin?"

The younger woman wipes at her moist eyes. "I wish he was still here."

"So do I, so do I."

The women clasp hands and sit in quiet. The sun warms their beautiful faces—so much alike, aside from forty years of age.

A few minutes later the children return. Fitzy leads the way with a smile as bright as the sun and a bundle of purple flowers clutched between his little hands.

It's pitch black as I sit up. My skin feels clammy. Wind rushes over me and I scramble frantically away from it. Bones clatter underneath me but my hands reach solid stone. I crawl forward on all fours until I've left all the bones and the pit and the vision behind. I feel one wall, then crawl to the other, just a few feet away. I'm back in a tunnel, and I start to cry.

My daughter. My grandchildren.

Their bones are back there. They never existed.

Susan told my daughter—the beautiful young woman who never saw life—that I had courage, humility. But it didn't happen that way. I decided to fight death with science instead of life. I still don't know how it ended, except now I'm sure there was no daughter, no Fitzy, no adorable little girl gathering purple flowers. *This was to be*…except I chose a different path.

A sound cuts off my crying.

"Hank?" My voice echoes down the narrow hallway.

"I'm here," he says softly.

I crawl forward and soon find him. He sits with his back to the wall, his arms clutching his knees close.

"You okay?" I ask.

"I saw things, Cipher."

"Me too. The pit does this. It shows what could have been, if not for what we did."

"It's terrible."

"You want to talk about it?"

"No. Please no. I want it all gone. I never want to think about it again."

I've never heard Hank like this. There's no joy in his voice. We can't just sit here. The darkness is too close, the despair too heavy, like it could crush us.

"Let's get away from here," I say.

"What's the point?" Hank mumbles.

"We have to go to Blue."

"Whatever."

I take his hand and help him up. "Come on, let's go."

He doesn't protest. We move slowly, careful with each footstep. I still can't see my own hand in front of my face. There could be a cliff, a drop-off, a dragon, anything. The path goes on and on. Time slips into footsteps. As my hand drags along the wall, I count steps to keep my mind under some kind of control.

When I reach one hundred steps, I feel like we have to be close to Blue's entrance. When I reach one thousand, I start to worry. I'm on one thousand four hundred two when Hank asks, "You still think we're going the right way?"

"Has to be," I say, failing to hide my doubt.

"What if we missed a turn, or stairs or something?"

"Let's go a little farther. We can always backtrack."

"Alright, man. Hope you're right."

When my count reaches three thousand steps, we stop to rest. Hank sits beside me in the darkness. We eat some bread that he brought, then march on. My hand drags along the wall. The count rises. Four thousand steps. Five thousand.

I'm considering turning back when Hank whispers, "Cipher, you hear that? Water."

Standing motionless, ears tuned, I hear a faint drip-drop like a leaking faucet. "Yes. Maybe we're close."

It's hard to judge distance underground, but it seems like we've gone far enough to be under the sea beyond the Blue Tower by now. Unless we've been gradually turning, maybe even going in circles, without me noticing.

"Look!" Hank says in a hushed whisper.

A dim light has appeared, like an opening at the end of the tunnel.

But then, like it never existed at all, the light vanishes and the perfect dark returns. Without that point in the distance, my center of gravity loses its fixed point. My head spins. Was the light really there?

A touch on my arm makes me jump.

"Hey, it's me." Hank sounds calm. "We have to go there."

He's probably right, but... "If it's a door, someone

closed it."

"I don't care what it is," Hank says. "It's light. That's where I'm going."

We continue down the tunnel, and soon the light appears again. This time it's much closer. I can even see Hank's dark form beside me. The light seems to be coming from around a bend. We move forward as silently as we can.

When we reach the bend, we stop and peer around a corner of the wall. Only a short distance away the tunnel opens into a huge cavern that smells of brine. And there, in the middle of the darkness, a small blue orb glows at the top of Abram's staff.

29

MY EYES SLOWLY adjust to the faint blue light, but not to the surreal memory of this place. Abram's staff moves slowly down a path, toward a boy who lies on the shore of an underground lake that looks like dark glass as it extends and fades into blackness. I shiver as I remember that a smooth wall borders the lake. It's where I woke up so long ago, without any memory, with no clue of what awaited me in these Five Towers.

Abram reaches the boy and holds out a robe. The boy rises slowly to his bare feet and slides on the robe. The two of them look like a pair of ghostly specters in the light of Abram's staff.

I see Abram's bearded mouth moving, but I hear no sound over the distance. The boy suddenly steps forward and wraps his arms around Abram, who pats his back. The two of them turn and walk away together, taking the glowing blue orb with them. The cavern goes black again.

The boy *hugged* Abram. Not me. I was afraid. The first thing I knew, I was treading water. Then I swam toward Abram's light. He met me on the shore. I didn't trust him.

Why was this boy so different? Maybe he's been in the Blue Tower a long time, but even then, wouldn't he have been wiped?

A distant shout interrupts my thoughts. It's a girl's voice, frantic. "Help! Help!"

There's a sudden motion beside me. I'd almost forgotten Hank was there. "Come on," he says. "Let's help."

"Wait." I reach out and grab a fistful of shirt. "It's a newcomer," I say. "Abram will come for her."

Hank twists out of my grip. It's easy to forget how much stronger he is. "What if she can't swim?" he asks.

The shouting stops. The only sounds are our breathing, the wind, and the distant waves.

Hank grunts in frustration. "Maybe she sank…"

"No one dies here," I say. "But we could be wiped if we're caught."

"Abram wouldn't do that."

"I hope not, but…" I think back. It's different in Blue. They don't always wipe new captures. Some of them become servants, with collars around the neck. That's not as bad as getting wiped, but it's not good. "Listen, we're here to find Emma. We know our way around Blue."

"You think we could just ask Abram?" Hank says.

"I don't know about that. The leaders stick with their rules no matter what. If we're caught, sure, we'll talk to him. But let's try to avoid that, okay?"

"Fine, but if someone yells for help again, I'm going."

"We'll see." I'd hate to hold Hank with the wind, but I

will if I must. He hasn't been the same since whatever he saw in the pit. Yet, as we sit quietly in the darkness, a hidden smile spreads over my face. Deep down I know Hank's right. It's still simple for him. Someone needs help. He might be able to help. So he will. I wish it could be that simple for me.

Eventually the faint blue light appears again. Abram comes into view, looking very small in the distance as he descends down the path, his staff and the blue orb bobbing with each step. The light reveals a small body on the shore. It's probably the girl who cried for help. If she's like me, she realized no help was coming and decided to spend her energy swimming. Now she's curled up in a ball. Her hair is long and black, splayed out behind her like a shadow on the sand.

Her eyes open, and I gasp. They are the dark eyes that first greeted me in the Blue Tower.

"It's Kiyo," I whisper.

"*Now* you wanna help?" Hank asks.

There's no time to discuss it. Kiyo has already been wiped in Blue more times than she knows. It's not right to make her start again. I could help her remember…

Abram is still a hundred paces away.

I summon the air and form a long, slanted wall between Kiyo and Abram. The sand begins to blow up the wall. In moments, thousands of grains of sand cover the invisible wall of air and make it look like an extension of the beach, blocking Abram's sight of Kiyo. I wrap her in a cocoon of air and lift her off the ground. She startles but I silence her.

I'll apologize later.

I rush her toward us, just above the ground, always hidden behind the wall. With a final flick of the air I pull her into the small cave opening where Hank and I stand. I weave countless threads to release the wall of air and sand so that Abram's view never changes, except that one moment Kiyo was there, and now she is not.

I turn and look into her eyes. She stares at me blankly.

Then the faint blue light blinks off, plunging us into total darkness.

"Follow me," I tell Hank quietly.

Keeping my hand on the tunnel wall, I hurry away from the cavern and Abram. I use the air to carry Kiyo behind us, like she's wrapped in a floating cocoon. Each footstep feels heavier, louder. I've only made it twenty steps when a dazzling blue light bursts into life. For the first time I can see everything in perfect clarity. The tunnel's stone floor and walls. Kiyo's curled up body and alarmed expression. Hank's fear.

And Abram. Standing right in front of us.

30

"YOU GO TOO far," Abram's deep voice booms. The blue orb on his staff points at my chest. His blue eyes blaze behind wire glasses, like an angry principal staring down a student.

I take a step back. "I'm sorry. I—"

"Silence." He swings the staff up, stopping right at my neck, and my words suddenly choke in my throat. The thread of power is yanked out of me. The force knocks me to my knees.

Abram moves to Kiyo and wraps a blue robe around her. He puts an arm over her shoulder, protective. He whispers something to her that sounds like, *it's okay*, then he turns back to me. His long beard does not hide his fury.

"Do you have any idea the danger you put her in?" he asks.

"She's been in Blue," I say, feeling very small. "I was…going to help her remember. We would come back. I thought…"

"Where were you taking her? Toward the *pit?*" His last word comes out like a curse.

"I—I've gone through it before. That's how we got here. I'd take care of her."

He shakes his head gravely. "Rahab warned you about the pit. Daniel warned you. And yet you need *another* warning?"

"I know it's dangerous."

"You know nothing!" His shout is a thunderclap, shaking the walls and knocking me back on the ground. I hug my knees to my chest, trembling. His voice comes softer, but still deadly serious. "To take one to the pit without a single memory, with the Colorless One growing and…well, I will speak no more of it here."

From my knees, my head bows. I can't meet his eyes. I am speechless, awestruck by his words and devastated by my mistake. Abram was the first leader I knew. Even after Rahab and Daniel, I still feel like he's the main leader. He has a power and a force that makes the others seem weak.

A hand clasps my shoulder. "Now you know," Abram says gently. "You will come with me. You, too, Hank. Though you may not be scoured of fear, though you may not know the Healer, you are welcome back with the Genius."

I stand slowly, knowing I have no choice. Abram and Kiyo step past me and head down the tunnel. I catch Hank's eyes. His face is pale, but he turns and follows Abram. I trail after them.

Abram leads us out of the tunnel and into the cavern with the lake where everything started. We walk past the spot where Kiyo laid curled up, and where I first put on a blue robe. The long spiral path up through the Blue Tower is just as I remember it. Cool stone beneath my feet. The hollow openness in the center.

We have not gone far when Abram opens the door to the kitchen. The stench of rotten fish wafts out. Two boys in white first-class robes are wearing collars and scrubbing dishes.

"Help them clean," Abram says to Hank and me. "I will return for you." He leads Kiyo away without another word.

Hank and I exchange a glance, then he goes in, as if resigned to whatever fate Abram gives us. The two other boys barely acknowledge us.

Stepping into the kitchen feels like stepping into an old dream. It's not a nightmare, but it's not great either. This isn't like before when Emma and I cleaned side by side and I had the playful joy of first experimenting with my power. This time I summon the wind, businesslike, and clean quickly.

By the time I finish, the two first-class boys have gone and Abram has returned with Sarai. She eyes the collar around Hank's neck.

"Still subject to Yellow," she says. "Who's the master?"

Hank tells her that it's Joan. Sarai tells Hank to follow her. Hanks nods goodbye to me and they walk along the path going up the tower.

Abram takes me the other direction, back down. We exit the tower toward the dock. A line of boats bobs up and down. The sky is as grey as ever. The wind and crashing waves thrum in my ears. The sea looks almost black, with frothy white tips of waves dancing erratically in the wind.

When we reach the end of the dock, with a dark cliff looming overhead, Abram asks, "How have you been, Cipher?"

His anger is gone. He sounds more like what I remember—wise, curious, and slightly amused. But I'm still cautious. "You probably know," I say.

"There is a difference between the things that happen *around* you and those that happen *inside* you," he says. "Not even I can know the latter."

"I've learned a lot about who I was."

"And?"

"I made a lot of mistakes. But things have been getting better."

"For you, or for Dr. Fitzroy?"

"Is there a difference?"

A faint smile softens Abram's weathered face. He turns toward the boats bobbing up and down by the dock. "One of these is still yours. Where would you go if I let you sail it?"

"I don't know. I came here for Emma. And now you have Hank and Kiyo, too."

"Hm, they were sad when you left them for Red long ago."

"That was a mistake," I say, remembering their eyes through the gate between the Blue Tower and the Scouring, before I went to find my mother. "I thought I could make it alone. I know now that I need them."

"Genius requires company to truly thrive. I'm sure you have figured out by now that your friends here are no coincidence."

"Yes. You sent Kiyo to me when I first came. And in my first assignment, you told me to capture Emma in the Scouring. Now we all bear these strange scars. Daniel called us the marked ones."

"Heed Daniel's words. He discerns patterns and numbers better than any of us."

"He told me that I had to figure out how the five marked ones got here, to the Five Towers."

"That would be wise," Abram says.

"So will you let me talk to Kiyo, and Emma?"

"Perhaps. What can you tell me of Yellow?"

"The king there—Emma's father—he is losing his mind," I say. "He sent me on a quest to find a coin, and he hid it with Max. He has captured Yellow's leaders. He is mining some kind of twisted gold. And he wanted to use me…" I glance at the dark water churning beneath us. "He planted the coin with Max, the same Max who was here in Blue and shoved me off this dock after our boat race. He told me Kiyo was a marked one. She was his ancestor. He said if I brought her back to Yellow he would give me the coin. But I don't want to go back."

"This coin…tell me more about it."

"It is large and made of gold, with a lion imprinted on it. The king has one just like it. He used it to wipe a boy's memories. He told me the coin allowed him to see anything the light sees. Yellow's queen said the king once told her that the coin showed him the truth, that Yellow's leaders were a problem."

Abram frowns. "Corrupted truth can be worse than a lie. What did you expect from the coin?"

"The real point was to join the king's guards, to help with Emma's rebellion. She has many allies. She wanted to overthrow the king, free the leaders, make things right again."

"Yet now she is here," Abram says.

"I heard you traded four from Blue for her. Why?"

Abram shakes his head. "I did no such thing. It was the leader of Blue's group in the last Scouring, Luther. Strange things have been happening in the Scouring. The gateway to the White Tower has gone black."

"Strange things are happening in Yellow, too. The four from Blue have not been seen. A friend in Yellow told me that they, and many others, are enslaved in the mine, digging for this gold. This is why Emma wants to remove her father from the throne."

"And you? What do you want?"

"You know the answer. It hasn't changed. I want to leave the Five Towers, like my mother. But if that's not happening anytime soon, maybe I could stay in Blue. I don't like Yellow. It is stagnant as dirt."

"Yellow was not always this way," Abram says. "It needs to change. You will not leave before it does."

His words sound like a threat, and I don't like it. "Let me guess. Once things are back to normal there, with

Emma and the leaders in control, we can bring Yellow into equilibrium. That's what you want, isn't it? One hundred forty-four in each tower?"

"This is necessary," Abram says, stroking his beard to keep it steady in the whipping wind. "But tell me, Cipher, how do you think Yellow's true leaders, Elijah and the Widow, have been held captive?"

"It's the gold, somehow. I'm not sure. I've never even seen them."

He looks toward the cliffs, and the Yellow Tower beyond them. "Do you think gold could detain *me*?"

"No. Probably not."

"The gold is a tool. The force that holds the leaders is more powerful than gold. It is as I feared…"

"What do you mean?"

He turns back to me. His blue eyes are somber. "The outcome of the Five Towers is certain, but the path is not. How long would you imagine half of eternity to be?"

"A long time."

"Long indeed, or perhaps only a blink," Abram says. "But any moment feels long compared to what awaits."

"The White Tower?"

"That is the key to be unlocked. But a powerful force acts against it. This force long concentrated its attention on Earth, but the planet we knew has ended. The how and when of this are not your concern now. What it means, however, is that the opposing force now shifts its focus here. The pit grows darker. It lures almost all who enter it. None may be taken, but they may be trapped. Some indefinitely. The darkness feeds on their fear and shame, and it taints the Scouring, the light."

"Daniel hinted at this…" I suddenly wonder if I will be permitted to say the words, since Daniel wouldn't let me in Green. "Is the force called…the Colorless One?"

Abram blinks and shudders slightly. "This is one name. A dangerous name."

"Is the danger only in the pit?"

"I'm afraid not. It began there, but the danger has grown. It has long cast its shadow over the Black Tower, where it spawns darker and darker visions. And it is spreading."

"What could it do?"

"Rahab told me you passed through it. You tell me."

"The pit is…full of bones. They are the bones of souls who never existed, because of what we did on Earth. It is terrible, shameful. I hate it, and I hate myself for it. The pit shows what might have been, if we'd made different choices. Maybe the world would have been better off without us."

"A lie, a terrible lie!" Abram shakes his head gravely. "Cast away such twisted thoughts, Cipher. Hold to the light. If this darkness were to spread through the Five Towers…"

"But you said the outcome is certain. We get to leave, right?"

He clasps my shoulder. "No soul here may be stolen, but this place is in between. It is not meant to be permanent. The Colorless One seeks to detain and delay and hold any soul he can, as long as he can. He will fight until the bitter end. This could be his final stand."

Abram's steady grip and gaze comfort me, despite his harrowing words. I want to leave through the White Tower. Everyone here does, but now this force blocks our way.

"How can we fight it?" I ask.

"With light, only with light," Abram says. "I must find Yellow's leaders. We will hold back the darkness for a time, but I admit, not even we leaders are strong enough. Some of us may be lost. Black's leaders have long fought, but they have been overwhelmed. One is trapped in the Black Tower, another has been exiled. This is why Black has grown so dark. As long as the Colorless One dominates there, equilibrium will not be possible."

I swallow in fear. "So we must fight Black?"

"It is the only way. It will be up to you. But you will need the other colors with you. Blue, Red, Green, even Yellow."

"But…if you and the other leaders are not strong enough to stop the darkness, we won't stand a chance…"

"Do not lose hope, Cipher. The time is coming when you must lead the towers."

"Me? But you are the leader. How can I—?"

"Not alone. Genius needs Passion. The Provider needs the Healer. Every facet needs the other. With perfect equilibrium, the marked ones can harness the full prism and the purest white light of the Five Towers."

"What would we do with it?"

Abram gazes back toward the Blue Tower and the Scouring beyond it. "The path to the White Tower goes through Black. You must unite the colors and stab light into the black heart of the Colorless One."

31

WE TURN BACK from the dock and the windswept sea. The Blue Tower draws my eyes upward as we approach. It stands so tall, so firm, against everything in this place. Here, with Abram by my side, it feels like things will work out, like I could be the same blank Cipher who woke up beneath this tower ages ago and started the slow journey of discovering who I really am. But it is not so simple anymore. The light is being twisted. The Scouring is being corrupted. And Abram is going to leave. I will need more than the strength of this Blue Tower to fight back.

Sarai greets us at the doorway, with her thin dark hands clasped. The wind blows her long white hair wildly.

"I have told Cipher," Abram says. "He is almost ready."

Sarai nods. "What news of Elijah and the Widow?"

"They have not been seen in Yellow. Cipher has heard they are underground, held captive. I will go after them."

She takes his hands and looks deep into his eyes. They are silent for a long moment. The mist and rumble of crashing waves are the only sound. It almost looks like a goodbye.

Abram releases her hands. He bows to me. "As the light scours you, so you must purify the Five Towers and bring perfect equilibrium."

He turns and we enter the doorway together. Abram heads down. Sarai leads me up the familiar winding path into the Blue Tower.

"He's going to the pit, isn't he?" I ask.

"If he must," Sarai says. "As you must focus on what's before you."

We pass a broad doorway that I recognize as the entrance to the underwater dining hall. Sarai does not slow down. I have to hurry to keep up with her long strides.

"Where are we going?" I ask.

"First you'll need a robe."

I'm still wearing yellow. "Do you mean I can stay in Blue?"

"Of course, in Fourth Class if you wish," Sarai says. "I trust I need not remind you of its privileges?"

A girl in a blue robe passes us with a white-robed servant behind her. The girl has three stripes at her sleeves. She glances at Sarai and me curiously, but does not slow down.

Fourth Class. I thought I'd have to start at the bottom. But this means my own quarters, a servant, and the Scouring. Last time Emma was my servant, until she joined Blue.

"I need to find Emma," I say. "And Kiyo and Hank."

"Many will wish to see you," Sarai replies. "One thing

at a time."

We rise higher and higher up the coiling path, almost to the top of the tower. Sarai stops at a door and tells me my robe is inside. I enter and realize it's my same quarters from before. The view over the dark blue sea is just as stunning as I remember. I slip on the robe. It feels heavier than Yellow's silks, but also steadier and comforting. I've missed Blue.

When I step back onto the path, Sarai says, "Much better."

She leads me to another familiar room: the classroom where we first met. My feet stop at the threshold. On Earth, things were constantly diminishing. A childhood home, revisited twenty years later, has shrunk. Food or wealth stored up for the hard times dwindles away. Even bodies shrivel as they near the end of life. The opposite is true here. The classroom looks twice as large as I remember it. The glass wall—revealing the Scouring and the other four towers—is still the grandest view I've had in this place. The pillars rise like the legs of giants. And I remain very small, in the same boyish body that I began with here, despite how my powers have grown after all that I've seen and done since leaving Blue. But this is where it started. This is where I discovered my power over the wind, and the Genius.

"As some of you may know," Sarai announces, "this is Cipher."

My attention turns to the students in the room. I was so caught up in the memory of this place that I'd hardly noticed them. But now they face me. Sarai says something to the class about how I am a former leader of the Blue, Red, and Green Towers, and a marked one. But my eyes are fixed on an elegant girl with blond hair and blue eyes— hoping, praying, she remembers.

Her face lights up. "Cipher!"

We meet halfway, embracing. I step back and notice two stripes on her sleeves.

"You remember me, and you're second class!" I say.

Emma smiles. "I have been treated well."

"I'm so glad I found you. Hank and I came from Yellow. I know where the coin is. But your father…"

"He traded me." She looks down, and as her head rises again, her face is pale. "Your foot. The fourth scar."

I gaze down at the scarred flesh on the top of both feet, small against the immense stone floor. "It's from Max."

"How?"

"We fought, and he did this. But he might help us. He has your father's coin. He said he would give it to me if I bring Kiyo back to Yellow." I glance again over the room. Many of the students watch me with blank, wiped eyes. A few faces look familiar, but there's no Kiyo. "Have you seen her?"

"Yes, but—" Emma begins, but Sarai moves to us and places a gentle hand on each of our shoulders.

"You may speak with Kiyo," Sarai says. "But she will not remember."

"She will soon," I say. "I will help her. We will go to

the Sieve."

"It is not our usual way…" Sarai sighs. "But things are changing. Abram and I leave this to you."

Things are changing. Yes, Abram has gone. Yellow's leaders are missing. And I will no longer be limited to a single tower's struggle. I must bring equilibrium.

I scan the students in the room, struck by an idea. In an instant I summon the wind and lift everyone at once, only a foot, then lower them gently. Their faces are startled.

"It's not as special as it looks," I say. "I'm stronger than most because I was worse than most who made it here. As you recover more memories, you will see what I mean. What matters now is that we are going to work together for the light. We are no longer against all of the towers. We must join with Red and Green. We must rid Yellow of its king, and we must unite to fight Black. It has grown too strong, too dark. Have any of you been in Black?"

Two boys raise their hands.

"Good, you'll come with me. Anyone else?"

No one else volunteers. Now we must find Kiyo, and anyone else who has been in Black. I will take them to the Sieve and learn whatever I can about the Black Tower. Then I will lead Blue again into the Scouring.

32

SEVEN OF US stand around the Sieve. Sarai, Emma, Kiyo, Hank, and the two boys from Black. The vast room is cold. The pedestal of water stands lonely in the center.

We decide Kiyo will go first, and that I will lean close to look in at the vision as Daniel did with me so long ago. We will both try however possible to guide the vision to what she experienced in the Black Tower. Sarai says it may be possible. Because we are marked ones.

Kiyo grips the edge of the Sieve with white-knuckled fists. The scar looks ancient on her right hand. When I gaze into the water, I see the vision that Kiyo told me about soon after I arrived in Blue—with her fleeing and hiding with her children in snow-covered mountains, finding shelter and peace, but then losing her oldest son when soldiers came.

The memory shifts and begins to race forward so fast I can hardly make out what's happening. A village by a rocky shore. Then a vast city with an enormous castle in its center, many stories high with curved tiles marking each level. There are flashes of battle at the castle, across the drawbridge, up to the battlements, swords clinging and fire raging. For a moment the scene stops.

Kiyo grips a sword almost as tall as she is. She slashes and a man falls before her. Bodies litter the ground.

She drops the sword and kneels. There is blood on her torn kimono. Her face is dirty. A man rushes up and takes her hand, where there is deep wound.

Again the vision blurs and races ahead, all the way to the Five Towers. I see Kiyo coming to me, in the Blue Tower. I see her fighting in the Scouring, then all goes black before suddenly she is walking away from the Black Tower along a road through the terraced hills to the village I visited. There is Kiyo's hard rural life. Rising at dawn. Wading barefoot through flooded terraces. Planting grains until dusk. Eating meager meals of rice, occasionally with a pale broth.

I see my visit, with Emma, when we stayed the night and fought Max and fled with my Mom. Soon after that a woman rides into the village on a black horse. She wears a robe that reveals nothing but her eyes. They are eyes that I will never forget—Samantha's. Except Kiyo calls her Khadija, and she orders Kiyo and Max to follow her. They walk behind her as she rides into the night and the darkness. When they enter the Black Tower the memory goes blank again, like a gap in the Sieve's recording. But then Kiyo emerges in the Scouring, and the memory is clear. Over and over she fights, helping Black capture many, losing only a handful. In one of the fights Kiyo sees me with Green, except she does not recognize me. That was the time Black captured Baron. In the last Scouring Kiyo is captured by Blue. By a boy I remember as Luther.

Our heads rise from the Sieve.

Water drips from Kiyo's long black hair into a puddle on the floor beside the pedestal. She shivers.

I take her scarred hand in mine. "You have survived so much," I say quietly.

"But there is still more to see," she replies.

"You have seen enough today," Emma says. "Come, I will build you a fire."

After Emma and Kiyo leave, the other two boys go next and I decide not to watch. What I saw in Kiyo's vision has left me reeling, and I don't even know these two. They deserve some privacy.

It takes only moments in the Sieve's water for them, but their faces show the weight of lifetimes. They tell me they saw nothing from inside the Black Tower.

I wonder what power Black—or the Colorless One— has to keep these memories blocked. Our group talks briefly, but no one knows. Even Sarai can only guess.

"Black has long been shrouded in darkness," she says.

As we make our way down the path through the Blue Tower, two boys stand waiting. Tom and Luther, each with four stripes on their sleeves. They greet me like an old rival.

"Took you a while to get back," Tom says. "You should have let Blue catch you back when we were Green. It was much quicker."

"That was not the way for me," I reply. "I believe there are reasons we visit the towers we do. When you were caught, I brought Helena into Green.”

“She was never strong enough,” Luther says.

“She is a marked one,” I say. “More powerful than both of you.”

“Meh, I watched her leave our boat and walk to Green’s shore. The group should have sent me. I would have brought you back, instead of just Tom.”

“*Just* Tom?” he says. “I was the President of the United States of America.”

“And I started a reformation, some good it did us. We’re both boys in robes in the Blue Tower now.”

“We’re going to find the way out,” I say.

“Cipher’s always dreaming big,” Tom says, and Luther laughs.

Hank steps toward them. He’s as tall as Luther. “Quit laughing,” he demands. “You have no idea what Cipher’s capable of.”

“Oh, we have an idea…” Tom rolls his eyes toward me. “What is it this time, boy wonder?”

“Listen, Abram is gone,” I say. “We have a new enemy, the Colorless One. And we have to be united against it.”

“Colorless, ooh, spooky,” Luther says, and he and Tom laugh again.

“This isn’t a joke,” I snap.

Luther sneers at me. “You’re a joke.”

Hank’s punch takes Luther in the jaw, and suddenly the two of them are on the ground, wrestling for control. I summon the wind, just as I see Tom forming blue ribbons beside me.

My power quickly overwhelms his. I wrap him and Luther and press them tight against the stone wall. There's fear in their eyes.

I take a deep breath. We can't continue like this, fighting against each other. In Green we had to work together to take over the forest. In Yellow we had to trade to get nine grains. If only they could see…

An idea flashes like a lightbulb.

"Follow me," I say. "I want to show you something."

I don't give them a choice. I keep them bound by the wind and tell Hank to bring Emma. I lead the way back to the top of the Blue Tower, to the Sieve.

When Hank and Emma return, I tell everyone to link hands and watch with me. They should be able to see what I see, just as I did with Kiyo. The four of them crowd around the Sieve. I force myself to focus on my memory of the pit, of the bones, of the visions. Then I plunge my head into the water.

A rumble grows and approaches and takes form as a voice, grinding in my mind: *You cheated. You coward. You arrogant, angry, envious loser. You were worth less than the carbon molecules that made you. The world was a worse place after you. It ended before you died. It might have lasted a lot longer if you'd never existed.*

The voice goes on and on. It's my own voice, turned against me, accusing. The darkness ahead of me takes on contours, bending back. It sucks and pulls at me until bones are clattering under my feet. I start to see things. Countless unspeakable things—wonderful things that never were, and terrible things that *were*. It feels like forever. It might be half of forever, and there's no sign of any relenting.

Until something squeezes my hand.

It feels so weak that I hardly believe I felt it. But I squeeze back, and then the grip tightens, almost pulling at me. Then I remember: it's Emma. Still beside me at the Sieve, holding onto me as I gaze into this horrible darkness. She pulls me back and back. In the vision I scramble over bones and away from the voice and the infinite blackness.

When the bones stop clattering and the ground feels firm, it is still dark around me. I am underground, at the pit's edge. I try to remind myself that this is a vision, that I'm not really here. But it feels so real, so dark. I flee as fast as I can. I don't look back. I don't use powers. I just run.

Until I hear faint voices, people talking somewhere. I'm tempted to keep running, but something about the voices makes me pause. I move slowly, silently, toward the sound. I find myself on stairs, going down. A few scattered flecks glitter like gold on the rock walls beside me. The voices are still far away, but clearer. They come from a tunnel that extends away from the stairs. I stop just outside the tunnel's opening and still my pounding heart and listen.

"...marvelous, quite marvelous," a boy is saying, and I recognize his voice. Neville, the boy who descended from Emma, who was my opponent in the search for the coin.

"Yes, it solves everything," another voice says,

sounding more like a hiss than a tongue. "They allowed the Scouring to grow very dangerous."

"Oh, indeed," Neville says. "People get hurt out there, even killed! But isn't this…against the rules?"

The hissing voice laughs. "Whose rules? The Maker abandoned this place. The leaders were never strong enough to maintain order."

"A sad thing," Neville says.

"Most tragic. But they are the ones who allowed this danger. With all their talk of colors and Scouring, they turned this place into constant war! It will be much safer without colors. I alone can provide this safety."

"I suppose you're right. Safety first!"

"It is good that you have joined your king," the hissing voice says. "His enemies have fled. But they cannot resist me. None can. One of them listens even now. Come, I will introduce you."

Silence falls. I'm already backing away, my heart racing. Do they know about me? How? I turn to race up the stairs. I do not make it far. Something snags my ankle from behind. I fall hard onto the stairs and twist around.

An ink-black tentacle coils around my ankle. It pulls me down, bumping on one stair, then another. Nothing is beneath me but darkness. A black hole.

"The Sieve is mine!" the booming shout comes from the stairs above. A blue light appears, and a bearded figure rushes toward me. Abram.

He stands over me, protective. "Out!" he shouts. "Out!"

His staff lowers through the darkness and the glowing blue orb at its tip touches my forehead.

My head jerks out of the Sieve. I fall onto my back, gasping for breath. Familiar faces surround me. Emma, Hank, Luther, Tom, Sarai. They stare at me pale-faced, shocked.

Sarai puts her hand gently to my forehead. "You almost drowned."

"How?" I ask. "What happened?"

"I do not know. The Sieve has never held someone under like this. What did you see?"

"Terrible things. Wonderful things that never were, because of me. Then I felt Emma's hand. It pulled me out of the pit, away from the bones. But I was still down there, just outside the pit. It was not like a vision. It felt real. There was a hissing voice, talking with Neville. It said the Scouring was dangerous, that it would be safer without colors. It knew I was there. It attacked, but I think Abram saved me. When his staff touched me, I was back here."

"It must be the Colorless One." Sarai sounds afraid. "The darkness could have touched the Sieve. You must not look into it again. You understand?"

I glance around at the others. They are staring at me like I'm a ghost. "Just me? Why?"

"The Colorless One may know the threat you pose. He will use whatever he can against you—the powers of this place, the past, and certainly the pit. If you had drowned like this...well, I do not know where you would have woken up."

"What about Abram?" I ask. "Is he really down there?"

"He will hold back as much of the darkness as he can." Her thin hand clasps my shoulder. "We must do our part to fight back. Time to get some rest. Then warm soup. You will need to recover for the Scouring."

33

THE TWELVE OF us stand before the Scouring gate: Emma, Hank, Luther, Tom, Kiyo, and six others Sarai helped me choose. The Blue Tower's strongest. Everyone but Kiyo has three or four stripes on their sleeves. She is second class here, but she is a marked one who knows the Black Tower. I want her with me.

Sarai leans against the gate. "You remember my advice?"

"Do not go near the center," I say, reciting what she has told me. After she had thought more about what happened with the Sieve, she told me the Colorless One somehow poisoned what I saw, probably because of how I thought of the pit before dipping my head into the water. She told me the darkness spreads aggressively, that the Scouring would be a grave danger, but she agreed that I had to go anyway, if cautiously. We cannot just hide. We have to work for equilibrium, to fight Black, to heal Yellow.

"Stay united," Sarai says, pointing to the chalk tally on the wall beside her. "If you must fight, bring back a few from Black."

"We will try." I study the numbers again. They are closer than they have ever been to equilibrium:

Black 222

Red 144

Blue 141

Green 137

Yellow 76

"Have you still not heard from Yellow?" Emma asks Sarai.

"I have sent three pigeons," Sarai says. "None have returned."

Emma's brow wrinkles with concern. "Perhaps they did not reach him. My father should have found the offer appealing."

"They have always entertained our offers," Sarai says.

"But my father has changed," Emma says. "The Yellow Tower has changed."

"Many things have changed," Sarai replies somberly. "Abram has always opened the gate to the Scouring, and now he is gone. But we are here. You must take great caution."

"We will go straight to Yellow and propose the trade," I say.

"They must accept it," Emma adds.

"We shall see." Sarai steps to the side. "Stay close out there. Stay smart."

"Respect the mind," Hank mutters behind me.

I turn and spot his infectious grin. I smile as I look

around our group. Maybe the Scouring will be more dangerous. Maybe darkness grows and Abram is gone and pigeons are lost. But we are together. We wear the robes of Blue.

"Respect the mind!" I say.

The others join the chant as we march out into the Scouring. We move left along the wall, rushing to Yellow. The other colors are just emerging. They are not a threat, yet.

The team from Yellow stands in a defensive formation in front of their gate. Their golden armor gleams in the sunlight. They can heal. They can see along the light. And our powers can't touch them.

We quickly reach Yellow's guards. I bring our group to a stop ten feet away. "We propose a trade," I say.

Emma steps forward beside me. "We offer Cipher, Kiyo, and myself. Three marked ones."

An armored guard in the center of Yellow's formation lifts the visor of his helmet, revealing the striking blue eyes of the boy-king, William Chamberlain.

"Daughter," he says formally. "I will not trade with you."

"Come now, let us not be hasty." She sounds plaintive, patient. "You have not even heard the small thing we ask."

"I will not hear it. You are an exile." He lowers the visor and crosses his golden-plated arms.

Emma looks left and right along the row of Yellow's guards. "Will any of you listen?" she says. "We ask only for safe passage to a corner of Yellow's land, and for a plot to each of us. We will wear the collars. We will comply with Yellow's law."

Her words are met by unflinching golden helmets. Each guard has a hand resting on the hilt of a sword.

Emma turns to me with an expression of such fury that I've never seen in her. "He defies logic! He is twisted!" She glances back to her father, but he does not react. "Let's take him, all of them. Maybe Blue will do them some good."

"I would not try that," says the helmeted boy-king as he draws his sword.

But Emma has already taken my hand and begun to weave her power. I glance across the Scouring and confirm the other teams are nowhere near. I feed my power into Emma's, giving her control. It is magnificent, pulsing in radiant light, capable of almost anything, except touching anyone who wears the armor. Her next move is brilliant. She hurls the power over the Yellow team and toward Green. She grabs their whole group before they know what's hit them. She pulls them with the air and drops them, frantic and fighting, right on top of the Yellow guards.

A familiar voice speaks loudly behind me: "Give your father more respect."

Just as I spin around, the figures appear through a cloud of smoke. They wear black. They wield spears. And the one who spoke has granite eyes.

Baron. A cloaked figure suddenly takes shape beside him. It is Samantha. He made them invisible so they could sneak up on us. He still has his power from Green.

But so do I.

Just before Samantha's dark cloud of smoke reaches me, I focus on the past. I remember Susan supporting me. I remember my research, my team, and our breakthroughs in understanding the mind. And, gripping Emma's hand and linking with our whole Blue group, we go invisible. We back toward the wall and veer toward our tower.

"Hold them!" Baron shouts.

The boys from Black respond immediately. And so do Yellow's golden guards. They fight through Green and form into a line with Black, with spears and swords out to block us from getting past, to pen us against the wall. Being invisible won't help. They begin to close on us.

We might be able to break through them. We have to try. We—

The fireball explodes.

It hits with such force and heat that I'm knocked back into the wall and collapse. Everyone is on the ground. Smoke is everywhere. Screams ring out. People roll to put out flames. I watch in disbelief as a Yellow guard, protected in his armor, kneels to heal a boy from Black.

Another fireball hits, but it's smaller this time. Then another.

Rising on my elbows, I follow the trail of fire to an approaching group from Red. The girl at the front of them is stunning—not only because of her long auburn hair and sequined dress—but also because she's Helena. She's not in Green anymore. She reaches back and hurls another fireball at the chaotic mess of bodies.

I scramble to my feet and find Emma. I spot Hank running with Kiyo along the wall, making a break for Blue. Tom and Luther have summoned the wind, but smoke drops on them and shuts it off. Black's boys form into a phalanx between us. Their singed shields rise and block the next fireball that hits.

We won't get past them. We have to go around.

Emma squeezes my hand. "Come."

She has made us invisible again. We move together by feel, hands clenched, weaving through the battle around us. We pass silently within a few feet of Baron and Samantha, who have turned to face Helena and the team from Red. Smoke pours forward from Samantha. Fire blazes from Helena.

When the forces meet, Black prevails. The fire is doused.

"Attack!" Baron shouts, pointing at the team from Red.

Emma and I run as fast as we can from the fight. Smoke races around us, but it can't stop us. Green's power evades the other powers, just as Baron passed through my wind long ago in Green's forest. But even invisibility has limits. The wispy black smoke shifts around us like a river current around a boulder. Samantha might notice this. I glance back. She looks straight to where we are, though her eyes do not meet mine. She points as she says something to Baron, and they charge in our direction with two boys from Black at their side. The look on his face shows he does not see us, yet.

We won't be able to use our other powers. The black cloud of smoke surrounds us. It is hard to see through it, but I spot a gap ahead.

"There!" I whisper urgently to Emma.

We rush toward the opening together. If we can get free of the smoke, even for a moment, we could soar up into the sky and go straight to Blue. The sound of clanking metal draws closer behind us. We are almost to the gap when Emma jerks my arm.

"No!" she shouts. "The center!"

But it's too late. I look down just as my foot crosses the line from the grey stone of the Scouring to the circle in the center, except this time it is not milky white. It is completely black. Emma's grip keeps me from falling into the abyss, but the darkness engulfs me all the same.

Words enter my mind, sharp and sinister: *The fire has tried your work, and nothing survives.*

I'm in the same hospital, the same room, with five people. Susan, kneeling by the bed, crying, looking so tired in her wrinkled grey dress. Samantha in nurse's white, standing by the door. But this time, instead of Benjamin on the hospital bed, it's me. I have no hair. Tubes are in my arms.

Benjamin comes to my side. He leans close and whispers in my ear, "I tried to tell you. Why didn't you listen? Daddy, if only you had listened!"

Tears streak down his cheeks as he backs away from me. I reach out for him, but the tubes and the pain hold me fixed on the bed. He drifts out of the room like a spirit.

Samantha steps forward. She clutches a clipboard to her chest. "The prognosis is not good," she says. "You will not be able to save yourself."

"But I saved millions of lives!" Dr. Fitzroy tries to shout, to scream this at the world, but the words come out faint as a breath.

"Sorry, what was that?" Samantha asks.

"My research! I saved millions! The brain is the source of life. I found its secret. We can enhance it, make it more powerful, make it live forever!"

Samantha glances at her clipboard, then sets it down on the foot of my hospital bed. "I'm afraid that is not possible. You will not be able to save yourself."

She turns to leave.

"Wait!" I shout, but my voice is so weak. She does not hesitate or look back before striding out of the room.

I look to Susan. The always patient, always forgiving Susan. "Will you stay?" I ask.

She stands slowly, wipes at her eyes. "You're not the same, Paul."

"But I am. Please!"

"I'm sorry. There's nothing I can do."

"Why not?" The question is a desperate plea, like a final gasp from Dr. Fitzroy.

"What you have done to your mind, and to so many others, cannot be reversed. You are no longer what you were made to be. You tried to become the creator, but you only twisted creation. You could never defeat death. And in trying, you lost life."

"I'll change. Please, I can undo it. The nanoparticles can take away the circuitry. My brain can be normal again. It won't be connected to anything. It will be…mortal."

She leans over and kisses my forehead, then turns to leave.

"No, please, Susan. You can't go."

She doesn't turn back. As she goes, it feels like she takes my will to live with her. I look down at my frail body on the hospital bed, the tubes, the despair. I'm finished.

The fifth figure steps forward. It must be a man. He's tall. I can't see his face. It blurs in the light. He had stayed motionless and silent in the corner, watching Benjamin, Samantha, and Susan as they left. Now he puts his hand over mine. My eyes fixate on his hand and its warmth and its criss-cross scar.

"You are not finished," the man says. "Wake up."

34

THE CEILING ABOVE me is the familiar slate gray stone of the Blue Tower. The room is long and narrow, with short columns. Out of the corner of my eye I see a dozen small beds in a straight line beside mine, like a hospital.

This happened before, the first time I entered the Scouring. But then the circle in the center had been white, not black. The vision had been of Benjamin in the hospital, not me. I had wanted to see more then. Now I want to run away from everything I've just seen. I could have died forever in there. I know it in my bones.

But the man told me to wake up, and I did.

Who was he? I never saw his face, only the scar on his hand. I've seen versions of the same vision before, but never him, and with me on the deathbed. What did he mean that I'm not finished? Finished scouring, dying, what?

Whoever he was, whatever he meant, he cast me out of the nightmare, the hospital, the despair. I'm thankful for that.

I am back in Blue. I will not panic, even as I cannot move. One thing at a time. First my pinkie finger, then my hands and feet. Slowly I am able to rise up onto my elbows and breathe a sigh of relief as I see Emma beside me. She stares wide-eyed at the ceiling.

"You okay?" I ask.

"I have been better," she says, and it makes me smile.

The last time this happened, she woke up beside me with a collar around her neck. Now neither of us wears a collar. We bear only the scars. I glance at her hands, folded neatly on her stomach, and I gasp.

"You have another scar."

"I am not surprised," she says. "This was the worst memory yet. I saw how I died. But it won't help me escape. The White Tower is dark."

"I think I was on my deathbed, too. But my thoughts were worse than that. It felt like a trap."

"Yes, I know."

We lay in quiet as our bodies recover their movement. Sarai comes to us. I fear her disapproval, because we did precisely what she told us not to, but instead she says only that we did as well as we could.

"The Scouring is no longer safe for you," Sarai says. "I have another idea of how to get to Yellow. It is time for a Hunting of a different kind. But first you'll need to eat."

We make plans around a table in the underwater dining room. The squid soup has never tasted so good. I clasp the bowl between my hands, feeling its warmth, watching in wonder as a sea turtle drifts below us. The sea seems so peaceful beneath the surface. Lucky turtle.

With Sarai's guidance, we decide not to send a full team of twelve to Yellow. She cannot bear to send all of Blue's strongest away, especially with Abram still gone. We agree that it will be Emma and Kiyo and me. Hank and Tom and Luther and the others will stay. They will enter the Scouring, as they must, but they will not venture far from the gate. In the chaos of the last battle, they managed to drag out six. Three from Black, two from Green, and one from Red—all injured remnants of the vicious clashes. Now they only need to preserve Blue's numbers.

I tell Emma and Kiyo about the cave where Max had a boat hidden. The ladder may not be there, but we can find a way up. We could fly up the short distance, if needed. We agree it is our best chance of sneaking back to Yellow's land undetected.

We finish the meal together. I sleep in my quarters.

In the morning, I change back into Yellow's garb and go to the docks. A huge group awaits on the wooden planks, as if everyone from Blue is there. We say goodbyes. Hank embraces me so hard that I feel my back pop. It feels good.

Emma, Kiyo, and I board my little boat, like the one Emma and I first sailed together. The wind pulls the sails tight as we ride away from Blue.

My confidence rises on the boat. The sailing has not changed. I still have the wind to guide us, to propel us up and down the large waves. The sky remains a steady grey, without the ominous black of a storm. We sail briskly past the ragged cliffs that form the border between Blue and Yellow.

Kiyo and Emma talk quietly. Emma tells Kiyo about the Yellow Tower and what to expect. She says it was once a pleasant, safe place.

"I'm not worthy of a pleasant place," Kiyo says.

"Not true," Emma replies. "Did Black tell you that? I won't believe it. Everyone who has come to the Five Towers can be scoured and redeemed."

"Even your father?" I ask.

"Yes. I still do not understand why he worked with Black. It is wholly unlike my father. I am more sure than ever that he has been contaminated. He no longer cares about the Scouring. He lets the people in Yellow atrophy and turn soft. Ever since the leaders disappeared, my father has allowed this to worsen. Now the place is nearly stagnant. He must be wiped and start again."

Kiyo asks me to tell her more about Max. She remembers now, after having seen him in the Sieve, that he was known as Lord and she as Rice when they were in the Black Tower together. She remembers him as a quiet, unhappy leader. She knows of no reason why she or Max should be in Yellow.

"Max was not quiet in Red," I say. "But the unhappy part is right. Maybe seeing you will cheer him up."

I tell Kiyo about what Max told me, how he'd learned that Kiyo was his ancestor. Kiyo grows confused at this, because she lived in Japan, and he in China. I don't have answers to most of her questions.

The cliff turns sharply to the right ahead of us. It's the corner of Yellow's land, near where Max's hut should be. Mist still lays heavy overhead, but far beyond we can see the suns shining down on the coast. As we arc around the corner, I see the immense stone, many times the size of our boat, that hides the entrance to the cavern ahead. Waves crash against it with sprays of white foam rising twice as high as the mast.

"That's it," I say, pointing ahead.

"Are you sure about this?" Kiyo asks. Her dark eyes look alarmed, studying the waves.

"Yes," Emma says. "We cannot go further, to the wall, or my father will know we have come."

"What would he do?" Kiyo asks.

Emma gazes toward the shore in the distance, basked in sunlight, then up at the dense clouds above. "He can see through the light. He would collar us."

"But we have far more power together," I say. "They have only healing and sight."

"And armor," Emma replies. "But if we must attack directly, we will. I would rather find another way."

The roaring of waves silences us as we sail closer. I made it out, so I should be able to sail back in. The timing will have to be perfect, even with the wind under control.

I release the air, studying the rhythm. A wave crashes, then undertow sucks back and reveals jagged rocks under the frothy whiteness. But there's a path that shows no rocks, unless they are hidden just beneath the surface. We have to try it. Just as a wave crashes, the boat will need to carve into the undertow sucking back into the next wave.

"Ready?" I ask.

Emma and Kiyo say that they are, and I begin to weave. Emma's power surges through me, vibrant yellow with ribbons of red and green and blue. Kilo's power threads through hers, blue and black like a bruise. And I merge it all into mine: forging the air into an inky force that propels the boat forward even as it lifts it on the water. The bottom of the hull hardly touches the froth beneath us as we race ahead, skirting through the jagged rocks. But then the undertow pulls back, and behind us a wave looms like a hammer over an anvil.

"Stop it!" Kiyo shouts, and the power is yanked away from me. A cloud of smoke engulfs us. It dissipates a moment later, leaving everything still. The wave has settled. The water stretches like dark glass around us.

Emma and I stare at Kiyo in shock.

"What did you do?" I ask.

"I—I'm not sure. It's Black's power…combined with yours. I got scared. I had to do something."

The glassy water undulates, picking up the force of more distant waves rolling in toward us. She still has the smoke. She could shut me down.

"Can I have the power back?" I say, politely.

Kiyo nods, and I channel the force to propel the boat through the still, calm water past the giant boulder and into the cavern. We are inside only a few moments before the sound of waves returns outside, growing steadily louder until it makes the same violent drumbeat against the rocks.

We disembark into the shallow pool, cross over the sandy shore, and reach the cavern wall. The ladder that Max had pulled away is back in place, making this easier than I had hoped. We climb the ladder, then follow the narrow path up along the cavern wall. The roaring waves grow distant behind us. We breathe louder as we advance.

Faint voices come from above, from Max's hut.

"…no one else is going up, so why fight?"

It's hard to be sure, but the muffled voice sounds like Neville's. But why would he be with Max? He must know about the coin. I motion for Kiyo and Emma to stay quiet. We huddle close in the faint light. Only a few wooden boards separate us from the hut and the conversation above.

"I'm done fighting," Max says.

"Exactly, there's no point to it," Neville says. "I've seen the Scouring. The White Tower is gone. There's a hole in the ground now. It just looks black down there. It's time to bring an end to the Scouring."

"How can we do that?"

"Who's to make us fight?" Neville says. "Yellow's leaders are gone, and the king would prefer to keep things as they are. He sends his guards only for defense. If you give me the coin, I will become a guard. I will convince the king to stop sending guards at all. If Yellow sends no one to the Scouring, the others will stop. There can be peace here. True peace."

"I'm still not sure."

"What is your concern?" Neville says.

"If there's no Scouring, how would I find others I knew before, on Earth? My daughter is here. How could I have learned that, and all she showed me, if not for the Scouring?"

"Ah, yes, a very wise concern. But trust me, the peace that we will bring will allow you to find anyone. Why even keep the walls between the towers? Why keep playing this useless, violent game? The leaders are gone. We may do as we see fit. And my group knows how to do it. We remove the troublemakers—all who refuse—and those who will abide in peace may come and go as they wish. So, the coin?"

"You still haven't told me how you learned I have it."

"Why, have you not considered that the king *wanted* me to get it? He let my hand be restored, after all. He of course prefers me to that other boy." Disdain drips from Neville's voice at the mention of me, the *other boy*.

"I've considered that," Max says.

"Have you seen him, by the way?"

"No." Max pauses. "Okay, I saw him once, but that was many days ago. Are you telling me the king told you about the coin?"

"His adviser did."

"Who's that?"

"He's the leader of our group."

"What's his name?"

"Why do you bother me with these questions? His name is irrelevant. What matters is that he is powerful. He gave me my hand back."

"I learned long ago never to trust those with power."

"Oh, but this is different! It's not power like that other boy's or the other marked ones. He only shows us how to bring peace here—like stopping the Scouring. He does not act with force. He would not do that."

"Why not?"

Neville does not answer at first. A chair slides across the floor, then another. The wood creaks at a footstep.

"Your questions are easier to answer by simply showing you," Neville says. "Come, give me the coin, and I will introduce you to our leader."

"But I can't leave this plot of land."

"Once you give me the coin, I will make sure that you can. The king does not trust many of his guards. He will allow me to be your master. I will set you free, and take you to meet the leader."

"You sound like Cipher…full of empty promises."

"No, I swear I will do as I say. Haven't I delivered your daughter as a neighbor?"

"The king assigns the plots."

"And he listens to me. I have done my part once, and I will do so again. Now it is your turn to live up to the bargain. Your daughter for the coin."

A moment of silence. "Fine," Max says. "Follow me."

Footsteps move out of the room. The door creaks open, then closed. There's a rustle of motion, then neighing and hoofbeats going away.

I listen carefully, count to twenty to make sure the way is clear, then lift the boards overhead and climb up into the hut. It looks different. Max has done some work. There are two types of grains, even a half-eaten loaf of bread that he must have baked.

"This is as bad as Black," Kiyo whispers. "So dirty, meager."

"Quick, look." Emma stands by the window, peeking out.

Across the field, Neville and Max are walking away from the hut. Neville leads his horse by the reins, with the hand that was once severed. They stop near the edge of the field, before a lush row of tall golden grains.

Max yells out something but it is too far to make out the words. Eventually the grains part and a girl appears, Li Min. They speak briefly and she leaves. Her dark hair looks like a raven flying just above the grains. When she returns, a tiny object glimmers in her hand.

The coin, I realize. *Max hid it with his daughter.*

In a flash Neville moves to her, seizes the coin, and raises his arms triumphantly. The sunlight glints off the gold. Neville turns on Li Min again. She says something as she steps back, and he responds with a punch to her stomach. Max lunges at them but slams helplessly into the invisible wall between the fields. Neville hoists Li Min's motionless body onto the back of his horse, then mounts and begins to ride away.

I rush toward the door, but a hand stops me.

"Let him go," Emma whispers.

"But he has the coin! And Li Min!"

"It is too late," Emma says. "You heard what Neville

said to Max. He even got his hand back. This force he spoke of, I believe it could only be the Colorless One. My father has been so twisted. There's no use joining his guards. We have to do this another way."

"What's that?"

"I didn't want it to come to this." She shakes her head, golden hair swaying. "We have to use force. It's time to attack."

35

WE DO NOT charge out after Neville. He no doubt rides with Li Min and the golden coin to the king, to kneel and be knighted. He will have armor and sight through the sunlight, which could have been mine. But we will take it another way.

When Max comes back, he stares at the three of us in shock, standing inside his hut. I expect anything from him—to fight, to run—but not the look of defeat in his eyes. His gaze settles on Kiyo beside me.

"This is Kiyo," I say. "You remember her?"

He blinks as if seeing a ghost. "It's been so long," he mutters. "I'm sorry, I gave away the coin. To Neville. He…took my daughter."

"We will get her back," Emma says. "Would you like to be free?"

Max says he would, and Emma tells him that he should summon his master, Joan.

"How?" he asks.

"She knows your feelings," Emma replies. "If there is enough change from recent days—surprise, maybe even shock—she will come."

"Then she will come." He sits at the small table and motions for Kiyo to take the seat across from him. She does, and Emma and I stand to the side, watching as they talk.

"Shall I call you Lord or Max?" Kiyo asks.

"Max, please. Should I call you ancestor?"

Emma and I listen as the two of them talk. The conversation moves forward in fits and starts, like a sputtering car. Max asks about Kiyo's children and grandchildren. She tells him part of the story she told me long ago, in the Blue Tower, about fleeing with her children through the wintry mountains of Japan. She lost her oldest son, but the others survived. They became like her royal guard. She became a rebel leader, a ronin. By the time of her death, Kiyo had killed a shogun, taken command of his castle, and bounced four grandchildren on her knee.

"What were their names?" Max asks.

Kiyo leans back, hands folded neatly on the table. "I hear you lived in China. So first tell me about your parents and grandparents and how they could possibly lead to me, in Japan."

So it goes, back and forth, like duelists circling each other, until the full story of Max and Kiyo comes out. Max had a grandmother who lived in Nanjing, China, at the time of a Japanese invasion. The Japanese soldiers devastated the city, killing thousands and committing countless acts of horror. Even Max—who had thrived in the violent passions of the Red Tower—winces as he speaks of it. He tells Kiyo that his grandmother had an illegitimate child whose father was a Japanese soldier. He claimed to be the descendent of a samurai. The soldier was more honorable than most, protecting Max's grandmother and promising to return and marry her. But his duties took him away from Nanjing, and the war took him away from earth.

"This boy, once my grandfather, is now in Black," Max tells Kiyo. "I met him after you left. He says he descended from a famous samurai named Musashi. It is a name you once said to me."

Kiyo bows her head. Silence makes the hut feel smaller. Max keeps his eyes fixed on Kiyo, waiting. She eventually meets his gaze. "Musashi was my grandson. I taught him a Way."

"I have heard of this Way." Max sounds genuinely excited. "Musashi wrote a book. It became very famous, the Book of Five Rings."

Kiyo smiles. "Ground, Water, Fire, Wind, and Void."

"So it's true," Max says. "I come from you."

"It is possible, I must admit," Kiyo says. "The first principle of the Way is: Do not think dishonestly."

Max rises and faces me with such energy that I expect him to attack, but instead he hugs me and thanks me for bringing his ancestor to him. He tells Emma and me that we will be his guests, that he will prepare a meal. He only wishes he could bring his daughter Li Min, but he will tell her all about it. As he rushes to the hearth and mixes grain in his pan to cook, there is a soft clank of metal outside.

Then a knock on the door.

We freeze, breathless. Emma and I ready our powers, though we'll need more than that if the boy-king has sent his armored guards. Emma eyes each of us, confirming we're ready to fight, then moves slowly to open the door.

Joan strides in wearing golden armor and cradling a golden helm in her arm. "A welcome sight!" she says.

I would still be wary if not for the smile across her face. "Why are you wearing the armor again?"

"Desperate times," she says. "I have always done what I must to topple a tyrant."

"Is everything ready?" Emma asks her.

Joan nods. "I brought three guards loyal to you. They'll keep watch outside." She turns to Max with a faint grin. "I felt some interesting emotions from you."

Max's cheeks flush. "This is Kiyo," he says, looking to her. "We were connected on Earth. We have had much to discuss."

"Mending the tapestry," Joan says. "It is the Healer's way."

The five of us settle into the hut. Max serves bread. I sit by the hearth and eat and listen. Max and Kiyo sit at the table talking of the past, of the long family line that connects them. Joan and Emma sit on the pallet of straw, talking of the tower and the king. Joan says that the king may be on alert after seeing her leaving the tower in armor. He will know where she is, but he has no reason to suspect Emma's return. Joan thinks he has likely been distracted by Neville's return. He may have even knighted Neville already.

By the time it has grown dark outside, we have agreed that we will attack the tower. We know the danger. The king's guards are strong in their armor. And if they win, we will be wiped and none of us will remember what has happened here.

Kiyo stays mostly quiet as we talk, but as we discuss our plan to focus the attack on the king, she tells us that her grandson, Musashi, was a master of strategy. "In all skills and abilities there is timing."

"What do you mean?" I ask.

"All is timing," Kiyo says. "Timing can be cunning. You win battles by knowing the enemies' timing, and thus using a timing which the enemy does not expect."

"The king's timing is in the future," Joan says. "This is what he fears, where his mind dwells."

"Then we should strike before dawn," I say.

36

WE LEAVE TOGETHER under the cover of night. The three armored guards flank us. Joan releases Max from his collar, allowing him to pass through the invisible wall around his plot. He moves with a bounce in his step, no doubt enjoying the taste of freedom.

As we cross other fields, Joan releases everyone we meet. We go to the huts like burglars, and each time Joan emerges with a serf—uncollared and wide-eyed. Like this we gather Sally, Simon, Drew, and many others.

It is good to see their familiar faces. They look as if they are still dreaming, unable to believe that we are walking away from the plots where they have toiled and slept for countless days, and toward the Yellow Tower that has forever loomed in the distance, out of their reach.

But our growing numbers start to worry me. I come to Emma's side. "You sure they'll all be on our side?" I ask.

Emma nods. "We set them free."

"Okay, but what if a few resist us? Minds are complicated. They might doubt. Even if some in our group have little power, each one adds to the complexity. You really think we can weave all this together and control it?"

"We did in Green," she says.

"But only after we had removed our rivals. This time we'll meet resistance."

"I am prepared for that. The palace may look delicate, but it is defended well. We have the advantage of surprise. We must strike hard and fast. And if my control over the power slips, you will be there."

Her confidence steadies me, slightly, as we advance the rest of the way across the fields. We reach the cottage of the stableboy just outside the Yellow Tower.

He welcomes all of us and invites us inside, with a look of wonder at the group crowded into the quaint room.

"So the time has come," he says, looking to Joan.

"We fight to change the Yellow Tower back to what it was meant to be," she says. "The king is not who he once was. All of us need to be wiped clean from time to time. Now is the time for him."

"Will you rule?" the boy asks.

Joan shakes her head and looks to Emma. "That responsibility belongs to her."

"The king's daughter? But that's just monarchy!" the boy says. "Why not let the natural leader lead?"

"I am," Joan says. "Emma has been behind this plot all along. She plans to rescue the leaders, Elijah and the Widow."

Emma puts her hand on Joan's shoulder. "We will find them. We must. I will not become like my father."

"That's what they all say," the boy mutters.

"My father has changed," Emma says. "He once ruled with an open hand. He has spiraled down and down in his pits of fear and worry for his future. Now he lives in terror. His fist has clenched."

The boy eyes her skeptically. "And who's to say you won't change like he did?"

I step forward. "Me. Emma won't change."

"I remember you," he says, his tone softening. "You rode Serenity. She liked you. Okay, assuming you're right, what makes you think you can find the missing leaders?"

Emma holds up her hands, baring her scars in the firelight. "These marks say."

The boy stares in silence at her hands, then looks to me. "He's got them, too. What do they mean?"

"We're the marked ones," I say. "The leaders of the Green and Blue Towers told us that there are five like us, and that we will bring an end to the Five Towers."

"How?" the boy asks.

"Lend us your support and you will see," Emma says.

The boy shakes his head, as if still in doubt, but he says, "Fine, worth a try."

We go around the room, one by one, until each person pledges support. Most are more eager than the stableboy. Their fear seems to have fallen away with their collars.

Emma and I explain our plan to weave the group's powers together. The others look at us with a measure of awe, and they agree to let us draw as much power as we can. Joan and the three guards will defend us from the guards loyal to the king.

When we leave the cottage, the full and clear moon has fallen closer to the horizon and the morning's first light touches the sky. We march forward with Emma in the lead. A cloud of dust spits up behind us, motes looking like stardust in the silvery light.

I summon just enough wind to hold the dust down, to hide our approach. Again I wonder where this place is—a distant planet, a parallel universe? If the world has ended, does the universe still exist as I knew it?

Emma stops within a stone's throw of the Yellow Tower. Her hand tightens around mine.

She whispers, "He knows."

Figures emerge ahead of us. They move stealthily among the tower's turrets, approaching like shadows. The light is still too dim to see the gold, but the shape of the golden-plated armor is unmistakable. The king's guards are coming, fast.

"Hold the line!" Joan shouts.

She rushes forward with her guards. They form a defensive stance in front of us.

Emma begins to weave. She draws the threads out of our group, lacing each person's power into a brilliant cord. Every color is there—yellow pulses the strongest, then blue and green and red and black. The black strands give the weave the same inky hue as when Kiyo stilled the ocean as we sailed into Max's cavern, like oil on water.

The first battle cries ring out. Swords clash nearby.

My attention stays fixed on Emma and the power, tense and ready. Everything I have is funneled into it. I've never witnessed such force.

Emma coils the concentrated power tighter and tighter, then swings it like a wrecking ball at the tallest tower—the one where her father should be.

Stones explode from the wall.

The tower leans, then starts to crumble.

Weaving with the speed of light, Emma disassembles the collapsing structure, grabbing shattered stones and dragging them out as the turret caves in. The hewn stones whip like leaves through the air.

Only seconds have passed. The tower is down. Dust and debris billow out like a sandstorm.

"It's empty," Emma mutters, but she doesn't stop. She pulls back the power and flings it again like a wrecking ball.

Ahead there's a golden flash. Guards fight amidst the dust. Two of them break free and race toward Emma and me, their armor reflecting the first light of the suns.

Joan chases after them, shouting, "Courage! Do not fall back!"

Emma ignores all this.

She pummels the tower with quick, striking blows. More spires fall, crumbling and collapsing and adding to the enormous cloud of dust that mushrooms out and over us, blocking my vision.

But I can still follow Emma's power. Feeling her iron grip on my hand, I trace the vibrant flow through us. Racing along the yellow weaves I see her searching and prodding through the wreckage, in all the places where her father should be.

She shakes her head, talking as if to herself: "He is not there. No one is inside. Where is everyone…and *what is that?*"

In the center, where the first tower fell, there's darkness. I can't see it with my eyes. I only sense it, growing and pulling. The dark force unravels tendrils of Emma's woven power, sucking the strands in like hairs pulled into a vacuum.

Exhaustion washes over Emma like a tsunami, hitting all at once and suffocating her weaves.

She falls to her knees on the dirt and gasps, "Take it."

I seize the power.

I stagger at the force of it—channeling the intense memories and emotions of everyone in our group—but also this new force, this darkness. I can barely see anything through the dust. So I do what I know best: blow the wind as hard as I can. It rushes past, making our clothes whip and snap, until the debris and dust clears.

Sunlight blazes over the devastation and chaos. Dozens are fighting around us. The king's collared servants against the rebels.

I glimpse Seymour, collar around his neck, wrestling against Drew. Closer to me, guards in golden armor lay still on the ground. Max's body is motionless among them. Only three guards remain standing, locked in a fight a few paces away. Two wear helmets. The other has jet black hair and a silver crown.

Joan. Blood on her cheek. Golden armor gleaming.

"There she is!" It's Neville's frantic voice. A golden

gauntlet points past Joan to Emma. "Kill her! And him!"

The two helmeted guards leap past Joan. I channel the air but it blasts harmlessly around the guards in their armor.

They close the distance in seconds.

I spin to lift Emma away. But she doesn't move far.

A guard barrels into me. The armor smashes my small frame like a sledgehammer. The power vanishes.

The guard pins me down, weighing a ton. The pain is everywhere, excruciating.

A sword rises over me, ready to plunge down.

Another golden blur suddenly knocks the guard off, sending a helmet flying. The two armored figures wrestle for control on the ground.

I try to rise, but there's only pain. My head spins. My shoulder is out of socket. My leg feels shattered. I gulp for air, desperately trying to stay conscious.

Joan gets the upper edge and raises her gauntleted fist. The other guard's helmet is off. It's Li Min, twisting in rage, trying to break free. Joan brings her fist down but does not strike Li Min's face. Instead she reaches to Li Min's neck.

A collar falls off. Li Min goes white with shock.

"So sorry, the king used me..." Li Min presses her hands against her eyes. "I was captured and...the guards..." She glares down at the silver collar on the ground. "I couldn't stop..."

"Not your fault," Joan grunts, as she surges up and dashes toward another armored guard.

The guard looms over Emma. She kneels with her

hands out, pleading. Her arm is bloodied. Her blue eyes are desperate and tearful.

Focus, Cipher. But the pain overwhelms me.

The guard above Emma pulls his visor back. It's Neville, her own heir, smiling wildly with his blood-soaked sword raised high.

Focus.

It's only a gust, but it's enough. I knock Emma over, flat on the ground. The sword swings and misses high.

Then Joan is there. Her sword clashes against Neville's, ringing out loudly. The two of them stab and parry, fighting desperately. Their armor deflects blows. Their faces are covered in sweat. It looks like an even match.

I glance to Emma, who is motionless. Between us lies a golden helmet. I use the wind to pick it up. I hold it ready, dizzy and clinging to the power, waiting for the right moment to fling it at Neville, to help Joan.

The moment never comes.

Joan moves to swing high, but at the last instant she strikes low, knocking Neville off his feet. She kicks his sword away and looms over him.

He rises slowly to his knees, arms raised in surrender, panting. "I only want peace."

"Sometimes you must die for peace," she says.

"No, please," Neville whimpers. "We must put life above all."

"That is a lie." Joan shakes her head. "To sacrifice what you are and to live without belief, that is a fate more terrible than dying."

Neville cowers back. "Nothing is more terrible than death!"

"You will thank me for this." Joan swings her blade in a brilliant, violent arc, and Neville falls. Her shoulders sag as she wipes her blade clean and sheathes it. She hurries to Emma, kneeling over her and pressing her hands down.

Emma surges to her feet. Joan points to me on the ground, and she and Emma approach. Emma's slender hands go delicately to my temples.

Coldness pours over me like an avalanche.

I blink and sit up, shivering, but feeling no pain. She healed me. The fighting has stopped around us.

"Thank you," Emma says to me, and to Joan. "We have won, but my father escaped."

"Where?" Joan asks.

"There," Li Min says, approaching us and pointing toward the Yellow Tower. "He was there."

My breath freezes at what I see. Where there once stood a glorious palace, there is only a mound of wreckage and a single, slender, black shard rising in the middle of the devastation.

The shard is like nothing I've ever seen. A spotlight, but inverted—darkness instead of light, sucking in the colors around it, hazy as a mirage amidst the fallen tower. It is the darkness that unraveled Emma's power. It is the only thing that withstood her.

Emma squeezes my hand, and I look to her. She gazes at the shard with intensity in her eyes.

"Take me to it," she says. "Quickly."

37

EMMA AND I soar like missiles toward the black shard, propelled by the immense power. We fly over the debris of the destroyed Yellow Tower, with the sun and wind at our backs. We land at the edge of the blackness.

The shard is only a few feet wide, rising like a lifeless tube to grey clouds overhead. At the base there's a round, black hole in the debris. The broken stones and glass that made up the palace are stacked high around the hole. It sucks in every color around it. I feel it pulling at me. It is unnatural, horrible.

"I don't like this," I say.

"We must go inside." Emma kneels beside me, close to the shard, eyeing a fragment of yellow stained glass in her hand. "My father is here."

"What? How is that possible?"

"He was not in the tower when it fell," she says. "He must be hiding. I think this is where he went before, when the tower stood and he went underground. I followed him." She motions to the debris around us. "This stained glass was in the room above the hidden stairs he used.

Maybe, before, the tower blocked this. Now it is exposed and projecting this—this darkness. He must be in here."

"But—"

"I'm going now. Will you help?"

The black hole reveals nothing, no clue, no hope. But I know Emma. She will go no matter what I do, and she needs my help.

I nod. "Lead on."

She reaches her hand forward, just as we reached into the White Tower's light so long ago. When her fingers enter the black shard, they disappear. She doesn't slow down. She reaches all the way inside.

"No barrier, and no pain," she says. "It only feels like air." She steps a foot inside. "Stairs, just like I remember. Come on."

She enters the blackness and pulls at my hand.

I follow, hesitantly, and find myself moving down a spiral staircase. I can't see anything. She's right. It feels like empty air, with no color inside. I use my power to prod into the blackness. I feel a smooth wall around us.

Emma moves steadily but quickly, keeping a hand on the wall and feeling no change or variation. It feels like we descend a hundred feet or more before we reach the ground. It's still pitch-black dark. There's solid stone beneath our feet, and a familiar musty smell carried on a gentle current of air.

"Are we in the tunnels?" I whisper.

"Yes." A flame springs to life, flickering above Emma's hand. She looks determined as she gazes up. A pipe-like cylinder of black runs along the dark stone overhead and turns up into the staircase we descended.

"Let's follow this pipe, whatever it is," Emma says. "Either my father ran away, or someone brought him this way."

She walks forward, following the black pipe along the ceiling, head swiveling alertly. Her candle-sized flame does not reveal the end of the tunnel.

After a few hundred feet, the pipe meets a wall of darkness. It swallows the light of Emma's flame.

Emma stops. "The pit," she says. "No more power."

"Let's get back," I say quietly.

"No." Emma sits cross-legged on the floor and presses at her temples. "I need to think."

Her fatigue carries through the link. As much as I want to get away from this place, I can't leave her. I sit and reach into a pocket and produce a few thin wafers of bread.

"Here, eat this." I smile, trying to beat back the fear. "Nine grains."

We eat in silence, thinking. My thoughts run in too many directions to follow. There are glimpses of my past, of golden nanoparticles circulating through the body to attack cancers. I feel like that now. Emma is gold, and this darkness—in the pipe above and in the pit ahead of us— seems like a cancer. It's not like anything else in the Five Towers. It has no color, no life to it. *The Colorless One,* Abram warned me, *focuses his attention here.*

A faint clatter makes me surge to my feet.

I hear movement, and then a voice, coming from the

blackness and straight toward us.

Emma joins my side. Our backs are against the wall. She places a finger over her lips for quiet. Her face glows in the light of her tiny flame.

"…will trap you," a voice says.

"No, no, I was protecting my tower." It's Emma's father, the king of the Yellow Tower. He sounds defensive.

"You're not listening," says the other, a deep, strong voice, closer than before. "Are you entirely infected?"

"Elijah was gone," the king says. "The Widow was gone. There was no one else to keep Yellow's land safe. There were so many things to fear. *Your* tower above all!"

"If only you had fought, you could have won."

"Fight! But why? To suffer, to hurt?" The king now sounds only a few feet away. "We should work for peace!"

"This place was not made for peace. It was made for scouring. That is the only way to reach paradise for those who come here."

"You speak of *paradise*. Bah, I say it's a lie!"

"So be it."

There's a loud grunt and a quick shuffle of movement. I summon my power, ready for anything.

An instant later a tall man emerges from the darkness before us, as if materializing out of nothing. A motionless body lays over his shoulder, with golden hair hanging down toward the floor.

"Father!" Emma cries.

38

"WHAT ARE *YOU* doing here?"

The moment the man speaks, I blast air at him. It's enough force to bend an oak, but the man doesn't budge. The wind blows harmlessly around him. Not even Emma's flame, the only source of light, wavers above us.

A smirk touches the man's hard eyes. "That's enough."

He sounds like a general, like a man to be obeyed. He looks like one, too, with short-cropped brown hair and a square jaw. He came out of the blackness at the end of the tunnel. He came out of the pit.

Emma rushes to the limp body of her father, draped over the man's shoulder. She takes her father's head gently between her hands.

"No, Father!" she says. "What have you done?"

The man stares intensely at Emma, as if deciding what to do. He can't be the Colorless One. He's a man, not a nameless, dark force. But he's clearly not just another boy from a tower. Maybe he is a leader, maybe from Black?

"Who are you?" I ask, releasing my power.

The man turns and looks me up and down. "Thought

you'd be bigger," he grunts. "Both of you, come."

He strides off down the tunnel, away from the blackness of the pit. He doesn't look back.

Emma and I exchange a glance.

"Black's leader?" I whisper.

"I hope so," she says. "Remember, before they came out of the pit, he asked my father if he was infected."

"And your father said he feared the man's tower."

"He must be a leader," Emma says. "Let's follow him."

I agree, still confused, but relieved for any reason to get away from the pit.

We run to catch up. The man moves quickly through the dark tunnel, with the force and discipline of a soldier. A sword hangs at his side, on the opposite side of Emma's father. He turns down another passage without hesitation, then another. Trying to keep up leaves me breathless, but something about the man's firm confidence gives me a flicker of hope.

After several more turns, the man pauses and faces the tunnel wall. It's cold, gray stone, identical to the wall stretching as far as we can see into the distance.

The man presses his hand against it, and part of the wall swings back. The hidden door leads to a stairway going down. It looks just like the stairway I saw in the Sieve, leading to the mine.

In the vision, the Colorless One was down here.

Emma begins to follow the man down, but I grab her arm. "Wait," I say. "Are you sure about this?"

The man turns back to us. He is several steps below,

making his eyes level with ours. He leans with one arm against the wall. The muscles of his forearm look like they could snap me in half.

"Who *are* you?" Emma asks.

"My name is Joshua. From the Black Tower."

I remember the name. Long ago Rahab told me that her friend, Joshua, led the Black Tower.

"Why are you here?" I ask.

"It's my duty," he says.

I look past him down the stairs. "Will this take us to the mine?"

He nods. "If you want your father healed, and if you ever want to leave these towers, this is the way. But if you'd rather flee back to Yellow with your tail between your legs, I won't stop you."

My throat is tight. This is not how the other leaders speak. I look to Emma. Her face is pale. Her blue eyes shift to Joshua, then to the body still hanging limp over his shoulder.

"So you can help him?" she asks.

"I'm taking him to someone who can."

I want to believe him, but this could be a trap. The Colorless One could be using him, just as the king was used. The Black Tower has long been dark, and Joshua came out of the pit.

"Is the Colorless One down here?" I ask. "How do we know you're not doing what he wants?"

"Bah." The man's face twists in anger. "If I didn't know about you Cipher, I'd wipe you right now for such blasphemy. I've been fighting the enemy long before you showed up in Blue." He shakes his head, then speaks more softly. "Abram said you were a curious boy, number 720, a marked one, and all that. So I'll tell you this. I have not been able to enter the Black Tower for a very long time because the Colorless One infected it, just as he infected Emma's father. Now, if you want to stop this darkness from spreading, and if you want him healed, come."

He turns without another word and moves down the stairs. Emma starts to follow, then looks to me.

Joshua's words tumble through my mind. It's worse than I thought in the Black Tower. Not even the leader can enter it? How are we supposed to fight it? We have to trust someone. I don't like it, but I won't let fear hold me back.

I join Emma as we hurry after him. We descend and descend, until I feel like we are deeper underground than the towers rise above ground. Eventually the stairs end at a flat platform.

Joshua turns to Emma. "More light."

Emma hesitates, but then does as he says. Her flame grows and the darkness retreats, like a curtain opening around us.

We stand on a ledge in a cavern unlike anything I've ever seen. The walls glitter with bright veins of gold. It must be the mine—the source of the armor, the coin, the corruption. Above and below there is only blackness. No bottom, no top in sight.

"So this is it…" Joshua says, gazing around. "Idol of idols. Come, we must move fast. They should be close."

Who? Why? I want to ask, but he's already moving.

He strides along the ledge, still holding the king's body over his shoulder as if it weighs nothing.

Emma and I rush after him, going up along the wall. When we reach the opposite side of the cavern from where we entered, there's an opening in the wall blocked by tall golden bars. It's too dark to see anything inside.

"Elijah! Widow!" Joshua calls out. "It's time."

A faint clanking of metal draws closer. Then two figures appear from the depths. A man and a woman.

"It *is* you! Really you!" Emma covers her mouth in surprise.

I have never seen them before, but as they come into the light of Emma's flame, I know who they are. Yellow's missing leaders.

Elijah has a beard as long as Abram's, but it's dark brown with peppered spots of grey. The Widow looks about the same age as Elijah, with almond eyes and strands of grey in her long, dark hair. They look similar, crouched over, tired and pale. Their robes are dirty, but yellow. Golden shackles bind their wrists and ankles.

"Bring him closer," Elijah says.

Joshua steps forward, so that the king's body presses against the golden bars.

Elijah and the Widow both reach out. Their shackles ping against the prison bars as their hands squeeze through and touch the king. Their eyes close, concentrating.

Emma places her hand on her father at the same time.

She suddenly gasps and coils back.

Her father's head lifts.

Joshua sets him down. "Undo the chains," he demands.

The boy who was the king, William, blinks innocently, then nods as if in a dream. He wavers on his feet and grabs hold of the golden bars for support. He meets Elijah's eyes.

Elijah smiles gently and nods. "Go on."

The boy's mouth opens, closes, and opens again. Sounds begin to come out of his lips—guttural, terrible sounds. They sound more like growls than words. The walls begin to tremble. Wind gusts through the cavern. Stones shake loose.

Then, all at once, the chains and the prison bars crumble to dust. With a great exhale, the boy collapses.

Joshua catches him. He hoists the boy's body over his shoulder again.

For a moment, the cavern falls completely silent.

"The others," the Widow whispers, stepping out of the prison, rubbing at her chafed wrists, and looking up along the ledge. "We must take all of them."

As she speaks, a group emerges from another opening in the cavern wall. Boys. Girls. Faces blank. Dozens of them. They step over piles of golden dust where moments before there were prison bars.

"Come, come," the Widow says to them.

They approach cautiously. I recognize one of the girls. She's Anna, the guard who removed my collar in Yellow's courtyard. She helped Emma, then she disappeared. She looked so powerful in her golden armor. Now she looks like a shadow.

A deep groan courses through the cavern. The walls tremor again, harder.

"He knows we're here," Joshua says. "Come, after me!"

His command has a force of its own, demanding obedience. We run in Joshua's wake as he charges back down the path along the wall. I glance back and see Elijah and the Widow waiting for the last of the other boys and girls to pass. Then they race behind us like their lives depend on it.

We reach the bottom of the path and gather around Joshua on the broad platform. He stares into the cavern like a captain staring down a storm, then turns to Elijah. "You'll take the wiped ones to Yellow?"

Elijah nods. "It must be me. Do what must be done."

"We will," Joshua says. "It should buy you some time."

"Follow me!" Elijah shouts to the group. He turns to go, but the Widow stops him with a gentle touch on his arm.

"Be careful," she says. "This is not Mount Horeb."

Elijah's bearded lips turn up in a grin. "Yes, this time we are below ground." He spins with a flurry and charges up the stairs. The other boys and girls run after him.

I take a step to follow, but the ground shakes violently beneath my feet, stopping me.

"You two," Joshua says, looking from me to Emma. "Destroy it." He motions into the cavern.

"What—the whole place?" I ask.

"It will collapse on us," Emma adds.

"Perhaps," the Widow says. "But we must stop this

evil."

"Yes. Now." Joshua points to the far wall. "Start there, blast it with everything you have. Then we run."

I gaze into the bottomless cave, with golden flecks sparkling in the firelight. It's dazzling but sickening at the same time. This is the source of the golden armor that blocked our powers, that led the Yellow Tower into atrophy and decay. The leaders are right.

"Okay," I say, summoning the wind.

Emma takes my hand, and I fuse our power together. We have every color but Black, and we slam it into the far wall of gold. Then we slam harder.

Wind whips around us, dousing the flame—our only light. The whole cavern groans. I hear stones knock loose. They fall soundlessly into the darkness.

"Again!" Joshua says over the groaning.

A light appears beside us. It's from the Widow's face, glowing. "We must go," she whispers.

"Once more," Joshua demands.

I slam the power as hard as I can into the wall. The stone platform begins to crumble under our feet.

"Now!" Joshua yells. "Run!"

He takes off up the stairs, bounding two at a time as if Emma's father weighs nothing on his shoulder. We race after him, with the Widow at our side.

The sound of the collapsing mine explodes behind us. Dust billows up the stairway, clouding everything. We don't look back. We run faster.

When we reach the top and dash into the tunnel,

Joshua slams the hidden door shut.

"It should be enough," he says.

"For now," the Widow sighs. "Let's find the others."

Joshua spins and hurries along the same tunnel as before. We take several turns and pass through another hidden door. I lose track of direction. I couldn't find my way back alone. Emma and I stay close to the leaders.

As we stride down another hallway, another figure appears and quickly approaches us. He's bent over, leaning on a gnarled staff.

"Joshua, Widow," the old man says, "and you brought friends." He stops and studies us with familiar eyes.

"Daniel!" Emma says, rushing to him. "You have to help my father! This man, Joshua, he brought him out of the pit."

"I suspect you saved him," Daniel says calmly.

"Yes," Joshua replies. "With Elijah and the Widow's help. And Cipher and Emma destroyed the mine."

The ground rumbles as if in response.

"A temporary victory, eh?" Daniel motions for us to follow. "We will speak more where it is safer. The others will want to hear of this."

He turns, heavy green robe spinning around him, and hurries down the tunnel with his staff. Joshua strides beside him with the body still on his shoulder. The Widow walks quickly by Daniel's other side.

Emma and I rush to keep up.

39

DANIEL LEADS THROUGH the tunnels, taking turn after turn after turn. He finally stops at a plain stretch of wall and looks to Joshua. "You ready?"

The tall man hoists Emma's father off his shoulder and holds the still body in his arms. "Can I put this burden down?"

"A heavier one's coming." Daniel winks and taps the wall with his staff.

The wall swings open and reveals a small room lit by a dozen candles. A low table is in the center, surrounded by figures sitting on colorful cushions. I begin to enter after Daniel and Joshua, but stagger back, my knees almost buckling, when I see the faces around the table.

It's the leaders. Rising to greet us.

Abram and Sarai in their blue robes.

The Hunter in his green cloak.

Rahab in her red dress.

"Welcome," Abram says, taking in our group. "Everyone take a seat. There is much to discuss."

We move toward the table. My legs are unsteady, but

my mind races. What is this place? Why are they all here? I find myself on a blue cushion beside Abram, with my back to the door. Joshua sets Emma's father down gently on the floor and sits across from me. The cushion underneath him is purple. Each leader sits on a cushion matching the color of his or her tower. It is surreal. The leaders look calmly and quietly to Abram, as if he is the principal in a teacher's lounge—making me feel like an eavesdropping student.

"Tell me what has happened," Abram says.

Joshua speaks up. "I saw a light in the pit. Only a flash like lightning, but a true light! Was it you?"

Abram nods. "Partly."

Joshua waits, as if expecting Abram to say more. "How? What did you do?"

"I did a little of what we all must do when the time comes." Abram sounds calm, but there's a depth, a trembling, in his voice. "We will speak no more of that. Tell me how you came here."

"Whatever you did in the pit, you distracted the Colorless One. I crossed and found William. He was stumbling, lost, totally dark. I saved him. Then, the moment I stepped out of the pit, Cipher and Emma were waiting. I'm sorry they saw me, but I enlisted their help. We went to the mine. We freed Yellow's leaders. We freed the slaves. Then we destroyed the whole damned place. There won't be any more gold unless the enemy wants to spend another thousand years digging." Joshua leans back with his arms crossed in satisfaction. "If you like, I can take them back now."

"Back where?" Abram strokes his beard. "They are marked ones. It seems the time has come for them to learn what must be done."

"Should we bring the others?" Rahab asks.

"You know we can't," Joshua says. "One is in Black."

"I could bring Red's," Rahab says.

Daniel shakes his head. "She has only just come to your tower. She had quite a romp among the tribes. Give her time."

"Helena?" I blurt out, unable to contain my questions any longer. "That's who you're talking about, right? Baron's in Black and—" I look to Rahab. "What do you mean that Helena is *Red's*? Does every marked one belong to a tower?"

A bemused laugh slips out of Rahab's ruby lips. "It is nice to see you again, too, Cipher. Have you missed me?"

"Don't toy with him," Joshua grunts.

Abram taps his staff lightly, quieting the room. "You have all seen what happened in Yellow." He looks tenderly to the Widow, who sits beside an empty yellow cushion. "It must have been dreadful. Where did Elijah go?"

"I imagine he is enjoying the sunlight," the Widow answers. "The darkness nearly broke us. Elijah fled with the enslaved ones to Yellow, where they belong. Never has there been such a need for healing. The Colorless One corrupted what was intended for beauty and light."

"What do you mean it nearly broke you?" I ask. "Could the Colorless One kill you?"

"No, no," Daniel replies. "None here may die."

"Only detained, as I have told you," Abram says. "But such a fate could be worse than death. It is very good that you have saved this one." Abram glances to Joshua, as he motions the body of Emma's father.

"The darkness had reached deep into him," Joshua says. "He had become gripped by the very vice he needed to scour."

"The gold twisted him?" Emma asks.

"No, the Colorless One did that," the Widow says. "He digs deep to prey on our weaknesses. But gold was one of the means. He will use anything at his disposal."

"Aye," Joshua says. "The golden armor upset the balance of the Five Towers. It allowed your father to hide behind his defenses, instead of fight and scour away the stains of the past.""

"I see, as it has been with the others…" Abram looks around the group, then his gaze settles on Joshua again. "You must continue your fight down here. Who knows how many we would have lost without you."

"Right, after I already lost a whole tower," Joshua grunts, then his hard eyes fix on me. "Did you know Black was not always black?"

"That's enough," Abram says. "We cannot barrage them with all that has transpired. They are not your infantry to command. You cannot treat them as such."

Joshua's head hangs. "My apologies."

"Understood. You are forgiven." Abram faces Emma and me, with his hands clasped neatly on table. "I will explain what I can. The darkness that you saw in the

Yellow Tower, the darkness that you followed down to the pit—it has been growing. As I told you, when the world ended, the enemy shifted all of his attention here. We have tried to hold him back, but he has always been too powerful. He is not like us. Not human. He rejected the light, and so he rejected color. He absorbs it, feeds on it, like a parasite. The Black Tower was originally made Purple, but the darkness wrapped over it long, long ago. We contained it—Joshua contained it—but our defenses have begun to fail. What you saw in Yellow was a grave and dangerous thing. This could happen everywhere. The darkness could swallow all the color, turn all black."

"But what about the White Tower?" Emma asks softly. "You said all of us could leave."

Abram nods. "And you will. But I did not say when. It will not be easy. It will take all of your powers."

"What about *your* powers?" I ask, looking from Abram to Rahab to Daniel. They've always been able to shut down my power. They're the ones who are strong. "If you can't beat this Colorless One, how would we stand a chance?"

"We are not fully present here," Daniel answers. "We come and we go, to ensure the process continues as it was created to. The power of this darkness is more than even we can withstand. I have told you, we do not know the future. But I can tell you this: the Five Towers were made to harness the powers of everyone who comes here—to scour you, unite you, then free you."

"So if we're scoured, we can leave?" I ask.

"This was once true," Abram says, "but the White

Tower has gone dark. The world has ended. Now no one enters and no one leaves until the towers are equal. And now you know that equilibrium must be perfect, with each person in the correct tower, and with a marked one leading each one. Then, and only then, may you leave."

"The way will find you," Daniel says. "I have no doubt."

"Yes," the Widow agrees. "Even as the greatest disruption stands before us, the towers ripen for harvest. It is the Healer's way." She smiles at Emma. "You will help us heal Yellow now, yes?"

Emma nods. "If you think that is best. What of my father?"

"Go, heal him," the Widow says.

The room goes quiet. Emma rises from her yellow cushion and leans over her father. She presses her hands to his temples. He suddenly gasps and surges up. Their blue eyes meet.

"Who are you?" he asks, looking from Emma to the rest of us. "Where...where am I?"

"A clean start, eh?" Daniel moves to Emma and, with a flourish, produces a small red fruit from his robe. I thought this might be helpful."

"Thank you, oh thank you!" Emma rubs tears from her eyes, then delicately takes the fruit. She holds it out to her father, who looks like her twin. He studies it curiously, then takes it and bites into the enticing flesh.

His eyes widen, then he swoops her up in a hug. "Emma! But how?" He steps back and notices the room for the first time. "Where are we?"

Her laugh is gentle, comforting. "It is a long story."

"You will have time," the Widow says, standing. "I will lead you back to the Yellow Tower."

Emma turns to me with a smile. "Cipher, come on."

"No, not yet," Abram says, tapping his staff against the ground, silencing the room. "The darkness grows mightily. We must proceed carefully before we send away these three. We must have a plan."

"I agree," Joshua says. "I cannot stand against the Colorless One. He cast his darkness over the Black Tower long ago, blocking me from entering. He will come for Yellow again. He will come for every tower."

"If we lose our colors," Sarai says, "the path to the light could grow very long, very dark."

"Come, would even we despair?" Abram asks.

Sarai bows her head. "Forgive me. The accuser grows very strong."

"This is why we must take the fight to him," Daniel says. "Before it is too late."

"Yes!" Rahab stands, with a hand on her hip. "We will attack! My girls could burn the Black Tower down."

"No," Sarai says, still sitting, her dark eyes like a calm ocean.

"We cannot attack," Abram adds. "The light is not yet pure. The Colorless One will find the imperfections and exploit them. He delights in strength, in twisting those with power. Only white can overcome black."

"Then what do you propose?" Rahab asks.

"Joshua, you know the way of Black." Abram clasps the strong man's shoulder.

"The Colorless One believes he can win," Joshua says. "This is our advantage. We must work from the inside."

"Inside Black?" the Widow asks. "You've seen what happened to Elijah, not to mention Black's other leader."

"He will *not* be mentioned," Abram demands.

"Of course not," the Widow replies. "The point is that we no longer have any power over Black. It is all we can do to keep the darkness from spreading."

"Hm, no one proposed a leader entering Black," Daniel says.

"Then who?" Joshua says. "A marked one? Several have come and gone. No one has been able to rise there, to change things."

The room falls quiet. The candles flicker.

The Colorless One delights in strength... I am strong only because of my weakness. As Rahab first told me, it's the vast gap between what I could have been on Earth, and what I was, that gives me power here. So if it must be from the inside, and it can't be a leader...

"What if it's me?" I say, my voice faint.

All the leaders turn to me. Daniel strokes his beard. Abram's icy eyes look full of sorrow. They don't have to say it. I'm right. I must go to Black. Samantha is there. Baron—Rockefeller—is there. The darkness is there. Everything has led to this.

"Yes," I say. "I will go."

Emma rushes to me. "No, you'll be wiped!"

"I know." Something swells up in me—remembering all from Yellow—and it is courage. This duty falls to me. This is what Abram hinted at so long ago. I look to him, seeking his assurance. "Even without the memories, I will be different, won't I?"

He nods. "Much has been scoured. You have four scars now. Do you believe you are ready for a fifth?"

I meet Abram's wise eyes. "I'm ready."

"Good," Abram says. "For the final battle comes."

40

THE RISING SUNS bathe the fields in gold. From the top of the wall, I can see all five towers. Behind me the sea stretches to the horizon, and the gentle, sandy coast gives way to cliffs to the left, arcing toward the Blue Tower. To the right, the beach is overtaken by the dense jungle of the Green Tower. Beyond that, vast mountain ranges rise beyond the Red Tower. The mountains form a sharp ridge between Red and Black. It's the ridge where I once huddled with Emma and my mom, freezing, just out of reach from Black's smothering smoke. The Black Tower stands straight as a steel rod, ominous as a spear over the other towers and the Scouring. That's where I will go today. That's where I will fight the Colorless One.

"Beautiful, isn't it?"

Emma's soft voice brings me back to the wall. She stands beside me, not looking toward the Black Tower, but at Yellow's awakening fields. Each square plot has its hut, its worker. The invisible barriers still separate the grid, but it's not the same as it was under her father the king. Only a few plots are dormant. The leaders have assigned the serfs with a purpose—to cooperate, to share, to overcome the cowardice of their pasts. They will grow their loaves of nine grains. They will advance. And they will be scoured.

"I see now why you belong here," I say.

Emma smiles and again we watch in quiet as the suns rise. It's the second morning since we emerged from the tunnels. The day before was a day of healing, of recovery. Elijah and the Widow have begun to restore order. At their request Emma and I used our combined powers to melt the golden armor—stripped from the king's former guards. We molded the gold into a single block and hurled it with the wind into the dark hole in the center of the Scouring. "It is the most we can do," Elijah said.

Then, using every ounce of power we had left, we rebuilt the central turret of the Yellow Tower. We forged the slender tower with stone and glass, then we collapsed. The Widow took us to our beds. We slept. We woke. Emma wanted to rebuild more, but the leaders told us to come here, to the wall. "You need rest," the Widow told me. "You'll need your energy for what's ahead."

Now the turret glistens in the morning light. Emma and the others will do the rest of the work without me.

"I will miss this light," I say.

Emma turns to me and presses her hand over my heart. "You will take some of it with you. Not even Black can take all of it away."

"And if I'm wiped?"

"Then you will remember again," she says. "You have four colors now. Nearly the full prism. Nearly enough to be white, to be pure." She pauses as she glances over the fields. "You know what happens here when a plant breaks or dies?"

"What?"

"The seeds fall and grow again. There would be no need to heal if there were no hurts, no sickness. But because there is, the Healer rebuilds and regrows and restores. This is how hope defeats fear. It is a belief that things can improve, that pain and suffering are not final. No matter what Black does to you, you'll grow back."

I want to believe her, but I shudder when I think about the dark tower that stands like a spear on the horizon. "But if I'm wiped, do you think Black will allow me to get my memories back? What if I'm stuck, like when I first arrived in Blue, without powers, without knowing who I am?"

"I have been thinking about that," she says, with her trademark look of determination. "You told me that on Earth you discovered a way to implant little chips inside a person's brain. What if I tried doing that now?"

"A chip?"

"No, light." She puts her hand gently on the side of my head. "Mind if I try something?"

"Um, okay…"

She closes her eyes. The yellow wisps of her power stream toward me, then *into* me. It feels soft and delicate as silk, grazing my thoughts. A light suddenly flashes in my mind. It is a memory. The memory that we saw together long ago in the flame at the top of the Red Tower—of going to college at Chamberlain Hall, the last moments with my mother, before the building that Emma's son, Oliver, had built.

"There." She steps back and grins with satisfaction. "We have this memory together. It is ours. It might help."

"How did you *do* that?"

"I found a place in your mind that felt familiar. I touched it, and there was so much energy, between us. So what would Dr. Fitzroy call that?"

"Concentrated neural activity?"

She laughs. "Sure, call it that. Wherever it was, I wove my power into it. Maybe it will help. Somehow."

"Hey, worth a try." It's not crazy. I remember from Dr. Fitzroy that a central part of memory is association—neurons moving in familiar, settled patterns. Dr. Fitzroy was a healer, after all. I don't want to forget him—who I was. I need to know the end of my story. I was on a hospital bed, like my son Benjamin, except with circuitry in my brain. Everyone one I loved was leaving me. But someone remained. He told me I was not finished. "Do you think in Black I'll learn how I died?"

"Quite possible," she says. "I learned of my death. It is not easy. But it is necessary. I believe I am mostly scoured, but still there is work to do here. My father must remember. And Neville. And others."

"So you can't leave."

"I want to stay in Yellow, to do what I can here. I trust what the leaders have told us. We will be trapped here as long as the Colorless One darkens the White Tower."

"I know." I gaze out across the fields and the Scouring,

at the straight shaft of steel looming in the distance. "Black will do everything it can to hold me back. Even if they accept Yellow's offer to trade me for eleven of them, and even if they do not suspect me at first, they will still see the scars on my hands and feet. They will know about me. Things could get very dark there. I'll need every bit of hope I can get. So will you promise me something?"

"What's that?" Emma asks.

"If you don't hear from me—or don't see any change in Black after 100 days—come after me, okay?"

She smiles brightly. "You have my word. I will come for you, with the united Yellow Tower behind me. Who knows, I have demolished one tower already. Might as well try another."

"It might not be so easy with Black. And you won't have guards in golden armor."

"We will have the light. But I do not think it will be necessary. It will not take you 100 days." She puts her hand gently to my cheek. "If anyone can bring light to Black, it will be you. Only you are number 720. Only you have four scars. Only you have brought four towers to equilibrium. Now there is one tower to go." She lowers her hand, leaving the feel of her soft touch. "The Scouring awaits. Shall we?"

I nod but feel unworthy of her confidence. Not even Joshua, the leader, could hold back the darkness from the Black Tower. But Emma is climbing the ladder down from the wall. She will go with me into the Scouring. She believes I can do this. So, with a final glance out over the sea, I follow her.

Our horses graze peacefully on freshly sprouted grains. Serenity neighs as I approach, then bends her head. I rub her soft, chestnut hair and mount the saddle. I'm going to miss Yellow's animals.

Emma and I ride side by side toward the tower. Serfs in the fields greet us cheerfully as we pass. We visit briefly with William, who tends a young field of wheat. Neville is on the plot beside his, growing corn. Emma promises to return every day to see them. There is still much they need to share from their pasts.

We also bring our horses to a halt when we see Max. He stands at the corner of a lush green plot, hoe over his shoulder, talking with Li Min and Kiyo. Kernel, the friendly dog, lays peacefully at Li Min's feet. Max's plot is the same one that he had when I first arrived here. The rye grows high in perfect lines. There's not a weed in sight. I tell Max his field looks good. I ask how the three of them how their nine grains are coming.

"I have seven already," Max says proudly. "And I've had the most amazing dreams. Lily and Kiyo have helped me learn much of the past."

The two girls bow graciously in response. They look like sisters—same age, straight dark hair, and intense gaze—rather than an ancestor and an heir from generations later. But only Kiyo's folded hands bear the familiar criss-cross scars.

"Father and I have learned together," Li Min says. "We have even seen some good, some healing."

I feel there is more to their story and how it connects with mine. Li Min had her perfect citizen score in China. Max paid for my research into neural enhancement. And somehow this led to the Chinese President being overthrown. "Have either of you seen more about how my technology was used?" I ask.

The smiles retreat from their faces. "Only one thing," Max says. "It was a contract. We were together when we signed it. The deal made me very rich." He looks away, sounding apologetic. "It was an exclusive license to a secret military unit. They planned to implant the chip in soldiers' brains. I know nothing more than that."

"I see." It is not surprising. Dr. Fitzroy had discovered the way to enhance the mind. It would only be a matter of time before others would try using this to their advantage. "The chips could have made soldiers very effective."

Max nods. "A dangerous thing."

"Whose military was it?" Li Min asks. "China's?"

"I doubt it," Max answers. "The contract was in English."

"English?" Kiyo speaks up for the first time. "What is this word?"

"A grand word for a grand country," Emma says, with all the dignity of a monarch.

"And a language," I say. "On Earth we spoke many languages, but only this one here."

"The five towers unite us," Kiyo replies.

They wish us well as we go, knowing it will be the last time they see me in Yellow. But I feel sure our paths will cross again.

Emma and I ride past more serfs working their fields, drawing closer to the Yellow Tower. There are signs of progress. Neat piles of rubble. Workers hauling supplies. The lone turret rebuilt and glistening in the sunlight. As we ride the path through the workers, a boy looks up and catches my eye in the distance. He has a broom over his shoulder, and his wide smile makes my lips turn up.

"Hey Drew!" I call out.

He waves and hollers back, "Go get 'em, Cipher! Show Black what we're made of!"

Another familiar voice calls to us from ahead. "Y'all plannin' to ride horseback into the Scouring?"

"I suppose not," Emma says with an amused grin.

We pull our horses to a stop as Sally hurries forward. She greets us with a bow, then takes the reins of our horses. "Guess who's the new stable master?"

"You wanted this task?" Emma asks.

"Oh, yes ma'am," Sally answers. "I always loved these amazin' creatures. Now, I didn't get to ride 'em much on Earth, mind you. But here, Elijah says I can ride any time, long as I take good care of 'em." She holds out both arms, with oats in her hands. The horses sniff at the food, then munch it. "See, they already take a likin' to me."

She leads the horses away, and even among the rubble of the tower's destruction, it all seems right. Elijah and the Widow have put so much back in order with their assignments. Sally as stable master. Drew sweeping as he did on Earth. Max and Li Min on neighboring plots. They even named Seymour head chef in the kitchens, making him about the happiest boy in the five towers.

We follow the path by foot to the central courtyard, with the gate to the Scouring looming in the wall. The courtyard has been swept clean of debris. Its patchwork design has squares of different shades of yellow, showing the names of the serfs who work in the corresponding plots. But now, nearly every square has a name. Many will get their nine grains. Healing will come to the Yellow Tower.

A small group has gathered near the gate. I count twelve of them—ten boys and girls who will enter the Scouring with us, joined by Elijah and the Widow. The leaders wear soft, yellow robes and look twenty years younger than when I first saw them underground.

Joan steps forward to greet us. "You look happy," she says to me. "Maybe too happy for someone who's about to do what you're going to do."

I smile. "It's been a good morning."

"As it should be," the Widow says. "The way is prepared."

"The terms of the trade have been accepted," Elijah adds. "Black sent the message by crow. No one signed it. They will trade eleven for you, Cipher. You must meet them near the center. The gate will open soon."

"As fine a deal as we could get," Emma says, turning to me. "You know what this means, right? With the boys and girls from the mine, our numbers are at 134. This trade will put us at 144. So, you have done it again. You have brought four towers to equilibrium. Only one to left to go."

"*We* did this," I say, but something about it makes me feel uneasy. I've needed Emma's help with every other tower. I take her hands and run my fingers over her scars. "I may need your help again."

"And you shall have it!" She wraps me in a hug. "You know this isn't goodbye," she whispers by my ear. "We are marked ones. We will be together again."

I want to believe her. I also want to stay in her embrace. But there's a low, cranking sound by the gate. It begins, slowly, to crack open. I glance at the numbers scratched onto the wall. What I did in the other towers has not lasted. Black still has over 200. That means Red, Green, and Blue have lost dozens. Two steps forward, two steps back. "They're still not equal," I say. "I'll have to stop Black."

"Yes, but remember," Elijah says. "The light's power has great strength in weakness. Black is very strong. If you try to fight it strength with strength, you will fail. Only light can defeat the dark."

"Here." The Widow places something small into my hands. "Your friend made me promise to give you this before you enter. It has all nine grains, of course."

I look down at the morsel of food. It has golden crust and dark jelly in the center. A macaron. A smile spreads across my face. "Seymour?"

"He says it's no use fighting on an empty stomach. Go on, enjoy it. Come, there's one for all of you." The Widow distributes eleven other coin-sized macarons. A snack before the Scouring. It's surreal but fitting—a last taste of nine grains.

41

THE GATE INCHES OPEN. It's yet another thing that moves slower in Yellow than in the other towers. Growth is slow. Healing is slow. Good things take time. But the Scouring, I know, will be fast as ever.

Joan orders our group into formation. I know only a few of them. One is the broad-shouldered girl who led the tower's managers. Another is Vincent, the painter, and Itzel, whose plot neighbored mine in the beginning. Joan and Emma stand at the front. The others cluster around me, protecting the one they will trade.

Once the gate is wide enough for two to pass through at once, we move out into the Scouring. The vast space is familiar but not. It is the same size. The ground is the same cool, grey stone. But the feeling is completely different. There is no adrenalin of battle. No hope of the White Tower. Dread grips me as I gaze at the center. A dark beam rises from the center, like a new offshoot of the one that rose from the Yellow Tower before Emma destroyed it.

We begin to cross the Scouring, toward the dark shard, toward the Black Tower. I glance around at the teams from the other towers. Red and Blue move along the wall toward Black, and each other. Green is nowhere in sight—they could have gone invisible already.

The twelve from Black come straight at us, moving fast. They circle around the dark shard and meet us in their typical square formation. We stand facing each other. Loose wisps of smoke settle around us like fog. It is so quiet I can hear the others from Yellow breathing nervously around me.

Suddenly Joan shouts out, "Lay down your arms!"

"You have him?" a girl calls out from Black.

"Cipher is here," Joan says. "But first, arms down!"

"No powers!" the girl from Black demands. Then a murmur, too quiet to hear, spreads among the Black team. In unison they kneel and set their spears and shields on the ground. Through the smoky haze they look like boulders on the ground.

"The girl," Emma whispers urgently to Joan. "Have them send the girl, and we'll send Cipher. I will surround the girl with my power, so her smoke will be contained."

Joan nods and shouts out, "Boys stay on their knees! Send the girl forward, and we will send Cipher."

Moments later a girl steps forward from among the ten kneeling boys. She is covered head to toe in black, with only her eyes revealed—innocent, hazel eyes. I do not recognize her.

Emma turns to me. "It's time," she says. "Light be with you."

I move forward as if in a dream. Emma clasps my hand

briefly as I pass. Then I'm alone, in the space between the Yellow and Black teams, under the looming dark shard. The girl and I walk past each other silently.

I stop before the kneeling boys. A girl stands in the middle of them. The haze shifts slightly, and I see her familiar green eyes. It is Samantha. I am not surprised, but I swallow in fear. She looks fiercely pleased.

"Now, the boys!" Joan shouts behind me.

The other girl from Black has reached Joan and Emma. They stand by her side, holding her arms. I see a shimmer of light—a translucent net of Emma's power around her.

"Go," Samantha commands.

The boys from Black rise in unison and race past me. The smoke weaves and bends around them in a blur. Through the haze Samantha takes shape right in front me. I reach for my power by instinct, but there is too much smoke. I can't summon it. I'm powerless.

"Look, Paul," Samantha says. "See what your friends will do."

I follow her gaze to the Yellow team. As the boys from Black approach, Yellow springs into action. They tie the boys' hands behind their backs. There is no resistance. The girl and the ten boys are Yellow's captives now. The fields of grain await them.

Something grazes my cheek, making me jump. Samantha is inches away, with her hands around my neck. I glimpse chrome. The metal clicks shut.

Samantha grins and whispers, "Are we so different?"

I cower back. I grab at the metal, desperate to rip it off

but knowing I can't.

Her command comes over me like a vice: *Attack Yellow with everything we have.*

I have no choice. I summon the wind, and as I do, I feel Samantha's power funneling into mine. It is black and blue and darker than any bruise. I slam it like a hammer down at the team from Yellow and their new captives.

But the hammer clangs away. A shield is there. Golden and bright and impenetrable.

Again, Samantha demands.

I obey, drawing more of the power. There's something odd about the black threads. The more I weave, the harder they are to control, as if they take on a life of their own. But there is more blue than black, and I slam the power down at Yellow again. It bounces away harmlessly.

"Enough!" Emma shouts, her blue eyes like ice. "The deal is done."

"Very well," Samantha says loudly. "It is done!"

Emma meets my gaze. She raises a scarred hand, presses a finger to her head, then points at me. I know what she means. She is with me. In my mind. Concentrated neural activity. She and the Yellow team, with their glistening shield of power still raised, turn and race toward their gate.

Stay by my side, Samantha commands as she strides swiftly in the opposite direction, toward the Black Tower. "Your friend is tougher than she looks," she mutters. "But she will be Black, too. Soon everyone will. Then the five towers will have true peace. Colorless peace."

"No, that's not—"

Silence, Samantha commands. "No words from you. I wish only to *use* you, Paul, as you once used me." Her eyes are amused and sinister. "Let Yellow go. But take Blue and Red and Green, all of them. To Black. Now."

Under the unrelenting force of the collar, I obey and summon the power. I forge a shield around us, then go after Blue. The smoke pours over them, dousing their power. Yet a small wedge of wind fights backs, dissipating the smoke. I blast my wind at it, and together with the black weaves it strikes like a tornado. Their group scatters like dust. I manage to seize half of them. In an instant I hurl them toward Black's gate and fling them inside.

I turn to grab the others, but flames suddenly erupt around me. Red. Fire. The heat is overwhelming, the blaze relentless. My shield bends as if it will melt. I pour every ounce of focus into the weaves. The shield holds, barely.

The Red team charges at Samantha and me in pairs. They come from too many directions, blasting more and more fire. My power drains fast. I can't hold them off.

Give me control, Samantha commands.

I relinquish the power to her. She weaves black and blue threads together, strengthening them into a protective cube around us. Then she turns to me and pats my cheek playfully, like I'm her favorite new toy.

"You're not as strong as I thought," she says. "You need Black's discipline. We'll make you hard, Paul. Hard and very strong."

She commands me to follow her. We move quickly

across the Scouring. Fighters from other towers come at us and clash against each other. I glimpse familiar faces. Helena in red. Hank in blue. Some of them call out to me. It doesn't matter. I have to obey, and none of them can penetrate Samantha's shield.

We approach Black's open gate, with only darkness inside. I gaze up at the straight, metal tower above. It sends a shiver down my spine. I am collared and captive. I am not as strong as Samantha thought…

But my mind is still free. Maybe Samantha doesn't understand strength. The leaders—Abram, Elijah, Rahab, and the others—they are right. It's my weakness on Earth that makes me strong here. Paul Fitzroy's failures gave way to change, to healing, to light.

I may be weak, I may be captive, but I will not be afraid. I am ready. I am not just doing this for myself, but for Emma and Kiyo and Hank and the rest. I am doing this for my son, Benjamin, and for my wife, Susan. They were strong when I was weak. I am Paul Fitzroy, and I am Cipher, filled with light, even hope, as Samantha ushers me into the Black Tower.

J.B. SIMMONS is the bestselling author of the *Unbound* trilogy, *The Babel Tower*, and *Light in the Gloaming*. He lives and writes outside Washington, D.C. To learn more about J.B. and his books, visit **www.jbsimmons.com**.

Don't miss *The Black Tower*, the sequel to *The Yellow Tower* and the finale of The Five Towers Series, available on Amazon and more.